Woven

This book is dedicated to all of the threads who came before me, and those yet to come. To my husband, Pat; our children, Elizabeth, Melissa and Ian and their chosen threads Brian, Aidan and Stephani; and to our grandchildren Sheamus and Elliott and whoever may come next...

Woven

Maureen Morrissey

Time
Human time
Passes slowly
Each day, week, month
And yet
Where did the time go?
How did the numbers,
My numbers,
Get so big?
Generations
Not just a word
Descendants
Not just a word
History
Not just a word
All stories
People's stories
That bring us to here
Bring us to now
Bring us to me
To you
To this:
Threads
Woven into a masterpiece
Are still threads

It was karma, it was kismet, it was magic. It doesn't matter how it happened, just that it did. -Shannon Hale

How do any of us know where the strands of our lives are interwoven? -Claire Duende

Introduction

Every American has an immigration story. Even those who were living on this soil when the Europeans arrived came from somewhere else, if you go back far enough in time. Each historic tale is unique- some traumatic, some sweet and fortunate; and each deserves to be shared.

Woven tells just four of these stories, which eventually become two and then one. In *His*, Cam's story begins with his great grandfather in Ireland during the Great Hunger and follows the generations in surviving and thriving through tough times in the United States. In *Hers*, Tessa's family suffers through the Holocaust, and the surviving family members experience the aftermath in different ways. In *Theirs*, Tessa and Cam forge a new life into twenty-first century America, taking these families into the future. While each of these stories merits a novel of its own, my goal is to explore how events and the passing of time shape the lives of people through the generations.

Although this is a work of fiction, the events are based on what actually happened during each of these time periods. It is both a cautionary tale and one of hope. A quote that has been paraphrased many times by people more intelligent than me says, "Learn from the past; plan for the future; but live for today." We are who we are today because of what happened to our families and ancestors; but that does not limit who we become.

Table of Contents

Part One: His

Part Two: Hers

Part Three: Theirs

Part One: His

1849-1979

Glen's Story

Padraig stood, filthy felt hat in his bony hand, about halfway back in the line from the door. The line moved a few meters, and he took unsteady steps, almost falling over his little brother who was crouched in front of him, with his head on his knees.

"C'mon, will ya, the line is moving," he said, but his voice was weak and Darragh did not hear him.

Padraig stepped around him and heard him scrabbling behind. There were hundreds of people in the queue, but the only noise to be heard was the low sound of listlessly shuffling feet. The humid air was rank with the odor of unwashed infectious, diseased bodies and rotting teeth, but no one paid it any mind. It was all they could do to hold on to the tin plates or small woven baskets as they waited.

The afternoon sun beat relentlessly on their heads. Just ahead of them, an elderly woman wobbled, leaned heavily on the stone building and slid to the ground, her small tin making a muted thump as it hit the dirt and rolled a meter away. The others trudged around her emaciated and dirty bare legs without a glance. A tiny girl fetched the tin and got back in line without a word.

When the boys finally stepped inside the dim low rectory

building, the overpowering reek of corn stew almost made them retch. The nuns in their black habits with large metal crosses hanging on their chests, stood in a row behind black iron pots. As the line moved through, they placed a steaming scoop of mush in each of the proffered pans, intoning, "God bless you."

The boys walked outside, carefully carrying the laden tins to the rocks by the river. Darragh scooped up a small handful in his grimy fist, shoved it into his mouth and swallowed. As soon as the first gulp was down, he did it again, and then again. The first solid food to hit his stomach in days came back up and out onto the ground.

"Slow down, Da," Padraig told him. "Do it like me," and he took a pinch between shaky fingers, chewed it a few times and swallowed. Then he waited to make sure it stayed down and took another pinch.

As soon as his tin was empty, the smaller boy put his face in the water to get a drink, but his brother poked him in the shoulder.

"Wait a minute for the grub to settle, Darragh," and, as always, he listened to Padraig.

The warm food in their bellies gave their mood a little lift. The setting sun stretched shadows over them, a relief from the heat of the day, and they took off their dilapidated hobnail boots to splash filthy toes in the water. They even played for a while, throwing rocks into the river.

The boys had been wandering Galway for days. The narrow cobblestone streets were filled with stinking garbage, rotting dog carcasses and hundreds of hungry people all searching for food.

Padraig and Darragh had left home after their father died, bent over and crying, by the last rotting potato plants on his plot of land. His heart and spirit had broken after loading a second son onto the death cart in just under nine months. After a year of fighting the blight that killed his potato crop and was slowly but steadily killing his family, Eamon Ó Cealláchain, the large man with the largest laugh in the county, had lost the battle of wills. Darragh, eight years old, had found him there.

"Go fetch your Pa, Darragh," his mother had said, looking down at the baby in her arms with worry lines creasing her forehead. "The wee one is not getting enough to eat. She can barely open her eyes. He will have to go back into town straightaway and see what he can find. You and Paddy go with him. Check the church and maybe the docks at the harbor. There has to be something."

Her lips were desiccated and cracked as she added wretchedly, "We can't lose another one."

She sent him off without looking up.

It had taken the little boy a while, but finally he spotted his father far out in the field and moved toward him as fast as his underfed legs could go. Now he stood staring at his father's unruly dark curls matted around the large head. The gaunt face was blackened with dirt and streaked with his last tears. His shirt was unbuttoned to the waist and ripped at both sleeves.

Darragh remained still for a moment, staring at his father's unflinching gaze, waiting for him to move; wanting him to jump up, grab the boy and throw him in the air and let out a loud guffaw like he always had, before.

"Pa?" he said, just once.

He waited another moment and when the man did not respond, the boy went to find his brother Padraig. It took some time, but he finally found Paddy dozing in the shade of their broken-down wagon and nudged him awake with his foot.

"Somethin's wrong with our da', Paddy. You better come see."

They walked back to the field where their father lay in the blazing haze of hottest noon, kicking up dust and dirt with their ragged shoes. Standing together over the motionless body, they stared at him for a moment. Padraig, older than Darragh by less than two years, was not much taller than him; but he radiated an assured confidence that came with being the oldest in the family.

"What do you think, is he dead, Paddy?"

Padraig crouched down, looked into the open unresponsive eyes, shooed away a pair of black flies, and shook his father's arm gently. When there was no reaction, he touched his father's hand. In the sweltering heat of the day, the skin he held was stiff, papery, cool.

"Dead, Darragh," he said, standing up.

Padraig hitched his pants over his bony hips and turned to his little brother. Darragh looked down at the ground, tears streaking his grimy thin face. The older brother felt his own eyes begin to fill, but he blinked rapidly to fight it before his brother could notice.

"First the little boys, and now Pa. And Mam says the baby is not getting enough to eat. What will happen to all of us? What are we gonna do now, Paddy?" the smaller boy sniffled, wiping his eyes with his ragged shirt.

"We better start by telling Mam," Padraig replied, and put his arm over his brother's shoulders as they walked to the shack.

They found her sitting on the floor with the top of her tattered dress down around her waist, struggling to nurse the infant she was holding to her flabby, empty breast. Two small girls lay on threadbare potato sacks on the bare ground, eyes closed. They looked to the boys like they were sleeping, but it was hard to really tell.

The two remaining sons of the family stood in the open

doorway of the crumbling shanty for a moment, taking it in. The furnishings, as poor as they had been, had been sold long ago; and the empty room was dark, humid, close. The boys often slept outside at night, despite the ravaging mosquitos that plagued them; at least they had an occasional breeze to keep them cooler. The large black iron kettle still held water from the pump and a few corn stalks that had been boiled to a pulp days ago. It was all they had had to eat in so long, their stomachs ached constantly with emptiness. Their mother gently wept as she crooned to the thin babe she held; an infant girl whose soft bleating was almost too faint to hear.

"Mam," Darragh said.

She did not look up, did not seem to have heard. She had been so kind, attentive, warm and fun in the time before. Their evenings had been full of music, dancing and laughter, Pa playing fiddle as the aroma of stew wafted through the small and poor but happy home. Even as the crop began to fail, their stores of grain were enough to carry them for a long while. Worry had crept in gradually, but Eamon and Cara had been able to keep up a charade of happiness for a while beyond that.

When hunger moved in, like an ill-disposed guest, the laughter had given way to querulous children clamoring for something to eat; and then, too quickly, to starvation and death. Eamon and Cara's souls became withered and beaten down. At night, Padraig and Darragh heard the sounds of quiet whispers of comfort between them, and that made it seem like all might still be okay.

The birth of their newest sister, on the floor of the shack with their mother's screams echoing off the walls and out through the open door, had come nine months before. Padraig took all of the others on a walk to hunt for a gift to welcome the new babe; wildflowers or pretty rocks or even a discarded piece of leather strap that could be braided into a bracelet. Padraig carried his slingshot in case they spotted a pheasant, grouse or ptarmigan. He was a good shot, and had often brought home some game for the cooking pot; but the birds had been decimated by the starving families and it was rare to find one these days.

Now they stood in the doorway waiting to tell their mother more bad news, very bad news, the worst news.

"Mam," Darragh tried again, tears sliding down his cheeks and neck.

When she still did not look up, the boys went to her, one on each side, and lay their heads on her bony bare shoulders. She leaned her head to the left and then to the right, gently touching their matted red hair with her own, now streaked with premature gray.

"Me big boys," she said, her voice low and weak. They wanted to stay there forever.

And then, "Darragh, did you find your Pa?"

Padraig turned to look into the haggard face, trying to find the young fresh one hiding just beneath. It was gone; and in his ten-year-old mind, he knew this news would bury it forever.

"Mam, we found him in the field. He was…"

He did not need to finish the sentence. Her eyes squinched shut, the crow's feet deepening to trenches; her mouth opened a bit wider and her shoulders shook. She cried almost silently, no tears wetting her slack cheeks. Both of the boys cried with her.

When she was able to contain the grief, gradually boxing it in with the already overwhelming hopelessness and fear, she let herself look up at the small children lying still on thin potato sacks, at the baby lying still in her arms, at her oldest sons, thin in the extreme but somehow still full of life.

"Paddy. Darragh."

She forced herself to say words no mother should have to utter to her children.

"I want you to go. Leave here and go to town. If you stay here, you will die, like…" she paused, searching for strength to continue. "Like your little brothers, and like your dad. You are old enough and strong enough still to find food and shelter there. If you stay here much longer, you might not be."

Padraig, head down as he listened, whispered, "What about you, Mam? What about the baby and these other two? We can't leave you here. I'm the man of the house now, I have to take care of you."

"I'm still the mother, Paddy, my love. I will get the girls to the poorhouse; at least there we will have shelter. The British and their king might suddenly decide to help fix this mess they made, *Go dtuitfeadh an tigh.*" Her tone turned bitter for a brief moment as she spat out the curse; *May your house fall upon you.*

"The poorhouse will be the first to get any help from them, and so we will go and take our chances there. At least then we would have a coffin to be buried in, instead of a paupers' pit."

At this both boys began to cry again, shoulders shaking with their sobs.

"This hell that we are in cannot go on forever, boys. You are the ones who will carry this family forward now. That is what a man of the house does, Paddy."

She put the baby down and gathered the boys in her gaunt, skeletal arms and hugged them with the last of her strength. The boys clung to her until she pushed them away.

Padraig and Darragh stood then and walked to the open doorway. For the last time, they turned and took in the sight of their mother and what was left of their family. Eyes blinded by tears; they waited for her to change her mind. When she did not look up again, they left the hut without another word.

They began walking the six kilometers into the city. In better days, they had often ridden with their Pa in the horse and cart to market and knew the way well. On the side of the road, they passed barren potato fields, dilapidated shacks resembling their own, and abandoned wooden carts, one still attached to the bloated and rotting carcass of a mule. A few other people were shambling in the same direction, carrying cloth sacks of belongings over their shoulders. A family, father and mother and four children, asked them for food or money as they walked by.

It took them most of the day to reach the outskirts of Galway, and they immediately began their search for something to eat.

The day they arrived in the city, they found an ear of corn with the kernels already eaten and chewed on it as best they could.

That afternoon, they passed a darkened storefront with a broken plate glass window, and went inside. Padraig spotted a cubby tucked back high over their heads. He crouched down so that Darragh could stand on his shoulders. As weak as he was, he struggled to hold his brother's legs long enough for him to reach inside. They were rewarded with a quarter bag of oatmeal which they mixed with water from a pump on the street and drank down.

They had lucked out two days ago with a small loaf of black bread they found behind some rubbish bins. Darragh had watched Padraig scrape off the blue mold and very carefully split the loaf in exactly half to share.

Nights, they dozed in alleys or along the banks of the river, keeping watch for roving thieves, kidnappers, murderers. Padraig kept his slingshot tucked into a ragged pocket in his pants, along with some small but sharp stones; ready if needed.

They had wandered past the poorhouse; shadowy, sinister and

bleak. Living skeletons squatted outside, shivering in spite of the blazing sun, half naked, slack-jawed with sunken black eyes. They all looked ancient, even the smallest and youngest of them; like the characters from a book about deepest Hades their mother used to read to them late at night by the eerie glow of the warm fire. The delicious sensations of delighted fear they had felt then echoed hollowly in the face of this real-life hell; where their mother was hoping to find aid.

They looked away and continued their quest to survive.

Now this morning, they had wandered by a long line of people at the back door of a church rectory. Paddy saw that the others held a pan of some kind and told Darragh to get in the line. He was gone for a long while, returning with two badly dented but serviceable small tin platters. They had been just fine to hold the corn mush the nuns gave them; and when they had been licked clean, the boys hid them in some bushes by the river.

When night fell, they found that the low straw shelter they had slept in the night before was occupied by a mother with four little girls. Ten large eyes in lean faces stared at them until they backed away.

The brothers meandered along the water's edge looking for another place to bed down.

Suddenly Darragh cried out and dropped to the muddy ground. "Look, Paddy!" he said, proudly holding up two snails.

"Well, that is a find, Da! This is our lucky day," Paddy said, and they each sucked a snail out of its shell with a satisfied slurp.

They continued along the cobblestone street, following the river. They stopped to watch two rats gnawing a dead rooster.

"Do ya think we could eat that?" Darragh asked.

"Nah, the rats are sick and look, there are maggots crawling under the feathers, see 'em there? That'll kill ya. We'll find something tomorrow. Didn't I get you some corn stew today?"

"You did. I wish it had bacon in it, and some potatoes."

"Don't even say that word, Darragh! Feckin' potatoes got us in this mess to begin with. Come on now, let's find a place to sleep."

As they came around the corner, they stopped short. They had wandered to the Port of Galway and, spotted, sitting alongside the wharf, several ships waiting to sail. Waiting, too, were hordes of human scarecrows, lying atop their grubby valises, trying to get some rest without losing their spot in line. The sail lines of the ships, towering high above the decks, were blowing impatiently in the night sea breeze.

Padraig grabbed Darragh by the arm and pulled him back behind stacked boxes that would be loaded in the morning. For a while he stared at the scene, working it around in his mind. Darragh sat still beside him, waiting for his big brother to speak.

Finally, he turned to Darragh and took him by the shoulders, looking into the tired eyes.

"We're getting on one of those ships, Da. I don't know where it's going, and I don't care. We have to get the feck out of here, and wherever we land, it will be better than this. Mam said we have to find a way to carry on and this is it. Are you with me?"

"Of course, am I staying here by me self? Where you go, I go."

They dozed sitting up against the boxes until a ship's horn woke them. It was still dark when the people began to move up the gangplank.

"Follow me," Paddy directed. "Hold me hand and don't say a word, no matter what. Got it?"

Darragh nodded. They wove through the mobbed dock until they were almost at the gangplank. Paddy searched around until he found what he was looking for. He started walking behind a mother-aged lady carrying a baby and holding a small child by the hand. Over her shoulder was strung a burlap bag with a few possessions.

As she stepped onto the gangway, Paddy quietly and gently took a corner of her skirt in his hand. As they moved up towards the ticket man, the crowd was forced into a narrow lane. Just ahead of them, shouting erupted from the mob of people jockeying to keep their places in line. The woman Padraig was hanging on to desperately held her babies and cried out as she was jostled roughly by two men in front of her. As the boys watched, one of the men raised a knife and stabbed the other in the arm. As tightly as they were packed in, the two men began to tussle violently. The other passengers helplessly tried to avoid them but had no room to move. Blood from the open wound splattered them all. The knife went up again.

Suddenly three sailors shoved their way down the gangplank and grabbed the fighters, forcibly dragging them off to one side of the dock. The people kicked at them weakly as they went by, grumbling and grousing feeble complaints to no one.

The ticket man, flustered, began to wave the travelers back into a semblance of a line.

"Come on, now. Keep yerselves movin'. It's all over now, let's go!"

He took the woman's pass with a cursory glance at her wretched face and waved her impatiently on board, unknowingly towing an extra couple of lads behind her.

The throngs of skeletal travelers moved into the lower decks, feet shambling along, looking for a space to claim. The boys separated from the crowds and searched the ship from stem to stern.

"Look at this, Paddy!" Darragh exclaimed over and over again, pointing to the masts, the jib boom, the captain's bell, the winch. The steering wheel fascinated them both, and they played at turning it until a sailor ran over and scolded them to get below decks and back to their Mam.

They descended the hatch and explored the rest of the ship, finally finding a place behind stacked crates in the hold where they could sleep unnoticed.

After dozing for a short while, banging and the sound of running feet awoke them. They climbed back up to the deck and watched, mouths hanging open, as the ship's crew yelled to each other, raising the billowing white sails, and throwing off the lines that secured the ship to the dock. The boys held tight to the rigging as the ship set sail, the wind whipping their red mops of hair around their faces.

The brothers spent their days on the deck watching the ocean steam past, breathing in fresh sea air. Each morning when they came out of the hold, they found the sight of the vast water startling and astounding; yelling reports to each other of racing pods of dolphins, breaching whales, and large gray shark fins swimming alongside the ship. A few times over those many weeks, the young sailors, not much older than Padraig, allowed them to climb into the crow's nest and have a look from high above the ship. The sea breeze and sunshine worked wonders on the boys.

Below decks, dozens of people lay mortally sick or already dead. Padraig and Darragh stayed as far away from the reeking odor of illness and death as they could. The boat had a galley which served a watery cabbage soup once a day to the passengers. Darragh proved good at spotting crumbs of bread or cheese left behind by some of the crew after their meal; and both boys became adept at stealing whatever morsels the deceased passengers had hidden in their belongings.

It was never enough, but it kept their spirits up.

They were on deck watching the seagulls circle, crying loudly, overhead when they heard the first call of "Land Ho!" A harbor on a small island came into view in the hazy distance. Beyond that a larger land mass covered with a maze of low buildings jutted out into the water, which was crowded with the masts, large and small, of ships and boats. Steamboats ferried back and forth across the river ahead of them.

"What is that?!" Darragh asked, pointing in amazement as they sailed towards the dock.

"I'm sure I don't know; I've never seen the like."

"'Tis the Land of Liberty, boys! A surely God-given sight for these sore eyes! Look well upon her, gents, she welcomes us to the shores of salvation."

An elderly man standing near them wiped his eyes as he spoke. He stood erect and proud in his worn suit; his black felt hat held tightly over his heart in gladness.

They waited in line to get off the ship, and then in lines to get inside a massive white and red building, and then in more lines to get to the bottom of a long, steep set of stairs.

"What kind of place is this?" Darragh asked in awe, as they gazed up past the hordes mounting the steps ahead of them.

"Let's see," Paddy said, pulling Darragh off to one side.

As they watched, men in white coats stood at the top of the staircase with clipboards. The people climbing the steps reached the men, who asked a single question, wrote down the answer and directed them towards the door on the left or the door on the right.

An older man, hobbling up and stopping to catch his breath

every few steps, made it to the top and was sent straight through a third set of doors. His family, who had already been directed to the left, tried to protest. To Paddy it looked like the men in white offered them the opportunity to follow the old man through the central set of doors. Weeping, they chose to continue left.

"That's the dread 'staircase of separation', lads," a voice said behind them.

They turned and found themselves looking at a young man in a uniform. "To the left, New York City, to the right New Jersey. Straight down the middle is detention. That's where they put you so they can decide if they're going to let you in or send you back. Are you going to New York or New Jersey when you get out of here?"

Darragh looked at Paddy, who did not know how to answer, since he had never heard of either place.

"No need to be shy, boys, it's my job to help you new ones and I'm proud to do it. Do you have people here? I'd bet New York is where you're going, that's where most of us Irish start out. Did that me self just ten years ago when I was about your age."

"New York," Paddy answered.

"Follow me, lads, I'll take you to the inspectors me self, then." He led them up the stairs to the left. As they walked, he pulled a chocolate bar and two pennies out of his pocket to hand to them.

"Is that Lady Liberty on tha' coin?" Padraig asked.

"That's right, clever boy!" the young man said; and wishing them luck, dropped them off on yet another line.

At the end of this one was an older man in uniform standing at a wooden podium. He had a book open in front of him and was using a feather to write in it, after asking each group of people many questions. The boys gobbled up the chocolate while they waited, licking their fingers, and wiping their hands off on their shirts.

"I hope New York has lots of that!" Darragh said with a contented brown-smeared grin.

After an hour, they made it to the front of the line.

"Name?"

"Padraig."

"Patrick," he said, writing in his book. "Hey Anthony, check it out, another Patrick. What are they, all named the same over there?"

He looked down at Darragh. "Is your name Patrick, too?"

"Darragh," the little boy said quietly, intimidated.

"Are you clearing your throat, son? Did you say Darren? Darryl? Daniel?"

"He's Daniel, Sor, that'll do."

"Oh good. Last name?"

"Ó Ceallácháin"

"Oh, for cryin' out loud, I'm putting Callahan. Patrick Callahan, Age?"

"Fifteen, Sor, and me brother is fourteen."

The man looked them up and down. "It's *my* brother, not *me* brother; you're in America now, son. But you look nine and he looks seven."

Paddy straightened himself and tried to look taller. "We look young, but we're grown men, Sor!"

The man shook his head and wrote more on his book.

"You got someone meeting you here?"

"Yes, Sor, our uncle Sluaghadhan is waiting for us right outside."

Uncle Slay..Slu...Slee...I'm writing Uncle Donald. Welcome to America and good luck, Daniel and Patrick Callahan, who are definitely not fourteen and fifteen. Next!"

The boys waited in one last line to board a ferry. It approached the mainland at a steady clip, neatly and with practice avoiding the other vessels that crisscrossed the waterways.

"I hope Land of Liberty means lots of food and a nice place to sleep!" Darragh said.

When they stepped off and walked from the dock into the city, they were immediately swarmed by old women and young girls hawking wares, asking if they needed shoes, baskets, live chickens and pigs, handkerchiefs, or apples. A girl, about the age of their little sister and wearing a ragged kerchief tied over her unkempt brown hair, held up a wretched wooden box and begged them to buy her matches

Paddy pulled Darragh over to stand against a brick building and take it all in.

"What are we gonna do now, Paddy?" Darragh asked, taken aback by the scene.

"Give me a second to think, Da," Paddy answered.

After a moment, he said, "Let's take these Liberty coins and get us a loaf of bread. There's a lady with bread and apples in baskets on a small table. See her? When we get up to her, you take a bread and give her the coins, okay?"

"Hey! Don't touch with your grubby grabby hands, boy! That loaf's five cents," the woman scolded Darragh.

He held out the two pennies, looking up mutely at her.

"Oh, for the love of God, you look like you just got off the boat and haven't had bread in years. Fine, give over the pennies and get out of here. I don't know why I feel sorry for you, there's plenty of other hungry urchins running around this godforsaken place. Go on, get out of here now before the other bairns get wind of my kindness and come begging."

"Thank you, missus," Darragh said, and the boys walked to

the river to eat.

As they sat down, Padraig pulled an apple out of each shirt sleeve and handed one to his little brother. They munched in happy silence, watching the clipper ships, oyster barges, ferries and small sailing vessels battle for a clear route up, down and across the wide river. Stomachs full and faces tilted toward the warm sun, they dozed on the grassy bank.

A swift kick to his side brought Paddy wide awake.

"This is our spot. You got any money to rent it? Otherwise, scram."

Paddy got up and stood in front of his brother who was groggily rubbing his eyes. He took in the three boys who challenged him: his age but taller, caps pulled low over their eyes, fists clenched.

"We were just leaving, boys. Come on, Da, we'll find us another place."

As they walked away, a man who was sitting on the bench nearby called them over.

"Why didn't you fight those ragamuffins?" he asked. "You look scrappy enough."

"I only fight when I know I can win, Sor. That was three to one, and they were better fed too."

The man laughed, nodding his head approvingly, and watched the boys walk back into the streets.

"We need to find a place to sleep tonight, and we need to find a way to make money, Darragh."

Padraig led the way through the maze of streets, still steaming as the sun set and the peddlers reluctantly vacated their spots for the night.

"There, Paddy," Darragh said pointing at an empty wagon with only three wheels abandoned in front of a warehouse.

They climbed in and used their shoes for pillows; and slept until the sun rose on another day.

A clatter nearby woke them, and they sat up to see a long wooden pole with some kind of brush tossed onto the cobblestones. They heard a curse behind them and saw a man, covered in black dust except for his bleary eyes, climbing out of the window of the warehouse.

The man attempted to brush some of the dust off his britches but gave up quickly with another frustrated curse. He stood up and caught the boys staring at him mutely. At first it looked like he was going to unleash a stream of profanity at them, but suddenly his face changed.

"Well, good morning, fellas! Fine couple of lads, aren't you?" His large smile showed blackened teeth.

Padraig and Darragh both raised a hand in greeting.

"I would be needing a couple of lads to help me with me work today. The boy I had just passed yesterday. Got a bit too big for the work, didn't he? But you," he pointed at Darragh. "You look like you'd fit in a chimney. I'd give you each a penny for cleaning out the coal soot and taking it to the farmers for their soil. I even have a loaf of bread in my bag I'll share for your breakfast. What do you say, boys?"

"Three pennies, and we'll do it, Sor!" Padraig answered back. "And the bread," he added.

"You drive a hard bargain. Three pennies and a loaf of bread it is. And if you do a good job, there'll be work for many days to come! Off we go, then," and he laid the pole brush over one shoulder and walked up street. The boys scrambled off the cart and followed.

Darragh barely fit inside most of the chimneys, even when Paddy pushed him from below. He breathed in more soot than they collected the first day. The man gave Darragh a patient lesson in scraping the coal dust into a small bag and squeezing it through down to Paddy, who would empty it into a tin pail and toss it back up. On the second day, they filled half the bucket. On the third, they filled it all the way before high noon, ran to the nearest farmer who would buy it, and then refilled it again.

The pennies bought them cheese, apples, and bread; but they were often too exhausted and coughing too hard at the end of the day to enjoy their supper. The man let them keep the bucket overnight so they could get water from the river to wash the black soot off their faces.

They did not notice that the man sitting on the bench near the river was the same one from their first day in New York, but he noticed them. He watched Darragh pour the bucket of river water over Padraig's head as he scrubbed at the dust, and Paddy did the same for Darragh. They sat listlessly and chewed their supper before walking wearily back to the wagon to sleep.

After they came to the same spot for the third time, the man came up to the dripping boys and took a minute to look them over.

"It looks like you found some work, boys. Good for you," he commented.

"It's dirty work, Sor. We are only doing it until we find something better. Cleaner, anyway," the older brother responded.

"I knew I liked you that first time I saw you sizing up those ragamuffins by the river," he said. "What's your name?

"I'm Patrick and this is me little brother, Daniel."

"Well, keep working hard, Patrick and Daniel. They say God helps those that help themselves."

"I don't know what that means, but we know how to take care of ourselves, Sor! Been doing it for a long time now."

"Here's a little something for you, then. For taking care of yourselves," the man said and handed them a small silver coin.

"What's this?" Paddy asked.

"That's called a half-dime, son," the man answered. "That's a lot of money, get you something good to eat. Or maybe some soap." He laughed quietly as he walked away.

In the morning, when the chimney sweep came for them, Padraig told him, "We'll be takin' a day off today, Sor. Me little brother's about sick to die from the dust."

The sweep let out a stream of curses, but Paddy, palming the half-dime, could not be persuaded. They both knew the man needed them as much as they needed him; and they watched him walked away, swearing.

"Come on, Da," Paddy said with a grin. "We're going to have us a well-earned holiday!"

They bought a small sliver of soap from one of the peddlers and found a place upriver where they could strip down and have a good wash. They scrubbed each other's backs, lathered up their hair and scoured the soot off their shirts and pants on the rocks jutting out of the riverbank. They chased each other through the streets to dry their clothes, laughing for the first time in days.

When their stomachs complained, they visited the market and made their way back down to the benches. Sitting on the grass and watching the boats, they gnawed on sausages, ham, dried fish, and cheese that they had bought from a tiny old lady in a kerchief who did not speak English. Their big smiles and bright red hair won her over; and she had been generous with the exchange.

"And here you are again!" a voice called from nearby. "At least I think it's Patrick and Daniel; hard to tell, as clean as you two are."

"It's us, Sor!" Padraig recognized the man who had given them the half-dime the day before. "We're havin' a holiday with the money you gave us and thank you for that very much, Sor! Took us a bath with real soap and we're having a regular feast. Would you like some, Sor?"

Paddy offered him a chunk of cheese, but the man raised his hand and shook his head.

"No thanks, boys. You enjoy that. A holiday today, and then back to the chimneys tomorrow, eh?"

That put a damper on the boys' moods, but only until the next bite of salty meat brought their smiles back.

The man observed them for another minute.

"Would you be needing a real job, Patrick and Daniel? My boss likes spirited young men like you. Might even have a place for you to lay your heads."

Paddy did not hesitate. "Oh, yes, Sor! We're not afraid of hard work. Take us to him and you won't be sorry, Sor!"

The man chuckled, shaking his head, and led them through the dingy cobblestone streets towards the middle of the island. They dodged horse-drawn carts, pigs running down the road, and women with small children holding tin pans and begging for money. They walked down a street with close two-story brick buildings and wooden doorways. A heavily made-up woman, wearing strong perfume that made their eyes water, called over to them.

"Not today, Donna darlin'" the man responded, and then they entered one of the doorways.

Inside was a dim and cool open space, surrounded by rooms. The man knocked on one of the closed doors and waited to be told to come in.

The biggest man either of them had ever seen sat behind a large wood desk. There was a cigar burning in an ashtray and a half glass of amber liquid next to a stack of papers. He was dressed like a dandy: bowler hat, tailored jacket, leather boots; and he took a moment to look them over.

"What am I supposed to do with these street urchins, Joe?"

"You'll like these two, Mr. Donahue. The big one's Patrick and right smart. Looks out for his little brother, Daniel, like a real man. I think they'll be an asset to your business, Mr. Donahue. I'm thinking they'd make a good pair of runners, to start with," he said, and left them with a pat on the head when Mr. Donahue waved him away.

"Patrick, is it? Got a last name, son?"

"Callahan, Sor."

"Call me Mr. Donahue, Patrick and Daniel Callahan. This may be your lucky day. If Joe says you're good men, I believe him. He hasn't steered me wrong yet, when it comes to new hires. Let's see how smart you two are. I'm getting hungry. Take this dime to the market and get me the biggest supper you can for it. I'm a large man, boys, and I like a large supper. Can you find the market and your way back here?"

"Oh yes, Sor!" Darragh spoke up. "Me brother's as good at finding his way as any man you ever met!"

"Well, then, off you go. Make haste, my belly is complaining," Mr. Donahue said, patting his middle.

"Yes, Sor!" both boys said, and took off at a run towards the river.

They went directly to the part of the market where they had been that morning. The little old lady was sweeping her area with a hay broom as people rushed by, ignoring her. Darragh took it from her and swept the dust and dirt off the cobblestones all around her table. Padraig began to hawk her food in loud, descriptive English, quickly drawing in a small crowd. The woman sold more in ten minutes than she had all morning, chattering happily in her strange language.

When there was a small break in the crowd, she hugged the boys in joy. Padraig held up the dime and she filled a basket to overflowing with her smoked meats and cheeses. She placed a small loaf of bread and a brown bottle of ale on top. Then, with an impish grin, she put her gnarled hand into the pocket of her apron and pulled out two small chocolate bars, which she handed to them, repeating "Danke, danke, gute jungs!"

"I'll pay you and your brother each a half-dime a day to run books for me around the Five Points. You can live here in the room at the back, there are mattresses in there. All the comforts of home. What do you say, boys?"

Mr. Donahue wiped the sausage grease from his lips with a linen cloth, took a swig of the ale, and burped contentedly.

"Oh yes, Sor, Mr. Donahue! We'll be the best book runners you ever saw, after you tell us what that is. Thank you, Sor!"

Mr. Donahue laughed. "Joe was right. I do like you. Patty, take these papers and find your way to the Bowery. See Liam Boyle at number 16. He'll give you some money. Bring it back here directly." He handed Padraig a folder.

He added, "And just to make sure you understand how this works, I'll keep Daniel here with me until you get back. You show me how smart you are, and before you know it, you'll be making some real money. Now, get, and don't be too long about it."

Patrick was back in an hour, and Mr. Donahue sent him on another errand. When he returned promptly from that one, the stylish man sent the two of them out to all sides of the Five Points through the rest of that day. They returned, tired and happy, at the end of the afternoon. Mr. Donahue gave them their half-dimes and showed them the room where they could sleep.

The brothers took their pay to the market, and bought fried fish, cheese curds and two small bottles of milk. The pennies they had left went into a little purse Darragh had found while they were doing their rounds that day. Sitting on the riverbank, they feasted happily.

"I think I'm going to like it here after all, Paddy!" Darragh said, sighing with satisfaction and patting his full belly. Padraig put his arm around his brother's shoulders in agreement.

That night, on the mattresses in the back room of Mr. Donahue's building, they had the best night's sleep either of them could remember.

Padraig and Darragh spent their days collecting money at the brothels and warehouses on the wharf. With their fine manners and contented smiles, they became favorites of the ladies, who gave them apples and cookies, and more than one kiss on the cheek.

The boys often carried pouches of cash through the streets back to the warehouse. Only once had a couple of toughs cornered them and tried to relieve them of their bags. Padraig casually mentioned how unhappy Mr. Donahue would be, and the would-be thieves backed away, apologizing.

Late one afternoon, they passed a large group of men in a circle yelling and cheering. Pushing their way to the front, they saw two men with their fists up, both bleeding from the nose and mouth.

"That's Tom McCann, never lost a fight yet," one of the men standing nearby said. "But this one looks like he might be up to the challenge."

The boys watched as Tom pinned his opponent down on top

of the burning coals from an overturned stove. His wool coat began smoking and the smell of roasting flesh reached the shouting crowd. Suddenly, he jumped up and cold-cocked McCann with a ringing left upper cut. Then he calmly took off his coat, stamped out the smoldering holes and put it back on.

The circle of men stepped over the prone Tom and began clapping the winner on the back.

"Old Smoke just beat the tar out of poor ol' McCann!"

"What a story this one'll make at the public house tonight!"

"C'mon, Old Smoke, I'm buying your first drink!"

And the men led away their new champion.

"Let that be a lesson for ya, Darragh- when you meet a tough one, you have to be even tougher!" Padraig told him as they headed back.

As they got older, Mr. Donahue gave them each their own territory. Darragh kept the west side collections, and Paddy was sent to the east side of Manhattan Island. Becoming known as Mr. Donahue's men opened every door, and they quickly developed self-confidence in their adopted homeland.

At the end of a solid day's work, Mr. Donahue called Padraig into his office.

"I have a feeling about Harlem, Patty. The new train line made it easier for working class people to move up there, instead of just the rich ones. Now that the moneyed people are moving upstate to Westchester County, there will be more regular folk heading north to Harlem. Those are our people, and I want to get in on the ground floor. Start at the Polo grounds and see what connections you can make."

Patrick made the right connections, and a bundle of money for his boss. He soon had a name for himself as a representative for Mr. Donahue, garnering respect and cultivating new business opportunities. Quickly, he established several gambling rooms at the back of public houses with regular clients who liked his direct and fair way of doing business.

Darragh outgrew his shyness through his work, encouraged by Patrick at every turn. He found a two-bedroom tenement apartment for them to move into. Every night, they had an ale and shared the day's news. On their birthdays, they had two.

As they celebrated Darragh's seventeenth, he clinked Patrick's second bottle with his own, and made an announcement to his brother.

"I'm going to be a Da', Paddy!

"What, now?" his brother said, thinking he must have heard wrong.

"Me, a Da', can you believe it? She's a fine lass, Mary is. Daughter of a fishing boat captain, and we're getting' hitched next week before her Pa finds out we're havin' a babe."

"Well, congratulations all around, Darragh Callahan! She's a lucky one, couldn't have picked a better man. Look at you! Who would have pictured this when we were starving little rats in the Old Country? Cheers, little brother!"

Patrick, by the time he was twenty, became one of Mr. Donahue's right-hand men, emulating his fashion tendency and his method of handling transactions. A magnanimous smile and a fair deal made on a firm handshake went a long way in their line of business.

He traveled to Boston to expand Mr. Donahue's operations. The first to open hidden gambling rooms after the state lottery became illegal, Patrick brought back piles of cash. There would be no competition for many years, and Boston became the source for Patrick's early wealth. He moved into a roomy apartment on the West side and stuffed his mattress with dollar bills.

He had written a letter to his mother over a year ago, hoping to hear that she was well, and he could send her money. Knowing it would take months for the mail to reach her and more months to get a response, he waited patiently; but there had been no response from the Old Country.

Patrick travelled to Atlantic City, which was becoming a popular resort spot for people who had money to spend, and opened another shop there. He invested money for Mr. Donahue in a harness-racing venture, purchasing ten acres and several horses. Over the next many years, this put Mr. Donahue on the map in New Jersey's rapidly growing gambling society.

At their morning business huddle on a warm June day, Mr. Donahue sat back in his new leather chair, hands across his expanding belly and looked at Patrick with satisfaction. Patrick knew better than to speak first and waited patiently for instructions.

"Patty, my boy, we are doing very well on the East Coast. A lot of that is thanks to you, and I want to show my appreciation."

"Thank you, Mr. D," Patrick said. "I learned from the best."

"I'm sending you to Chicago, son. When the Civil War was on, money started flowing out there. New banks, new factories, and Union soldiers on leave; all with money to burn. There are some gambling houses getting big now, and I want a piece of the action. You should plan on staying out there as my representative. I want you to leave by the end of the week. Is that a problem?"

"No, sir. I'll get a ticket for the train as soon as I leave here. I'll make arrangements with the men to take over Atlantic City and Boston."

"Make it a first-class ticket, Patty. You deserve it. Here's the information you need, and I will expect to hear from you once you're settled. Best of luck, I am counting on you, son. You're going to make us a lot of money out there in Chi-town."

In a rare display of emotion, Mr. Donahue came around his desk and gave Patrick a strong handshake and a firm pat on the shoulder.

Patrick found a vacant building on West Monroe Street in downtown Chicago and set up shop there. On his first night in town, he visited two gambling houses to get the lay of the land. By the end of the week, his own small operation was up and running.

By the end of the summer, it was growing to be a well-known hangout. The men who frequented his place liked his New York Irish straight forward way of doing business, and Patrick let them win enough money to hook them into becoming regulars. When the other gambling houses got wind of the newcomer's popularity, they sent the welcome wagon over and tried to rough him up. But Patrick already had his devoted group, all of whom stood up and showed them the door.

"Drinks on the house," Patrick said, pouring generous amounts of whiskey into their tumblers. The men raised their glasses and saluted him loudly.

The room was humming busily on an October night, the two barmaids keeping the patrons happy as they emptied their pockets onto the tables. Patrick sat in a corner, surveying his place with a sense of satisfaction. It was well past midnight, and he expected the action to go on through the night.

Suddenly, a tremendous explosion shook the building, rumbling on as they all sat, stunned. After a moment, they jumped up and ran outside to the corner.

"Look!"

One of the men pointed south and as they turned in that

direction, smoke began pouring up Market Street. The surging black smothering cloud was followed by a twisting vortex of flames shooting a hundred feet into the air and coming rapidly towards them.

One of the barmaids screamed, which spurred Patrick into action.

"Run! We have to get across the river. The train tracks are up the street. Go!"

As the others charged up Market Street towards the train bridge, Patrick ran back inside and collected every cent from the till and the tables into a canvas bag.

As he raced out to make his own way across the river, he nearly tripped over a prone body lying just outside the door. Her skirt was blackened, and she was missing a shoe. Her long red hair had sprung loose and framed her smoke-smudged face.

`Patrick squatted down and saw she was still breathing. He slapped her face hard twice and she coughed, retching.

"Come on, now, up we go. We have to get out of here or we'll both be Ulster Fry. There we go, one foot in front of the other, miss. That's the way."

She leaned heavily on him, and when they reached the train tracks, she made him stop so she could remove her other shoe to make crossing over the river easier.

"I'm okay now," she told him, but she took his offered hand as they started across.

The blaze, whistling, crackling, and chuffing loudly as it consumed building after building, towered behind them and spilled into the river itself. Just as they reached the western bank, they heard a tremendous *boom clang* and turned to see the great bell of the courthouse crash through the air and onto the ground as the tall cupola collapsed.

They ran north along the river until they felt fresh cool air and then sat, watching Chicago burn for a long, silent time.

"Thank you for helping me, um…?"

"Patrick," he said. "I thought you were a goner. You looked at least half dead lying there."

"I would have been if it weren't for you. Look," and she pointed to Monroe Street which could no longer be seen through the searing conflagration devouring the city.

"Well, shite, that sure is something you don't see every day," Patrick said.

"And thank goodness for that," responded the young woman. "My name is Nora."

"Well, Miss Nora, let's get you home so you can change into something a little less burnt. What do you say?"

He stood, gave her his hand, and pulled her up. They walked the mile to her parents' flat, talking the whole way, the yellow-orange reflections of the burning city on the river behind them.

At the door, he said, "Good night, Nora. It was nice to save you."

"Good night, gallant Patrick. You got your nice jacket all dirty doing it."

She shook his hand and went inside.

He found a room at the YMCA to spend the rest of the night in, although by then it was early morning. After a couple of hours' sleep, he shopped for clean clothes, took a long hot shower, and headed back downtown to survey the damage.

There was nothing left of the neighborhood but piles of ash and broken glass.

Once the flames were out, a different type of fire started. The rebuilding of Chicago began on the very day the last burning building was extinguished.   By the end of a week, the asynchronous hammering and sawing could be heard ceaselessly around the clock, as new wooden and steel frames rose out of the ground.

Patrick's new two-story brick building had an expansive bar, a nice apartment on the top floor, and a large open basement for storage. It was reopened by Christmas, and his regulars, who had survived because of his quick thinking, came back with all their friends to celebrate.

Almost exactly a year after he arrived, Patrick traveled back to New York City to tell Mr. Donahue of the Great Chicago Fire; and to hand him a large suitcase of cash.

"Patrick, my friend, you have done well, as I knew you would."

They sat on leather chairs in Mr. Donahue's large new office, holding glasses of fine amber Scotch and smoking cigars. Mr. D admired his protégé for a moment.

"You have come a long way from that vagabond mudlark that Joe brought in all those years ago. Look at that natty suit and those fine leather shoes. Patty, my boy, here's to you!"

"To you, Mr. D, I couldn't have done it without you."

They clinked their glasses and took a warming sip of Scotch.

"I don't know about that, son; I don't know about that. Now what you need is a missus to take care of you and make lots of little Patricks. My Mrs. Donahue is a treasure, and I could not be happier to go home to her and the little ones after a day's work. Find a lass and marry her up, Patty. You're not getting any younger!" and he stood to give Patrick a back-pounding hug.

Before leaving New York, Patrick stopped in at Darragh's place, now a three-bedroom apartment on the Lower East Side. The door was opened by a little boy with a mop of curly black hair, who let Patrick into a raucous scene: there were children everywhere, running, yelling, and happily playing. Mary, with a baby on her hip, was cooking up a roast; but stopped to give him a hug. He found his brother on the floor, under a pile of kids.

"It's Uncle Paddy, children! Say hello to your Uncle Paddy!" and suddenly Patrick was pulled down onto the ground next to Darragh and covered in children as well.

He stayed for dinner, commenting with a laugh to his brother as Mary laid the platters on the table, "Potatoes, Darragh?"

"Potatoes killed our family, but they also brought us here to the New World, and I started a new brood with Mary! Isn't it a crazy world?"

As soon as he returned to Chicago, Patrick found his way back to Nora's flat across the river. As he raised his hand to knock on the door, it opened. She stepped out, dressed in white from head to toe.

"Well, that is a change from the charred mess you were the fateful night we met. You clean up rather well," he said, looking at her tightly wound bun and spotless uniform. "You even have two shoes on."

"Patrick! You look pretty good yourself. Are those wingtip shoes on your feet?"

"Not the kind my Grandda' wore on the farm, but yes, they are. Do you like them?"

"Very fancy. Can you walk a mile in them? I have to get to the hospital for my shift."

As they walked, she chattered on about her job. "I've been working there since the 60's and it's been so hectic from the first day! There are a lot of shootings now downtown, but we even had a constant flow of patients during the Civil War, all the way up here in Chicago! One day a whole crop of Confederate prisoners of war from Camp Douglas were brought to us in bad shape. I know they were the enemy in the fight, but honestly, the Southern soldiers were being starved to death at that detention camp."

She talked about the work she was doing all the way to the hospital entrance.

He held the door for her but stopped her as she stepped inside. "What time does your shift end, Nora? I'll be here to take you to dinner."

He took her to dinner every evening after that for weeks. Then he started coming to take her to breakfast before her shift, and finally when he knocked on the door one day, it was opened not by Nora, but by her father.

"So, you're the young man distracting my daughter. Come in son, and let's have a look at you. Then I'll let you know if she'll be available for any more of your distractions."

Nora's father admired his fashionable clothing and his confident demeanor. He was not thrilled about Patrick's line of business but was won over by his Irish charm and frank story about his humble beginnings.

"You're a man after my own heart, Patrick. Self-made, honest, hard-working. But make no mistake, Nora is a special girl, and I won't have some young jackanape turn her head and then break her heart."

"Sir, Nora is special to me too. I swear on my family name and the heads of my many, many nieces and nephews, that you will never have to worry about her heart or a hair on her head." His firm handshake set the man at ease.

Within the year, Nora and Patrick were married in a ceremony held at her family's church; and bought a large flat of their own not far from her parents.

Nora gave birth to Patrick Jr., Ronan, Brigette, Ryan, Cian, Conor, Daniel, Maeve, Cassidy, Erin, and finally Tiernan. It was a noisy, happy household Patrick came home to every day and he felt once again, that Mr. D knew what he was talking about.

Patrick's business hit a snag early on when Michael Cassius McDonald came to town and opened his first gambling house on Monroe Street. When Mike's good friend Harvey became Mayor Harvey Colvin, Patrick knew he needed to make some decisions.

This was a new way of doing business. Mike took a piece of everything; and in exchange, his goons became Patrick's goons, if necessary. If he didn't get his cut, Mike's toughs would not be so friendly; and a lot of them were cops in uniform. Patrick, in typical form, handed over his monthly contribution with a smile and a handshake. He knew there was enough to go around; and had seen what Mike's henchmen did to those who were less than cooperative.

For the next ten years, even with the vig he gave away to Mike, Patrick became wealthy beyond his wildest dreams.

Junior and the other five Callahan boys followed their father into his business; but Tiernan, the youngest, shied away from the loud, rough brothers, preferring to sit quietly, and read. They made fun of him, calling him "Professor", but he could not be cajoled into joining a game of catch or a wild night on the town. When one of the boys came limping in from roughhousing, Tiernan would help his mother wrap the injured limb as she would say with a patient smile, "Heat and ice make the ankle feel nice."

As he got older, his brothers changed his nickname to "Teetotaler Tiernan" and none of the family was very surprised when he announced his intention to go to college.

Patrick often talked to his regulars about his smart son, buttons bursting as he said, "We had to try six times but finally got a boy with real brains! Not like his old man and knucklehead brothers, is our Tiernan!"

The farewell celebration was a proud one for Nora and Patrick, whose wide smiles and misty eyes gave Tiernan the courage he needed to actually get on the train.

When Tiernan set foot onto the campus of the University of Iowa, he found himself surrounded by young men and women, all with a drive and focus for learning as strong as his own. He was swallowed up into college life, found a room in a boarding house on Clinton Street and attended the Freshman social with a measure of awe. He felt, for the first time, that he had found an entire society of kindred spirits.

At the orientation meeting, where the Deans of each of the colleges introduced themselves and touted their specialties, he felt overawed with the choice he had to make. He was shaking his head to clear it during the sixth presentation, when the woman next to him laughed into her hand.

"I know," she whispered to him. "It's difficult to decide what to do, isn't it? My mother wants me to be a nurse, my father says I should have been married years ago, and I have no idea what I want."

"I'd say it's almost too much of a good thing," he responded, and she nodded her head in agreement.

He took all the literature back to his room and read every detail of every paper. It took him two full days to get through it all, and he only stopped to get a bite to eat, or to sleep.

At the point where Tiernan felt completely confounded and overwhelmed, he took a walk around campus. He stopped in at the Halls of Liberal Arts, Engineering, and Natural Sciences to see if they drew him in. He visited the School of Dentistry to have a look around. He walked into the Old Capital building and took time to read the historical information, and admire the art gallery and the Senate Chamber. It was all very interesting, but none of these specialties truly appealed to him.

Once outside, he headed towards the Iowa River.

As he passed the football field, he heard the coach running practice exercises and the players huffing and puffing around on the grass. He stopped to watch for a while, thinking of his brothers and missing his family.

Off to one side, he noticed a bench where a player was being attended to for a leg injury. He walked down and stood nearby as the player's knee was being manipulated by a man who was carefully watching the movement of the leg he was holding. At one point, the man put his ear down to listen to it before wrapping it in a linen bandage and standing up.

"My mother used to say, 'heat and ice make a knee feel nice', every time one of my brothers limped home from a game," Tiernan said to him.

The man laughed and said, "She's not wrong about that, son. Are you a Freshman here? I haven't seen you before."

"Yes sir, just arrived on campus this week from my home in Chicago."

"Stick around for a while if you want. There will be more injuries that need attention, and clever sayings."

Tiernan "stuck around" for the rest of that practice, and for every practice that week. Within that time, he got to know all the players on the team, and the coach, Jesse Hawley, and the physical therapist he had met that first day. After just a month, he was wrapping injuries and applying iodine and mercurochrome to minor cuts and scrapes himself. Quite by accident, he had found his path.

Over the next four years, Tiernan slept little, read voluminous tomes on the human body, and spent every second he could with the athletes. From the basketball players, he learned about jammed fingers and foot fractures. The tennis players taught him about shoulder, wrist, and elbow problems. The footballers hurt every part of their bodies, and Nora's "heat and ice" rhyme became a team chant.

The field hockey women always took care of themselves, but he liked attending their practices and competitions to see their focus and passion for the game.

It was there that he first spotted a blonde player helping a hobbling teammate off to the side. After getting an ice pack and a cup of water for her, the blonde ran back out onto the field and picked up the game without missing a beat.

He asked the injured player her name and rolled it around in his mouth: Ilse.

He had never known anyone with such a name or such a platinum ponytail, swinging left and right in rhythm to her running feet.

After that day, he came around at the end of every field hockey practice to check on the players, making sure that they all knew his name. It took weeks for him to approach Ilse. He watched her wipe sweat from her neck and forehead. She dumped a small cup of water on her head and shook it off, drops catching the bright sunlight.

"That's a good idea to put water on your hair when you are overheated," he finally said.

"I know."

"Your name is Ilse."

"I know."

"I'm Tiernan."

Then she turned to him. "I know."

She looked at him, appraising. "Do you want to ask me out?"

"I do," he said, taken aback by her direct gaze and bluntness.

"Well, then, what are you waiting for?"

"Can I take you out for dinner tonight? I have to study until around seven but after that I have a few hours."

"So, you can fit me in? Good. I live at the Kappa Kappa Gamma House. I will be waiting inside. The sorority sisters will want to meet you to make sure you are a gentleman. They need to approve of you before we can go."

Having grown up in a house with four girls, he knew how tough this would be. He showed up precisely at seven in his best suit, holding a small bunch of daisies he had just picked on the walk over. The door was answered as soon as he knocked.

"Tiernan Callahan, I presume? Right on time. Follow me."

She led him to an armchair at the end of a long table, at which six young women were already seated. Ilse was not in sight. He sat up as straight as possible, looking at each of them and wishing each a good evening. They did not introduce themselves.

"Where are you from?"

"What does your father do?"

"How old are you?"

"Where are your parents from?"

"Do you drink?"

"How many siblings do you have?"

"What are you studying?"

"What religion do you practice?"

"How are your grades?"

"What are your intentions with Ilse?"

Tiernan fielded each query with honesty, although he was a bit ambiguous about the family business. He was not sure they would approve of an ale house funding his education and told them his father was in entertainment.

He guessed that he passed their test, as Ilse was brought out from a room nearby. The sorority sister who had answered the door walked them out.

"Back by ten," she said.

"Don't worry, he has to get back to his books. He could barely fit dinner in," Ilse answered back.

"I approve," she said, and closed the door as they went down the sidewalk.

"Whew, I feel like I just underwent a job interview," Tiernan said, pretended to wipe sweat from his brow.

"Oh, you did," Ilse said, slipping her hand onto his elbow.

Through dinner, Ilse told Tiernan the story of her name- her grandmother who had left Germany in a hurry. She was one of the *Acht-und-vierzigers*.

"Ahh…too…ooo?"

"*Gesundheit*, bless you!" Ilse said, laughing. "I see the Chicago education system was strong in world history. Here's the nutshell version: In 1848, a revolution was brewing throughout Europe. The 'forty-eighters', acht-und-vierzigers in German, wanted more human rights and a more democratic government. When they failed, most of them left the continent bound for North America. A lot of them went to Canada or Texas or Ohio, but my grandmother wound up in Milwaukee, of all places. They brought beer and wine and a rebellious nature with them. I guess it's appropriate that they named me after her, I am not the quietest sweetest little thing you ever met."

It was true; Tiernan had never met anyone like Ilse. Over the next year, between semesters and during holidays, he courted her in unusual ways, to get and keep her attention.

He took her on a hot air balloon ride, hanging on for dear life while she put her hands up in the air and leaned so far out of the basket it swayed; and he almost fainted.

They took a ferry ride up the Miami-Erie Canal to see where some of the other *Acht-und-vierzigers* had settled.

They went to a small Oktoberfest celebration in Cincinnati, where he tasted his first beer. His grimace told her everything she needed to know about his drinking habits.

She introduced him to non-alcoholic German beverages, such as *apfelsaftschorle* apple spritzer and *kinderbowle* fruit punch. When they shared a *schlammbowle* ice cream float, his huge smile and white-cream mustache told her everything she needed to know about his love of sweets.

When he nervously mentioned he was thinking of taking her to Chicago to see the city and meet his family, she gave him a soft punch in the arm.

"Are you embarrassed to introduce me to them?"

"Just the opposite," he said. "I'm not like my dad and my brothers. They are a little 'over the top.'"

"Ha! Just like me! When do we leave?"

Tiernan had nothing to worry about. His mother and sisters loved her and took her shopping for hours. His brothers did not behave themselves, and embarrassed Tiernan by saying Ilse was more like them than he was. Ilse loved them all.

When, later that year, he got on his knee in a rowboat on the Lake of the Ozarks, with the dazzling tangerine sun setting behind him, she said, "I have only one question, Tiernan. Will you always have adventures with me, or was this just courting and then we will have a boring married life?"

"I think you have spoiled me for 'boring,' Ilse. Will you escapade with me for the rest of our lives?"

She said "Of course."

He took over as physical therapist at the University, and she began teaching history at the local public high school. Every vacation week, they traveled around the country, and ventured once to Germany and once to Ireland.

When she became pregnant for the first time, Ilse said, "Well, here's a real-life adventure we're undertaking."

The baby girl, whom they named Alice, became a walking-talking version of her mother by the time she was a year old. Tiernan called her his "little lass."

The next three daughters were calm like Tiernan, studiously watching the world as they learned their way around it.

Ilse and Tiernan took the girls camping across the northeast, stopping to see Niagara Falls and the Finger Lakes of New York. On a starry night after the girls had gone to sleep in the canvas tent, they made love by the crackling fire.

"I think you just made me pregnant, sir," Ilse said, lying close to him.

"If it's a boy, we should name him Glen, since he was conceived in Watkins Glen State Park."

He had, it was, and they did.

From the very day of his birth, Glen was a mirthful flirt. Everyone who stopped to admire him in his baby buggy stayed to coo at him. His sisters fawned and fussed over him; fighting to hold his bottle, or his hand when he began to walk. All he had to do was point at something and the girls ran to get it for him. He learned to speak early from their constant chatter, commanding attention with his little-boy voice and rapidly growing vocabulary.

His first-grade teacher told Ilse, "He won't stop talking during lessons. When I raise the ruler over his hand, he smiles up at me and I just can't do it."

At the playground, he scampered to the top of the monkey bars with Alice while the other girls played happily in the sand. He and his oldest sister had competitions to see who could swing higher. She often won because of her much longer legs, but this just made Glen try harder. It did not take him long to match her at swinging or any other contest they contrived.

At the end of each, Glen would smile and say, "Next time, you'll beat me, Alice. That was just lucky."

The summer that Glen turned eight, Tiernan put him on the train to Chicago to visit his grandparents and meet his scads of cousins.

"Let's see…" Tiernan said, sitting on the edge of Glen's bed the night before he left, the little bag packed and ready by the door.

"My brother Patrick Jr. has Patrick III, Mackenzie, Rory, Kevin, Tim, John, Cara and Margaret. Ronan has Daniel, Dermott, Dillon, Donal and Declan. Brigette has Ian, Aidan, Brian, Brennan, and Patrick. Ryan has Melisa, Bethan, Siobhan, Ailin and little John. Cian has John, Tim, Patrick, Margaret and Moyra. Conor's wife has been trying for years but so far, no luck, poor thing. Daniel has Sheamus, Elliott, Jamesina, Elspeth, Nora, Mary and Lilias. Maeve has Patrick, James, Rose, and Milly. Cassidy has twins Nolan and Niamh. Erin just got married, but I'm sure she'll be adding to the brood in a year or so. Do you want me to write them down?"

Tiernan looked down at the boy, who had his eyes closed, head turned to the side, snoring gently. He tickled his son, knowing Glen was faking it and added, "Just call them 'cousin' and you should be fine."

Glen learned the names of his cousins in the first week. It

helped that there were so many Patricks and Johns. He also learned his grandfather's business.

"Glen, my boy, Rory and Dermott will show you around the city. Since you'll be here for the summer, you'll be a working man, just like I was around your age. You can't tell your Da' though. He would not approve."

The first summer, Glen was a lookout in the back alley as trucks unloaded spirits into the cellar at Patrick's place. If a Prohibition federal agent came nosing around, Glen charmed him until his cousins could lock up the hooch.

He also stocked canned food items in the store front Patrick had put in to hide his real money maker. The well-dressed ladies and gents who came to "shop" late at night walked through an unmarked door at the back of the store, always with a pat on the head or a coin for Glen.

The second summer, Patrick brought him into the hidden nightclub and introduced him around. Glen was intrigued with the low lighting, soft jazz, and smoky environs; and would work any hours he could just to be there.

Glen would ride along in the Model A truck with his cousins when they picked up the whiskey and moonshine from surrounding states as far away as Kentucky. The year Glen turned twelve, Patrick let him drive by himself to pick-up points at farms in Illinois and Indiana.

That was also the first summer Patrick called him over to have a "manly drink with his old Grandda" at the end of the workday. Glen developed a taste for whiskey and women early on.

Late one night in the speakeasy, the band struck up a rousing version of Benny Goodman's "Sing, Sing, Sing." A reveler with bobbed hair in an intricately beaded dress that almost showed her knees, grabbed his hand. "Come on, Glen, come Jitterbug with me!"

He became a dapper dance partner, impressing the flappers with his Charleston, Fox Trot and Black Bottom moves.

Glen loved his summers in Chicago and dreamed of one day moving there permanently. When his parents asked how his summer went, he responded as his grandfather suggested: "It was fun. The cousins took me to the lake every day to swim and fish."

The economy crashed hard around them. While breadlines of destitute families formed all around Chicago, Patrick's business, which catered to both the working class and the wealthy, continued to make bundles of cash. Since the Valentine's Day Massacre there was a new boss in town, but not much changed for the easygoing Callahan patriarch. He just paid his protection money to Frank Nitti with the same smile and handshake as always. His generosity with his neighbors, as he gave away products from his storefront to starving families, made him more admired than ever.

Listening to the radio one morning, Patrick, Nora, and Glen heard an interview with Senator Morris Sheppard of Texas, known as the Father of Prohibition, who stated confidently, "There is as much chance of repealing Prohibition as there is for a hummingbird to fly to the planet Mars with the Washington Monument tied to its tail."

"Either way, we win, my boy," Patrick said, rubbing Glen's head with a calloused rough hand.

When Franklin Roosevelt, running for the "wet party", won the election, he introduced the only constitutional amendment ever to repeal a prior one; and Prohibition was over.

Glen helped his grandfather and uncles build a public house in the store front and hang a sign over the door: Callahan's Pub and Ale House.

During the other three seasons back home in Iowa City, Glen's charming smiles opened doors everywhere he went. His talents opened even more.

He taught his sisters and mother and father to dance, playing jazz and big band music on the gramophone in their living room. Although his sudden interest in the latest dance craze made Tiernan suspicious about the fishing story his son had told him, Glen explained it away: "The cousins over in Chicago taught me all the dances. The girls said they needed a partner to practice with, and since I wasn't doing much else, I was it."

His skills with the latest crazes on the dance floor made him a favorite at school sock hops. His name was on every girl's dance card, and he barely sat to eat. Every time a song ended, a group of girls came running over waving their cards at him and waiting to be chosen. Glen's good-natured smile won them all over.

His junior high school teachers noticed his excellent writing skills and encouraged him to join the journalism club. He took over the columns on school sports and social events.

Glen could talk his way out of any difficulty, a skill honed on the principal of the high school. He became a member of the debate team when the principal gave him a choice: "Put your argumentative prowess to work, or plan to spend many afternoons in detention with me."

He began playing football in high school and made a name for himself as a linebacker who was short enough to get underneath and neutralize the offensive lineman's size and strength. The whole town turned out at football games, and the Callahans were no exception. Ilse would yell louder than anyone every time Glen blitzed the quarterback.

Like his mother and oldest sister Alice, he loved adventure, and hankered for the next daring feat or new opportunity for exploration.

Near their home, the local kids spent time at the rock quarry, camping out every chance they got. Glen would always be the first to leap the thirty-foot drop into the water, usually with a flourishing flip or swan dive. He led the charge in the swimming races across and back. He made the biggest bonfires; and sitting around them, told the kids entertaining stories about Chicago, careful to leave his grandfather's business out of them. It was a small community, and he did not want anything getting back to his parents.

He drank himself into a tizzy, but still managed to wake up in the morning energetic and raring to go again.

Glen began to take over planning their family road trips, to Ilse's delight. The first journey he planned, at the age of thirteen and using that year's "Rand McNally Official Auto Road Atlas of the United States," took them south to the Gulf of Mexico, following the Mississippi River all the way down. They crisscrossed over the river as they went, to explore both sides before seeing the vast waters of the Gulf for the first time.

The next year, he took them out to the Rocky Mountains of Colorado to hike and camp among the breathtaking peaks. Glen, Alice and Ilse scared Tiernan and the other girls by walking out onto the edge of cliffs and sitting with their feet hanging over the abyss, or by climbing sheer rock faces like mountain goats. The girls would cover their eyes until the three came back to safety, laughing and exhilarated.

The following year, they rode all the way out to San Francisco and took the coast road up into Canada. Glen's trips were magical adventures for them all.

The economic depression raged around them. Due to Ilse and Tiernan's secure jobs, the family did not feel the effects or suffer as much as many of their neighbors. It did, however, bring out Tiernan's practical side in new ways. He began taking Glen on drives out to the farms in rural Iowa.

"Son, these are hard times for so many. We're going to buy what we can, both to help out the farmers and to get very good deals," he said on their first trip.

They would drive for an hour or two until they saw hand-made signs advertising produce or dairy or meat, and then pull into dusty driveways up to ramshackle houses. There would usually be a child or two sitting listlessly outside the place, watching them get out of their car, no curiosity on their lean faces.

Tiernan would make his deals, stuffing boxes of goods into the trunk and backseat of his Chevrolet Master. He always gave the children a peach or apple or piece of cheese from the box, and a kind pat on the head, before driving away.

On one of their drives, they came up to a small but well-kept farmhouse in a town so rural there was only a gas station and a general store, both closed. A girl a few years younger than Glen was sewing on the wooden step at the front door.

"Well now, that is a very nice doll's dress you're making there!" Tiernan said to her. "Do you sell your doll clothes? I have four daughters who would love them."

"Can I help you?" A man came to the door, his bib overalls worn and patched, but clean.

"Yes sir, I think you can. My name is Tiernan Callahan." He held out his hand and was pleased with the firm grip he received.

"James Wilbur, pleased to meet you, Mr. Callahan."

"This is my son, Glen. We live in Iowa City and we are out looking to buy products from you farmers who have fallen on hard times. I was just admiring your daughter's sewing and would love to take some of her handiwork home to my girls. Do you have other goods for sale, Mr. Wilbur?"

They left with a small box of doll's dresses, a large wooden crate filled with apples and corn meal, and two freshly baked pies, still warm.

By the time Glen started classes at the University of Iowa, all four of his sisters were married and having baby after baby. The little ones kept Ilse and Tiernan busy and happy. "Grampy T" as they called him, continued to enjoy finding deals by the boxload and now was thrilled to have a growing family to share them with.

Glen joined the Beta Theta Pi fraternity and moved into their house on campus. The initiation ceremony, which he was told to keep secret at the risk of his membership, lasted two weeks. Several other young men dropped out or were kicked out in humiliation. Glen relished it all and raised the bar for future hopefuls. At the installation ceremony that made him an official fraternity member, he had memorized the Obligation and Oath scripts and delivered them with a panache that impressed even the high Betas. His drinking abilities impressed them as well, over the weekend-long celebration.

Glen chose to follow his mother into teaching history. His special interest was in world leaders and their involvement in wars. He spent time in the library studying how tactics from the Trojan and Peloponnesian Wars in the B.C.E. period were used in the American Revolutionary War. He soaked up facts about the mad King Henry VI in the War of the Roses, and the brilliant, if murderous, tactics of Genghis Khan.

He devoured newspaper articles and radio programs about the current battles happening overseas in Europe. The newsreels showed Germany plowing relentlessly through Poland and Czechoslovakia, and making back-door deals with Russia while

England and France looked on, reluctant to start a second world war. It seemed to him a continuation of World War I; just a different set of despots with aspirations. He and his frat brothers constantly expounded and debated on whether the United States would wind up getting involved in this conflict.

Glen hoped so. He was itching to be part of history.

On a Saturday night just before Autumn semester final exams, the Betas held a "Party to End All Parties". Hundreds of young men and women in their finest attire attended, eager to have one last celebration before buckling down to study.

Glen took over the gramophone and played dance music that got the party going. He directed everyone to the open space where the brothers had removed furniture and led a Conga line around the room.

Then he took over bartending, pouring Gin Rickeys and Sidecars for the men, and Green Dragons for the ladies. The party was still going strong when the sun came up, and finally petered out just before noon.

The Betas were doing some preliminary clean up before hitting their beds, when the radio crackled out a nervous announcer's voice: *"Hello, NBC. Hello, NBC. This is KTU in Honolulu, Hawaii. I am speaking from the roof of the Advertiser Publishing Company Building. We have witnessed this morning in the distant view a brief full battle of Pearl Harbor and the severe bombing of Pearl Harbor by enemy planes, undoubtedly Japanese. The city of Honolulu has also been attacked and considerable damage done."*

The fraternity brothers nearest the radio yelled, "Stop! Shut up! Shut up!" and within a minute the house was silent, all of the young men gathered around listening tensely.

"This battle has been going on for nearly three hours. One of the bombs dropped within fifty feet of KTU tower. It is no joke. It is a real

war. The public of Honolulu has been advised to keep in their homes and away from the Army and Navy. There has been serious fighting going on in the air and in the sea. The heavy shooting seems to be . . ."

There was a little interruption, then the announcer continued. *"We cannot estimate just how much damage has been done, but it has been a very severe attack."*

The news reporter began listing casualties and damage, as the reality sank in: The United States had been attacked on its own soil, caught completely unaware.

Although no one spoke about it as they listened, they knew it meant that the country would be entering the war.

Hours later, stunned mute, they finished cleaning the house and lay in their beds, nerves humming and sleep evading them all.

The next day, after listening to the president officially declare war, the entire fraternity walked downtown to the recruiting offices and chose a branch of the military in which to enlist. Glen stood in line at the Army office, signed the paperwork for the Air Forces component and, shaking hands solemnly with his Beta brothers, wished them Godspeed.

Then he walked to his parents' house to give them his news.

Lillian's Story

Margaret was just pulling the last linen bed sheet off the clothesline when she heard the crunching of James' work boots coming up the dirt and gravel driveway.

The quiet morning, with the slight breeze blowing unobstructed across the homestead, was her favorite time of day. Breakfast had long since been cleared away. She had prepared two pie crusts, filled them with apples and placed them in the oven as soon as James left to attend to the lowing cows. Now they sat cooling on the windowsill. After washing the bedclothes and hanging them, she had gathered a dozen eggs from the henhouse, and chosen the young chicken she would roast for this special occasion.

As he appeared around the side of the house, they simultaneously wiped sweat from their brows; he onto the bandanna he removed from around his thick neck, and she onto a small linen square tucked into the pocket of her apron.

"It will be a long ride into the city," he said in his gruff voice, unaccustomed as he was to lengthy conversation of any kind.

"I have lunch in the hamper ready," she responded. "Do you think they will have what you are looking for?"

"We'll see. I hope so, I could sure use the help."

He rinsed his beefy arms at the pump and changed into clean clothes that she handed him from the woven basket at her feet. He brushed his dark hair to one side with wet fingers, rinsed the bandanna and wiped the sweat-streaked dust off his face.

They climbed onto the wagon seat behind their best horse, and set off, leaving a trail of dust that rose lazily and then moved sluggishly across the open fields. The endless rows of corn and the low green lines of soybean plants were flanked on one side by low outbuildings housing everything from livestock to farming implements.

Margaret and James were among the more fortunate of the young couples that had decided to leave Pennsylvania, and everything they knew, and try their hand on the unknown frontier. Owing to both brain and brawn, innate talent that was probably what drew them together in the first place, they built their acreage into a working and earning farm in just two years.

The stock market crash had now begun to affect many of the neighboring farms. Up the road, two families had filed for bankruptcy, abandoning the land to try their luck in the big cities. Margaret and James had been able to scrape up enough money to keep things running; but they knew that they had to do something, or they would be forced to follow in their neighbors' footsteps.

Pride was not in their makeup; nor was bragging. They were of the ilk "work hard", and not just as a means to an end. Well before sunrise and well after sunset, the two of them labored through the sweltering hours in the Iowa summer, and the bitter cold of deepest winter.

This ride into the city, which began as the sun had just fully breached the horizon, could make or break the harvest this year and long into the future. The risk they were taking by forsaking a day's work for the journey had to pay off.

They saw almost no one else on the road until they were just outside Ottumwa. As the farmland turned into a small, densely populated city, other wagons loaded with goods or tools, as well as the occasional gas automobile, began to fill the thoroughfare.

James guided the horse towards the steeple that rose above the one-story buildings and tied her to the post outside the low red brick structure that spread out behind the church. The rusted stake beside the door held a wood sign hung on a short decrepit chain, the black peeling paint of the words barely legible: *Catholic Services Orphanage.*

James' knock on the door brought a long moment of silence. As was his way, he waited. Hefty hands at his side, his large frame matched that of his wife as she stood beside him. She, too, seemed built for farm life. As the sun rose to high noon above them, its strong light showed that the work clothes they wore were well-worn, but not poor.

Clean and proper, tall and sturdy and solemn, they stood outside patiently.

Finally, the door creaked open. A small elderly nun waved them inside to a dimly lit room that had one window and a wooden desk that took up most of the space. She bade them sit in the two folding chairs on one side of the desk, as she sat herself across from them.

"I am Sister Abigail," she stated.

Out of a drawer, she took a single sheet of paper and a quill pen. Without looking up, she asked them:

"Names?"

"James and Margaret Wilbur."

"Address?"

"Town of Tama, Sister. We own a homestead out there."

The nun looked up. She peered into their tanned, unsmiling faces, their serious eyes, their tense straight posture.

"What can I do for you, Mr. and Mrs. Wilbur?"

Margaret leaned forward and placed both hands on the desk.

"Sister, we can't have children. We've been trying for several years, and it is just not happening. We figured by now we would have at least a couple of little helpers running around."

She smiled at the thought for just a moment, then pushed away the bit of sadness that tried to seep in.

"We are here to bring home a boy who needs a family. He will be well fed and well cared for, Sister. With the way things are right now, we can't afford to hire hands on the farm, so he will be expected to help out around the homeplace and learn how to be a farmer. We are hoping for a big strong boy to call our own."

James made a grunting noise to voice his agreement.

The nun, her erect posture causing her to appear taller than her tiny stature should have allowed, responded, "Mrs. Wilbur, the oldest boy we have is just seven. Bigger boys don't last that long in the orphanage these days. He is tall and strong for his age and gives us no problems around here. He was dropped off two years ago by his father after his mother died. He goes by the name of Benjamin. That is all we know about him. Do you want to see him?"

The Wilburs looked at each other, knowing exactly what the other was thinking: seven was younger than they hoped for, but they did not want to go home empty-handed.

"Yes please, Sister," answered James for the two of them.

She stood, and they stood, and followed her through a door at the back of the room.

They entered a dining hall filled with well-worn long tables, each surrounded by eight chairs. The room had windows on two sides, which were all open, allowing a small draft to cross the otherwise very warm room. The hall was empty, lunch already having been served, consumed and cleaned up. The odor of chicken soup and fresh-baked bread still wafted lightly through the humid air.

The diminutive nun led them through another door, which opened to a small yard. The sounds of children playing and running drifted through the air as they watched the scene in front of them.

The majority of the twenty or so children were small, no older than five. They wore identical blue jumpers, and were all barefooted, as they whooped and hollered. Two more nuns, much younger than Sister Abigail, were trying to quiet the little ones; but not very seriously.

Crouching off to one side, drawing with a stick in the dirt, a boy had his back to the Wilburs. Judging by his size, they knew this must be Benjamin.

A small girl came up to him, as they watched, to see what he was doing. He put a stick in her chubby hand and showed her how to make a picture in the dirt. Margaret felt a flutter in her chest, and James' grunt showed his approval.

Just as Sister was about to walk them over to meet Benjamin, the sound of a baby's laughter pierced the scene. It was answered by a joyful belly laugh and followed by squeals of delight that seemed to echo off the brick wall behind them.

Margaret turned and caught sight of twin girls, around a year old, making faces at each other and laughing with utter abandon. Their white cotton bonnets covered dark curls, tied underneath round red cheeks. Their identical sturdy little bodies stood wobbling, each holding the finger of one of the nuns with her fat little fist.

Margaret was struck dumb by the sight. She watched them take tentative steps, fall on their bottoms laughing and haul themselves up to try again.

Next to her, James watched the babies and his wife. His eyes wrinkling slightly, his version of a smile, he walked over to the babies, bent down, and lifted each one easily in his arms. The delighted girls chortled and reached for his nose, his hair, his chin. One of them grabbed the ear closest to her and yanked hard enough to bring a tear to his eye. He turned with his armload of babies and said, "These two are spunky."

"Yes, sir," said a voice behind him. "They are my favorites of the babies, full of piss and vinegar."

"Benjamin!" scolded the youngest of the nuns. "What have we said about saying such things? Where do you even hear that kind of language?"

"Sorry, Sister. It was in the book I was reading this morning. It just means they are very spunky, sir." He looked up into James' face and smiled.

"As are you, young man," said Margaret, finally finding her voice.

She turned to look at her husband, and he nodded slightly.

"Excuse us for one moment," she said.

Margaret and James stepped aside and had a quiet conversation that lasted less than a minute, the babies wiggling in his broad arms.

Then she turned backed to the elderly nun and said, "We would like to take all three home with us. I think we would make a very good family."

She looked down into the boy's brown eyes. "What do you think, Benjamin?"

Benjamin took one heartbeat and one breath, and quietly said, "Yes, ma'am, I think we would."

"That settles it then. Sister, what do we have to sign? We would like to get on the road as soon as possible so we can get back to the farm before dark. Benjamin, have you ever been to a farm? We have sheep, cows, pigs, chickens, and corn and soybeans. It's a lot of work, but you don't look like you are afraid of work. Are you?"

"No ma'am, I am not," he responded seriously, standing up taller still, with a tone beyond his years. "I fix the Sisters' bicycles, and I help look after the little ones too."

The new family walked back through the dining hall, Benjamin carrying one of the babies, James still holding the other. They went into the small front room, which now seemed very cramped, as Sister Abigail explained what she knew about the girls.

"They came from somewhere in Eastern Europe, with a group of other children brought over by the Missionary Sisters of the Blessed Trinity about a month ago. After they arrived in California, the children were brought by train to different orphanages around the country. We received these two. Their exact date of birth is unknown. Their names on the papers said Ula and Wera."

Margaret and James both winced.

"We will be changing those," said Margaret, determined to give her girls good strong names.

Turning to James she said, "How about Lillian and Lucille, after your grandmother?"

He nodded assent, as Sister Abigail drew up the papers.

On the ride back, Benjamin sat up tall beside his new father. Margaret made a comfortable nest in the wagon for the babies, who immediately curled up together and fell asleep. Once they were out of the city and headed back on the country road, James handed his boy the reins and quietly gave him instructions. As the sun began to set, Benjamin guided the horse and wagon to the side of the house and stopped her with confidence. He looked up to see James smile with satisfaction, and then went to help

Margaret get the babies down and into the house.

He came back out to help James unhitch the wagon and drag it into the shed. They fed the horse in companionable silence and then Benjamin asked, "Can I explore, sir? I promise not to break anything."

"Call me dad now, son. And yes, go explore. Just listen for when your mother rings the dinner bell. She does not like to be kept waiting at supper time."

He patted the boy on the head and added, "I hear there's apple pie and ice cream for dessert."

"Yes sir! Dad! Yes, Dad!" Benjamin yelled, and he took off running toward the barns.

All three children quickly fit into the fabric of Wilbur family farm life.

Benjamin shadowed James around whenever he was not in school. He loved watching James at all the farm chores and jumped in to help as often as he could.

One day, James handed him a metal bucket and showed him how to milk a cow. Benjamin took the bucket and, shooing away a barn kitten, sat on a low stool. He reached out to get started while James watched. The cow was less than patient at his fumbling yankings. Benjamin tried to massage the udder with one hand while pulling the teats with the other the way James had shown him, but nothing came out. He pulled a bit harder, afraid to hurt the cow, and still nothing. He took a deep breath, tugged, and was rewarded with a solitary drop of milk.

James stood behind him trying not to laugh at his obvious frustration and said, "You have to grab the top of her teat just near the milk bag and clamp down really firmly, like I showed you, son. Want me to show you again?"

"No, sir!" Benjamin replied, determined to prove to his dad

that he could do it himself.

He grabbed just under the bag and pulled down harder than he thought he should. As he did so, the teat angled up and a long stream of milk shot out and hit Benjamin square in the face.

He fell backwards off the stool into the hay on the floor, sputtering. James lost his battle with himself and let out a hoot that the girls could hear in the chicken coop. He slapped his knee and grabbed his middle and stamped around the barn, alarming the cow. She lowed her complaint as he came back to look into Benjamin's dripping hang dog expression. James tried to rein it in but couldn't help himself, and this time when he guffawed loudly, he was pleased to hear Benjamin join in.

As soon as the babies could walk without wobbling too much, they began to help collect eggs and feed the chickens. When she was around three, Lillian dropped an egg, and as it broke at her feet, she let out a cry of anguish. She would not allow Margaret to clean it up, taking the hand broom from her, and clumsily brushing the sawdust and broken egg into the dustpan. Once she had done so, she looked at Margaret with tear-stained cheeks, holding the slimy dustpan out with evident sorrow.

It was all Margaret could do not to laugh at the sight of the tormented face, but she knew she had to make this a lesson. With the way things were, even one egg was important. She bit her tongue and gently but firmly scolded both girls; Lucille had reassuringly patted her sister's back as she cleaned up the mess, and now stood next to her with an identical devastated expression.

"Girls, you have to be more careful if you are going to help mama with the eggs. I cannot have you breaking them when we need them to eat and make our bread. Do you understand?"

Solemn nods from both, with black curls bobbing dramatically, almost sent Margaret over the edge, but she did not let them see her restrained mirth.

"Here, feed the chicks while I finish up," she said, handing each a small light basket filled with corn meal. The delighted girls giggled as they threw the feed to the fluffy yellow babies tumbling over each other to peck as much as they could before it was gone.

Yet, even as they found ways to have fun together, the world around them continued to fall apart.

News on the radio spoke of runs on banks, causing them to shutter their doors; and of unemployment and breadlines in towns across the nation. Despite the help of the children, everyone working every possible moment, the money ran dry. There was little market for the corn or apples, and none for the soybeans.

They began to burn dried corn on the cob for cooking and heat; and they were not alone. On cooler mornings, the whole countryside smelled like popcorn.

Margaret taught the little girls how to do basic needle work as soon as their tiny fingers could hold the wool and fabric steady. They both caught on quickly, and one morning when Margaret awoke with the sun, she found Lillian sitting on the dining bench near the window, with her little tongue between her teeth, carefully and slowly stitching up a tear in Lucille's favorite skirt. She was whispering over and over to herself the phrase they had heard on the radio news the night before: "Use it up, wear it out, make do or do without!"

The clothes they all wore began to fray, and soon tattered and fell apart, no matter how much mending they did. Margaret and the girls made rag dolls, which they tried to sell at the market; but the neighbors needed food, not toys, and they came home discouraged. They began to use the rapidly emptying feed sacks to make simple dresses and pants for the family.

The family learned to stretch their stores of food, grinding dried soybeans into flour for griddle cakes or dumplings, and boiling chicken carcasses to make a thin broth. Margaret and James skipped a meal when there was not enough for five to eat; and there never seemed to be enough. Not knowing how long this misery would last, they were frugal almost to the point of starving.

The bank still expected to be paid, and the tax bills kept mounting. Benjamin, at ten, offered to leave for the city to find work and send money home. Two of the neighbor boys, just a little older, had left for Chicago a week before. James and Margaret wouldn't hear of it.

"We stay together, son," James told him firmly. "You belong here with us, and we will work until this thing sorts itself out."

"It can't go on forever," Margaret added; and then glanced at James to see if he agreed. He nodded, and Benjamin did not bring it up again.

Lillian and Lucille did everything they could, as four-year-olds, to help. Lillian never complained, and when her twin whined occasionally about being hungry, she would distract her by making mud pies and decorating them with straw and pebbles.

James and Benjamin returned from town one steamy afternoon with news they had heard from neighbors. Many farmers were downright disgusted with the way things were going and were planning a strike. The prices of corn, soy, milk, and pork had dropped to levels that did not even pay the telephone rentals each month. The farmers planned to burn or dump everything instead of selling it for consumption. James and Margaret had a different idea, and set to pickling, canning, and preserving everything they could. In this way, the family could survive another winter, if need be.

The folks in town were also talking about the upcoming presidential election. Most of the farmers supported Hoover, saying this was not his fault and he was doing everything he could. A few said it was time for change, and Roosevelt was their man. On the day of the election, an early blizzard closed the roads into town, and James and Margaret could not even make it to the polls to cast their votes.

News that Roosevelt had been elected did not produce half of the excitement in the locals that the new Vice President did. Henry Wallace was an Iowan and knew about farming. Less than a year after coming into office, he had pushed through a Farm Bill that gave money to the farmers who cut down their yield; and James and Margaret's worries ended just like that.

Over the next eight years, the Wilbur farm expanded, and then expanded again. With the government money, they were able to purchase more dairy cows, and to hire men to work the fields. Having survived the Great Depression, their farm was now one of the largest in the area.

Lillian, Lucille, and Benjamin were able to concentrate on school much more, even though they were up with the dawn to do their chores. Lillian excelled in all her subjects, and often tutored Lucille. And one time, only because he wouldn't allow it again, she even helped Benjamin when he got stuck on a word in his reader.

Lillian, when she wasn't in school or doing chores, would usually be found fixing a bicycle, or tending to a hurt sheep or sickly chick. She baled hay with Benjamin, sweating alongside him in the muggy afternoons, and learned to run the smaller machinery. She always invited her twin along, but Lucille preferred to sit in the shade and sew new clothes for her dolls.

"You could sell these, you know, Lu," Lillian told her more than once, admiring the detailed ruffles on a dress or the tiny buttons down the back of a blouse. Lucille would just shrug, smile quietly and keep her needle moving.

In the evenings, after supper, the family would sit around the radio, James and Margaret in the overstuffed chairs, the three children on the floor at their feet. It was the best time of the day: all work done, supper dishes cleaned and put away, everyone in their cozy pajamas. Sunday night's show was Lillian's favorite; and this Halloween evening was no exception.

"Broadcast into your homes from the Columbia Broadcasting System, tonight we bring you the Mercury Theatre Repertory Company's "First Person Singular", featuring Orson Welles!" the announcer theatrically made the weekly introduction. The orchestra struck up dramatic music and Lillian could barely contain herself.

"The Columbia Broadcasting System and its affiliated stations present Orson Welles and the Mercury Theater on the Air in 'The War of the Worlds' by H.G. Wells!" followed by more symphonic music. Then, finally: "Ladies and gentlemen the director of the Mercury Theater and star of these broadcasts, Orson Welles…"

His deep, serious voice quietly and gravely began: "We know now that in the early years of the twentieth century, this world was being watched closely by intelligences greater than man."

At this the girls squealed and grabbed each other, hugging tight and holding on until the entire hour ended. The air in the room hummed with drama and delight as Orson Welles wove his tale of alien invasion and utter panic.

"That was the best story ever!" Lillian sighed with complete satisfaction, and everyone agreed.

Lillian and Lucille were in their last year of school when the teacher suddenly sent them home in the middle of morning lessons. Puzzled, they arrived quickly and found James, Margaret, Benjamin, and several of the farmhands gathered around the radio, still wearing their winter coats, listening intently.

They walked in to hear the somber voice of President Franklin Delano Roosevelt: "Mr. Vice President, Mr. Speaker, members of the Senate and of the House of Representatives...Yesterday, December 7th, 1941 — a date which will live in infamy — the United States of America was suddenly and deliberately attacked by naval and air forces of the Empire of Japan."

He went on for seven minutes, voice cutting through the thick silence in the room, ending with; "I ask that the Congress declare that since the unprovoked and dastardly attack by Japan on Sunday, December 7th, 1941, a state of war has existed between the United States and the Japanese empire."

"War!" Lillian exclaimed.

There was a long moment in the room when no one spoke, as it sank in.

"I'm going to enlist," Benjamin broke the silence, and looking at the other men, added, "Right now. Who is coming with me?"

All three nodded, and they climbed into the truck and drove rapidly away from the farm towards town.

Over the next months, after Benjamin left for the front, Lillian and Lucille did everything they could to help the war effort. They ran scrap drives to collect pots, pans, farm equipment and even children's metal toys for bombs, ammunition, tanks, guns, and battleships. They got neighbors to donate tires, raincoats, hot water bottles, boots, and floor mats to be made into gas masks, life rafts, cars, and bombers. They collected nylon stockings from women for miles around, and drove two hours to Fort Des Moines to drop them off, to be made into glider tow ropes, aircraft fuel tanks, flak jackets, shoelaces, mosquito netting, hammocks, and parachutes.

It was during this trip that Lillian saw, for the first time, women in uniform.

That night a thunderstorm raged outside her window, as she lay in bed trying to fall asleep. At some point, she dozed and then fell into a deep slumber. The lightning became gunfire; the thunder, bombs dropping out of the sky. Smoke obscured the scene before her, but then cleared and she saw trenches filled with young men, ducking then jumping up to shoot. A soldier stood tall, shooting repeatedly at unseen targets across a field. Suddenly a loud *zing* and he was hit. His body was thrown into the air momentarily and then fell face up into the dirt at the bottom of the trench: *Benjamin*.

She awoke gasping for air, her heart hammering in her chest.

As soon as she had taken care of her morning chores, she told her sister that she was going to visit a friend, got in the car and drove to Des Moines. The recruiting office had just opened, and there was a line of young men waiting outside the door. When she finally got in, the man at the desk looked her up and down.

"What can I do for you, doll? Can't you see these men who are waiting to sign up and fight, I don't have time for silliness." he said.

"I want to join the Army," Lillian stated. "I am a farm girl, not afraid of much. My brother is on the front lines, and I want to do my part."

The man sat up straighter. "Unless you can fly a plane, most dames in the Army are nurses. The nurses are at the front, with the men."

"A plane?" Lillian asked.

"Women's Flying Training Detachment at Hughes Airport in Houston, Texas. They're doing important work down there, relieving the men to go fight in battle. But you're too pretty to fly a plane. The men overseas could use a pretty face to take care of them. What do you say?"

"Where do I sign, sir?" was Lillian's response.

After the initial shock on her mother's face, many tears from Lucille and a proud hug from James, Lillian packed a suitcase and moved into an apartment with three other trainees, a block from the Mercy Nursing Hospital in Des Moines. The training was rigorous, and one of her roommates dropped out in exhaustion after just a month. Lillian had seen her share of blood and injuries on the farm; had spent sleepless nights tending to sick animals. Nothing fazed her and she impressed her superiors with her willingness to do anything they threw at her.

The year of nursing classes was followed by specialized military training. Lillian learned how to read military maps and passed grueling physical endurance tests. She and the others in her cohort learned how to set up hospitals complete with kitchens, operating rooms, and laboratories.

Part of the training included viewing newsreels from the front. One night, she sat in the darkened room watching the story of nurses arriving in North Africa.

"Early in the morning of 8 November 1942, sixty nurses attached to the 48th Surgical Hospital climbed over the side of a ship off the coast of North Africa and down an iron ladder into small assault boats." The announcer's voice-over, accompanied by dramatic music, explained the black and white film showing the action.

"Each boat carried 5 nurses, 3 medical officers, and 20 enlisted men. The nurses wore helmets and carried full packs, gas masks, and canteen belts. Only their Red Cross arm bands and lack of weapons distinguished them from fighting troops. They waded ashore near the coastal town of Arzew and huddled behind a sand dune while enemy snipers took potshots at anything that moved." narrated the announcer.

"That evening they found shelter in uninhabited beach houses. From there, they were sent on to an abandoned hospital and began caring for those injured in the fighting. They worked without electricity or running water, holding flashlights so the doctors could perform their life-saving surgeries through the night under near constant sniper fire."

Lillian watched, partly in fear and partly in admiration.

On another night, the newsreel featured the Italian front.

"The HMS Newfoundland, a hospital ship assigned to the Eighth Army, while en route to deliver over one hundred nurses to the beach in Salerno, Italy, was bombed on 12 September by a German fighter plane. The intense battle on shore kept the ship anchored out to sea, waiting for a break in the fighting to deliver the nurses. Several near misses aimed at the Newfoundland caused the captain to sail out forty nautical miles from shore. That night the ship was attacked, destroying the deck and setting fire to the lower decks, sending all on board over the sides into life rafts. Luckily, there were no casualties, but several injured nurses were evacuated to North Africa."

Less than two months later, Lillian was on her way to join these nurses in their important and harrowing work.

She sat on the lumbering C-54 airplane with twelve other nurses and a dozen medics, holding on to the leather strap tightly. She could barely hear the four propellers over the storm that raged outside. They should be arriving in Bari in the next hour to begin evacuating the soldiers injured on the front line in Sicily. Suddenly, the plane nosed up sharply and climbed with great effort. It breeched the storm cloud and flew above it for several moments.

"Bari station, this is the 807th Med Air Evac, do you read?" the pilot barked into the radio.

Static.

He repeated his call four times, punctuated by several curse words.

"Our instruments are down," he shouted to the crew and the medical personnel on board. "We are off-course. I'm going to aim for the beach north of Sicily, and we'll radio from there."

The plane descended roughly through the thunderheads, coming out almost directly behind two German fighter planes.

"Hang on!" the pilot yelled and pulled back the stick to find cover up in the storm.

For the next thirty minutes, lightning lit up the skies, showing mountain peaks all around them as the pilot fought for control. Erratic, violent jolts shook the plane as the passengers hung on to the straps with both hands. Some of the cargo broke loose and began sliding around them.

The pilot hollered over the racket, "Ice on the wings, we're coming in. Prepare for crash landing."

Lillian had time enough to think of Lucille, of James and Margaret, of Benjamin; and then, with a jarring, bouncing, metal screeching, cracking that went on for long minutes, the plane came to a stop.

As they looked at each other and did mental counts and checks, the door of the plane opened. Three men, armed with rifles but wearing civilian clothes, hurried in, and frantically waved them out.

Lillian grabbed her pack and, along with the others, climbed down. They followed the men, crouched over and scuttling through dark hills. They moved in silence for an hour, until they reached several shacks well-hidden among the trees.

The men took them inside, and lit fires in the fireplace. Lillian and the other nurses crowded into one of the huts together, and sat on top of their packs, rubbing their hands together to warm them. The man who stayed with them gave them a welcoming smile and began brewing a pot of coffee.

"Miresheareshiperi," he said to them. "Shiperi," he repeated, pointing around.

None of the women understood his words, but they knew he was not speaking Italian, or German.

The pilot came in soon after, holding a steaming cup. His face was set grimly as he spoke.

"Our radar went down. We crossed the Adriatic, and we are in Albania; lucky to be alive and lucky to have been found by these men. They are resistance fighters. They will help us get back to Italy."

He paused before continuing. "It is eight hundred miles through the mountains to the coast of the Adriatic. We leave in the morning. Go through your packs. Take canteen, tent, sleeping bag, rations. Put on all the gear you can. Do you girls have boots?"

Lillian looked down at her feet in despair. She wore lace-up leather shoes, as did all of the nurses. She took a deep breath and then said, "This is it, sir, but we can do it."

"Be ready at four hundred hours, then," he said, and left to go see the medics in the next hut.

In the darkest part of the night, they set out. The snow-covered hills made for treacherous footing as they made their way west. They hiked in single formation, Lillian and the other nurses behind the three guides and the flight crew.

As she climbed a nearly vertical stretch of the mountain, using icy rocks as hand holds, her foot slipped and she hung on with her bare fingers, working to find purchase. From below her, she felt a boost on her shoe and found a place to put it so she could continue on.

The first night, they pitched their tents on a flat area under trees, ate cold rations and slept little. Conversation was minimal, encouraging each other and themselves, as they rose with the gray dawn and set out again.

The next night, a blizzard raged, trapping them on an unprotected rock face. They took refuge in crags, curled up in tight balls to protect their exposed eyes and skin until it subsided. Using the guides' ice picks, they were able to climb to the top; but it took almost the entire day to get the whole group reassembled.

By the end of the week, one of the medics and two nurses were suffering frost bite on their faces. They all fashioned face coverings from one of the layers of socks. Their humid breath instantly froze on the improvised masks, but the extra insulation managed to protect their wind-whipped skin.

They caught a break in the weather the second week and were able to make better time.

After a month, the nurses' shoes began to wear out. They took their knives and cut apart a flap from their uniforms to wrap around their feet.

During another blinding snowstorm, the group stopped to camp and wait it out. As soon as it ended, they dug themselves out, began to quickly form up and prepare to move on.

"Wait," Lillian called, looking around for the nurses who were usually right behind her on the hikes. "Where are Judy, Len and Kay?"

The others dropped their packs and began searching. Their voices echoed off the mountains as they called the nurses' names. The guides took one of the crew and they walked back down the path they had taken.

When they returned without the nurses an hour later, the pilot commanded, "Form up, we cannot waste more time."

As they summited the next peak, Lillian could see only more mountains on all sides, and sent up a prayer for her friends.

It took months to reach the coast. During that time, Lillian treated one of the crew for pneumonia with the small amount of penicillin she carried in her medical musette bag. A medic came down with dysentery, and they spent two nights camping out waiting for his misery to abate. Two of the nurses suffered from jaundice, which they treated with iron supplements.

Several times, German fighter planes spotted them crossing peaks during the day and unloaded endless rounds of ammunition at them. After the first bout, the Luftwaffe was on the lookout for them, and they were forced to travel only in the darkest part of the night when the moon was not full. It slowed them down and made the going even more treacherous.

Helping each other along, they made it through, arriving in Bari with the beginning of 1944 to finally begin their service.

The majority of the soldiers' injuries at Bari were devastating enough to warrant that they be sent on hospital trains and ships to North Africa for treatment. Several of them suffered from symptoms Lillian had not seen or heard of before: blistered skin, severe respiratory distress, blindness, uncontrollable vomiting. These men took priority on the hospital planes.

For several months with little sleep, so much blood and death, and endless surgeries, Lillian returned to her cot every fourteen hours to get some rest before getting back to her patients. It became an incessant, overwhelming repetition of horror and exhaustion. She managed one letter home to let her family know she was well, giving them few details about her work. Before her eyes closed, she always got on her knees and sent up a prayer, for the wounded, for her family and for her lost friends.

One evening, on her way back to the hospital, anxious and distracted but determined to show confidence to the soldiers, she heard a familiar voice shout, "Lillian!"

Thinking she must be mistaken due to exhaustion, she turned and saw heading toward her Kay, Judy, and Len.

They all had wide smiles on their faces as they ran towards her. The little group hugged tightly, Lillian still in disbelief.

"After we got separated, we found our way to the town of Berat," Kay explained. "The Germans had Berat surrounded but the resistance kept us hidden for months. Finally, they were able to get us local identifications, we dressed like Albanian women, and we drove to the coast, right under their noses!"

Lillian's steps were a little springier that night as she went about her work. She was reading the clipboard of one of the injured Air Force gunners when she heard a voice from the other end of the bed.

"What are you smiling about today, Second Lieutenant Wilbur?"

She read his name off the chart before responding, "It's a good day, Airman Callahan. A good day."

"For me too," he said, "because your smile lights up the whole place. Please call me Glen, all my girlfriends do."

Lillian covered her mouth with her free hand to keep from laughing out loud and disturbing the hushed ward.

"Airman Callahan," she said, "Get some rest. You need it to heal those wounds properly. And, apparently, to keep up with all your girlfriends."

She moved on as he repeated, "Call me Glen!"

The rest of that night was a nightmarish series of emergency procedures for a fresh batch of fighters rushed in from Sicily. Lillian held up the intravenous bags while the doctors performed surgeries on limbs and organs. She tightened tourniquets, did the closing stitches on gaping wounds, and held the hands of two young soldiers as they died.

By the time she made it back to her cot, her face was haggard, her hair disheveled, and her eyes were nearly swollen shut. She slept for four hours, changed into a fresh uniform, and headed back to the hospital.

After the rush of the last twenty-four hours, things were thankfully quiet once again. Lillian checked on those who had come in the night before and discovered that four more had died. She helped prepare the men who were headed to North Africa by plane or train, speaking softly and reassuringly to them; and then did her regular rounds.

"Good morning, Second Lieutenant Wilbur," she heard, as she reached Airman Callahan's bed.

"I'm fairly sure it's the middle of the night, Airman Callahan," she responded, wiping her hand across her forehead to brush a wayward lock of hair out of her eyes so she could read his chart. "You seem to be feeling better, and your vitals are improving."

"You're vital," he responded in an earnest tone of voice.

"When I see you taking care of all the men, taking care of me, I'm awestruck. Even when you look a mess, like you do right now, you're still the prettiest thing in here."

"If I look 'a mess' it's because of what a mess you all are. It is a little hard to worry about if my make-up is done right when my face is covered in blood, Airman," Lillian said, and went to the next bed as he called after her, "Glen!"

For the next four months, a whirlwind for Lillian, the one highlight of her day became stopping to check in on Airman Callahan; "Glen."

He was dogged in trying to get a smile or two out of her each day, even more so when she thought she could not stand one more minute of the pain and devastation she witnessed without end. She would sit on the end of his bed for a few minutes, listening to his tales of missions over Europe and Africa; and sharing her own misadventure in the mountains of Albania.

Glen's wounds healed slowly. Shrapnel embedded in his legs from German anti-air guns caused several infections. At one point the doctors planned to amputate his leg, and it was only the extra care that Lillian gave him that saved it.

Late one night, when the ward was quiet, Glen said to her, "Lillian, I knew the first time I saw you that I was going to make you my wife."

"Is that right?" she said, smiling. "Won't all your girlfriends be disappointed?"

He took her hand. "The war can't go on forever, and the doctors are not sure if I will be combat ready again. Let's get married. Right here. Then we can plan the rest of our lives together."

Lillian gave him a measured, studied, long look; and then smiled her assent.

A week later, with nurses and medics standing around Glen's bed, the Army chaplain performed the marriage ceremony. Kay took a photograph, with her Kodak Six-20, of Glen sitting up as tall as he could, holding hands with Lillian as she stood next to his bed. Her uniform was sharply pressed. Her hair and make-up were perfect.

Glen was given a medical discharge and sent back to the states a few months later. His wounds had healed, but the limp would be permanent, disabling him from further service. He left his Purple Heart medal with his new bride, to hold until they were reunited.

As soon as he arrived back in the states, he went directly to Tama to introduce himself to his new father-in-law and the rest of the family. He limped into the house, gave James a firm handshake and promised to be a good husband to his daughter. His twinkling blue eyes made Lucille clap her hands in approval; and Margaret made enough food for the whole U.S. Army. Glen stayed with them at the farm while he made arrangements.

By the time Lillian returned at the end of the war, Glen had a job at the University of Iowa teaching history and was finalizing plans on building a new home a block away from the campus.

Lillian became pregnant one month after she returned to Iowa. They had just moved into the new house when she gave birth to a boy at the university hospital. They named him Sam, as a tribute to the military that had brought them together. They had a family portrait taken, and Lillian placed it on the sideboard next to the wedding photo Kay had taken.

Four months later, Lillian became pregnant again. She seemed to have more trouble with this pregnancy, becoming large very early, and needing bed rest as much as possible. Glen hired a nurse to care for her and to help with Sam, still an infant.

When she went into labor, Glen brought her to the hospital, where they administered the usual morphine and scopolamine to put Lillian into "twilight sleep" for the birth Glen stayed in the waiting room, pacing and drinking coffee that the nurses brought him.

Hours passed before the doctor came to see him.

"Twin boys, Mr. Callahan! Both healthy, and Mother is doing fine. She will sleep for another few hours and then you can see her. Congratulations!"

A nurse handed him a cigar, which he lit, puffing proudly as he strode to the maternity window to look at his new sons. Another father was already standing in the large window in front of the rows of infants.

"That's my girl, my first!" he said, indicating a bassinette with the smoking end of his cigar.

"Congratulations," Glen said. "Those are my boys there. Already have one at home named Sam, for Uncle Sam. I'm going to name these two after my father, Tiernan. Tom and Terry, those are my boys!"

"Congratulations to you, too! Did you serve in the war?"

"Twelfth Air Force gunner Callahan at your service!" Glen responded.

"Eighty-eighth Infantry Division, enlisted. Corporal Garret Morse," the man said.

They shook hands, and then Garret added, "What do you say we celebrate, Airman Callahan? I think you get a drink on the house at the American Legion when your wife has a baby. Since you have twins, you might even get two."

Garret was right. The first two were on the house, and the next ten were bought by the other veterans in the lounge.

Two of the men at the Legion were fellow Betas. They exchanged tales of harrowing missions and sad news of lost comrades. Glen, reeling on his feet, had to be brought home by one of the other men, and poured into his bed.

When Lillian came home from the hospital, it took months for her to get back on her feet. She was nursing the twins every two hours, and Sam, who had been moving on to the bottle, suddenly wanted her breast again, too.

"I've never seen such hungry babies," Margaret exclaimed, when she came to help. "They never seem to stop eating!"

The more they ate, the more they grew; and before a year was out, all three were on running wild around the house. Lillian decided she needed help from above and joined Saint Patrick's Catholic Church.

"My grandmother would have approved," Glen told her.

She would not have approved of you spending so much time with your vet friends at the Legion, Lillian thought; but did not say aloud. She had once confronted him about his worsening habits, on one of the increasingly infrequent nights he was home and sober.

"This is not how I thought my life would be," he said shortly and bitterly. "Besides, it's a man's right to do as he pleases, so go cook some dinner. Or do I need to get something to eat at the Legion?"

Just a month after the twins turned one, Lillian found herself pregnant again. The ladies at the church were beside themselves, calling her a good Catholic and baking casseroles for the family.

Lillian embraced her church community. It gave her something she had been missing since her days as a military nurse: camaraderie. She walked the boys every day to morning Mass and stayed to help with charity work. She joined the Catholic Daughters of the Americas, and with her group of friends there, often prepared meals for the poor or collected items from the area to donate.

She became a religion teacher for the littlest of the children. Although she used storytelling to keep it fun, she was a strict taskmaster on the toddlers; a well-placed smack got everyone's attention pretty quickly.

It was a running joke among the church ladies that she was related to almost all of her students, and it was largely true: owing to Glen's sisters there were already many cousins in town. Her current pregnancy would become number thirty-one.

Of all the church activities, her favorite days were bake sales. Her hummingbird cakes and apple gingerbread pie were famous in the church community. At Christmas, the church ladies themselves fought over her sugar cream pies and yule logs before they even made it to the sale tables.

"You're a miracle," her friend Ginger said to her one morning, as they sat under the shade of a tree after Mass.

It was an Indian Summer day, one of those unexpectedly warm times that made Lillian think of the summer just past, and the bitter winter that was on the way. Sam, Tom, Terry, and Ginger's four boys ran wild around them.

"You always seem so calm and focused. How do you do it?"

"I guess the military training really helps," Lillian said, laughing. "I run my boys like an army troop. I wish I could run Glen like one, too," she added.

"He stops off at the Legion almost every day after work. Sometimes he is drunk when he gets home at dinner time. Sometimes, he doesn't get home until late at night."

She paused and then added, "Sometimes, he smells like perfume."

Ginger became instantly uncomfortable.

"The men will do what they will do, Lillian. 'Wives, be subject to your husbands as you are to the Lord. For the husband is the head of the wife just as Christ is the head of the church.' *1 Corinthians 14:34-35.* You are lucky God brought you to him, remember that."

It was the last time Lillian brought up her worries to anyone.

The baby came right on time, another healthy boy they named Joseph.

Her next pregnancy came right on time, too, when Joseph was just three months old.

When Cam was born, little Joe would not leave him alone. He was fascinated by the baby, patting his belly when he cried, and bringing him toys to entertain him. As soon as Cam could walk, Joe would hold his hand and take him to explore a sandbox or a swing at the park. Lillian loved to watch all her boys at play.

"No, not like that!" Sam would command, if any of them stepped out of line when Sam had one of his many plans for their games. "I am the Army captain. T's, you are the Germans. Joe and Cam, you are my soldiers. Now, form up, men. We are getting ready for the battle of Big Tree Hill!"

Lillian loved her boys, but secretly hoped the next baby would be a "little lass", as her father-in-law would say. When they went to City Park in the summer to swim, she enviously watched the small girls playing in the shallow end in their pink ruffled swimsuits, long strawberry blonde pigtails swinging around their heads, loudly chattering away.

When she became pregnant, she knitted pink booties and bonnets; and sent up a prayer every day at Mass. Five months into the pregnancy, she awoke just after midnight in terrible pain. Gritting her teeth to keep from screaming, she shook Glen; but he had just gotten home and was clearly not going to wake up.

She called Ginger, who lived two houses down. Ginger answered the phone after nine rings, her voice sleepy and alarmed at the same time. Ginger threw a coat over her pajamas and came to pick Lillian up to drive her to the hospital. When the nurse took Lillian, writhing and bleeding, away in a wheelchair, Ginger paced in the waiting room. Barely an hour later, the same nurse came back to talk to her.

"I'm sorry," she said. "Your friend lost her baby. She also lost quite a bit of blood and will have to stay for a day or two until she regains her strength."

The next day, Ginger rallied the church ladies, who once again plied Lillian's family with casseroles and Bundt cakes.

When Lillian returned home early the following evening, she found utter chaos in every room of the house. Cam and Joe were sitting on the kitchen table, eating out of cold baking dishes with their hands. Glen was watching television, holding a beer and a cigarette.

"So, you lost our baby," he said, his voice slightly slurred. "That's okay, the next one will stick. Get me something to eat, and another beer. And clean up the mess in the kitchen. Those boys are animals."

Lillian, seething but too exhausted to even respond, did as he told her. She then put the boys to bed and climbed in to her own. She heard the front door close as Glen left; and when he returned after several hours, she felt him climb into bed and push against her insistently.

"The doctor said to wait at least a month." She pushed him firmly away.

"Fucking doctors, what do they know," he said, but he rolled over and was snoring long before she fell back to sleep.

Two months later, she missed her period. She felt a mix of hope and fear when it did not come after a few more weeks. She did not say anything to Glen, or to anyone else, except in her prayers. Three months in, the cramps came hard, and heavy bleeding soon followed. Lillian took care of it herself.

A few months later, the same thing happened. This time, Lillian went to her doctor and told him. He did a preliminary exam, pronounced her healthy and sent her on her way.

Lillian found she did not bounce back quickly like she had before. Over the next year, she did not feel much like eating, her energy level was low, her back was constantly crampy; and when Glen bothered her at night, she had to bite her tongue to keep from screaming in pain.

Her menstruation did not return after the last miscarriage. At first, Lillian thought she was pregnant again, but the pain and discomfort continued for almost two years. She confided in her mother, who tried but failed to get her to go back to the doctor.

One Spring morning, as she was helping to load boxes of donated clothing into the church truck, she swayed noticeably.

"Are you okay?" Ginger asked, placing a steadying hand on her friend's shoulder.

Lillian sat wearily on one of the boxes.

"I don't know," she answered. "I haven't been well for a while. The doctor said it was nothing."

"This does not seem like nothing to me. You are gaunt and pale; you haven't smiled in months and you're tired all the time. Call the doctor and tell him you are coming right now."

This time while he examined her, the doctor's faced changed. He frowned as he moved his fingers around inside her, pushing on her abdomen with the other hand. She winced at each prodding and let out a small gasp several times. Finally, he pulled his rubber gloves off with a resounding snap and helped her sit up.

"I want you to go to the hospital," he said.

"Okay," she responded. "I have to make dinner for the boys, get the laundry done and finish labelling some boxes for the church drive. I could be there tomorrow around four…"

"Now," the doctor said.

"But Glen and the boys…"

"Now," the doctor repeated.

She looked at his serious and unwavering eyes, battling with herself for a moment. Then, she went.

When she left the hospital that afternoon, her face was ashen. She recalled sitting down in the large warm office to hear the diagnosis: *cancer*.

For the next few months, Lillian told no one. She took care of Glen, the boys, the house, the charity work; stealing away hours in between to take the chemotherapy treatments in secret. She was able to hide her constant vomiting and cover her head with kerchiefs when her hair began to fall out. Her weakness and lack of energy was harder to cover up, but Glen never noticed.

On a rare night Glen came home from work early, and they had a nice family dinner. She put the boys to bed, cleaned up and joined him in front of the television to watch the latest episode of Gunsmoke. He put his arm around her shoulder and pulled her to lean against him.

"This is nice," he said. "We should do it more often."

Lillian put her face in her hand and began to cry. Glen sat up and turned towards her. In the background, there was shooting and yelling as Marshall Matt Dillon once again tried to maintain order in Dodge City. Glen waited for her to get control of herself.

Once she was able to speak, she said, "Glen, I have ovarian cancer."

As he watched, she slowly removed the scarf from her head. He gasped at her nearly bare scalp.

"Shit, Lillian. Since when? What did the doctor say? Are you going to…" he couldn't finish.

"I have been doing chemotherapy for months. It doesn't seem to be working. The cancer has spread to my liver. He wants to do surgery next, and then more chemotherapy. There isn't much else that can be done."

"Surgery? When?" Glen asked. "We can hire someone to help you with the kids and house for a while, but honestly, money has been a little tight. The Dean cut my classes back, I'm only teaching part time now."

"What? Did he say why, Glen? That doesn't seem fair, you've been there for years now. I don't understand."

"I guess some of these stupid kids have been complaining about my classes. They just want everything handed to them easily. Not like when I was in college. You respected your professor, no matter what. Anyway, let's get you well so we don't have to worry about paying someone else to do your job, right?

"Yes, Glen," she responded, and he pulled her down to lean on his shoulder and finished watching the show.

Lillian and Glen did not tell the children that she was going into the hospital for a week; only that she would be away. One of Glen's sisters took the children into her home. Thinking of her six nieces and nephews and the five Callahan boys spending a week together, Lillian was in a hurry to get this over with and get back to her family.

It did not go well. After she returned from the recovery room, the doctor stood next to her hospital bed, looking at Glen as he spoke.

"I'm sorry, we got as much as we could, but it is too advanced. We will step up her treatments to try to stop more spread. I can't promise you that it will work. She will be in and out of the hospital for the next several months. Then we will re-evaluate her progress and go from there."

"Shit," Glen muttered, as the doctor left the room.

"I'm sorry, Glen," Lillian said, still groggy from the medication. "I'll do the best I can."

Lillian came home but could not keep up with the housework or the boys. She spent much of her time in bed or on the couch, scolding the boys and urging them to do their part to keep the house orderly. Sam and the twins would usually ignore her, slamming the door behind them as they left to shoot some baskets at the University field house. The younger boys made an effort to help, but the place very quickly got out of hand.

Glen had let the housecleaner go, and Lillian's church friends and sisters-in-law did what they could; but they all had their own households to maintain. At least there was always food in the refrigerator.

Cam and Joe made her Campbells' Tomato Soup and a grilled cheese sandwich every day for lunch.

"Thank you, my good boys," she would say weakly, touching their cheeks.

"Are you sick, mama?" Cam asked one day, as Lillian nibbled a corner of the bread.

She usually waited until they left the room to hide the sandwich uneaten, but today Joe and Cam had questions. She gave them a small smile that she prayed would reassure them.

"I don't feel that well, boys. I should be better soon, but for now I thank you for taking such good care of me."

She nibbled another small corner and worked to swallow it without gagging. Each of them gave her a careful hug, and then they too went out the door; and Lillian was left alone with her thoughts.

After another year, it became clear that Lillian's treatment was no longer working. She went into the hospital, where the doctor made her as comfortable with morphine as possible. Glen came to see her almost every afternoon, sometimes smelling of booze.

One morning he came on his way to the University.

"You're here early today," she said.

"Big night tonight. After the Hawkeyes' final, Coach Lute Olson is coming back to the Legion to celebrate. It's going to be a late one."

"Glen," she said to him, her voice weak but urgent. "I'm not going to make it. The doctor said so. You have to take care of the boys. They need you. You have to stop drinking and get work full time and find someone to help you. I don't know how much longer I have, and the doctor says I am not coming home. I'm begging you, please, tell me you will take care of them so I can rest in peace."

"Sure, I will, Lillian. They'll be fine, don't you worry. They're big strong boys, quite a little crew. Now, I have to go, but I'll bring the boys tomorrow, okay?"

He patted her arm gingerly and left.

When Glen showed up with Sam, Tom, Terry, Joe and Cam the following afternoon, Lillian's eyes were closed, and a nurse was adjusting her bedding.

"She's very tired now, boys," said the nurse in a quiet tone. "You keep your voices down, hear?"

They all gathered around her bed. Cam and Joe took her hands, which roused her awake. She smiled at each of them as best she could.

"You boys take care of each other no matter what happens," she said to them all. "I want you to promise you will grow up to be good men, good husbands, good fathers. Will you promise me?"

They all nodded, and Cam said, "Yes, Mama.

That evening, Glen was home stirring up five boxes of Kraft macaroni and cheese when the phone on the kitchen wall rang.

"Hello? Oh. Yes, okay. I see. Ten minutes ago? Okay. Yes, I know. I appreciate it. Thanks, goodbye."

He slowly hung up the receiver, and then turned towards the living room, where all five of the brothers were piled on the couch watching a Rin Tin Tin cartoon.

"Boys!" he called. "Come here. I have something to tell you."

Cam's Story

The cop was right behind them as the four boys dashed down the narrow dark alley.

"Split up!" shouted Mike, veering to the right with Cam on his heels. They turned the corner and crouched low against the brick wall as the crunching steps and heavy breathing approached. The police officer paused for a moment, deciding which two to chase. In that moment, Mike stood up, raised the flashlight he was still holding with both hands and, sneaking up behind the officer, brought it down on his head hard enough to make a solid *thunk*.

"Shit!!" yelled Cam.

Both boys were laughing as they raced back down the alley and out on to the street. They ran full bore into the side of another police cruiser that had just pulled up. Mike bounced off, spun around and sprinted away. Cam hit so hard, it knocked him to his behind on the street. By the time he tried to get up, two cops were standing over him. One dangled a shiny, clinking set of handcuffs. The other hauled him up and held Cam's wrists as the cuffs were snapped closed. They were heaving him into the back seat when the officer came walking out of the alley, rubbing his head, and looking pissed. They rode back to the station in silence, then pushed Cam in the door and plopped him down at a desk.

The officer at the desk turned his chair, looked up, sighed and said, "Again, Cam? What is it this time, stealing more radios out of cars?"

The cop still sullenly rubbing his head said, "Clocked me a

good one trying to get away. Him and them other boys were ripping off radios at the same parking lot as last time. Pretty stupid, going back to the same place twice in a row. Gonna call his dad, Sarg?"

"Are you the one who thumped Officer Johnson here?" the sergeant asked.

Cam gave him a tight smile in response.

"Loyal to a fault. That'll get you nowhere fast," he said, shaking his head as he picked up the heavy plastic handset of the black telephone sitting on his desk.

He had to untangle the cord before he could dial, which gave him time to look at Cam and sigh again. Cam could hear the rings come through the receiver, four of them, before his father picked up.

"Hullo?"

"Glenn? Sergeant Joe, Iowa City PD."

"Oh, for Chrissake, which one this time?" the overly loud slur came through the line clearly.

Cam rolled his eyes and slumped down in the chair.

"It's Cam. What do you want me to do?"

He stood up and walked as far away as the cord stretched and listened. "You got it. See you later."

Hanging up, he said to Cam, "In the cell you go. I'll drop you off after my shift. Sit there and think, Cam Callahan. You're a smart fella. I know you're sixteen and think you'll never get any older, but you will. What are you going to do with yourself? Do you want to spend a lot of time in a cage? 'Cause that is where you are headed if you don't get your shit together."

Just after eleven o'clock, Sergeant Joe dropped Cam off in front of his house.

Before he unlocked the door to let him out, he turned to the back seat and said, "Smarten up, Cam. I know you haven't had it easy, with your mom passing and all. My daughter says you're at the top of your class. You should use that brain of yours more."

As Cam got out of the car, Sergeant Joe yelled after him, "Get your shit together."

The houses on the quiet street were all dark, except for his. Lit up like Christmas as usual, Cam thought as he stood on the sidewalk and geared himself up for what waited inside. Squaring his shoulders, he walked up to the door and stepped in.

His father sat in front of the television staring at the vertical rainbow test pattern as if there were still a channel broadcasting a show. A bottle of Smirnoff vodka, two thirds empty, and several open beer cans sat on the table in front of him. His bleary eyes left the television set and landed on Cam at the sound of the door shutting.

Without warning he launched himself at the boy, fist flying in hard and catching Cam just below his eye. Cam staggered back but did not fall. He came at his father with his own fist cocked and caught him in the same spot.

Glen's feet couldn't hold him, and he lurched back, tottered, and fell over the table, narrowly missing the T.V. screen. He snorted once and then lay there, out cold.

Cam rubbed his bruised knuckles, took a long swig from the Smirnoff, and went to bed.

When Cam woke up mid-morning, his father was gone. The now-empty bottle of vodka was laying on its side on the table. Probably at the Legion having a seven course Irish breakfast- a six pack and a potato, only minus the potato, Cam thought; or picking his next girlfriend off a barstool, or buying a round for Sergeant Joe, Iowa City PD.

He was standing in the kitchen slurping down his bowl of

Froot Loops when he heard footsteps behind him and felt a solid smack on the back of his head.

"Hey, little shit, whoa…" his brother Joe whistled when Cam turned around. "Dad tuned you up again, huh? Come on, man, you know how he gets. Just stay out of his way, for crying out loud."

"Yeah, what's wrong with you?!"

"Dumb ass!"

"Stupid shit!"

The three older brothers came noisily into the kitchen, shoving each other to get at the cereal box first. Sam grabbed Cam's bowl out of his hand, tilted his head back and poured the multi-colored O's and brownish milk down his throat.

"Thanks, little brother," he said, putting it back in Cam's hands, which were still up in bowl-holding position.

Sam wiped his mouth on his sleeve and walked out the door. They all heard the revving motor of the '65 Mustang Sam had rebuilt in their garage, as he drove off down the street, tires squealing.

Tom and Terry, the "T Twins" as they were called by their teachers, were wrestling over the box of Froot Loops. They each poured as much as they could into their mouths, and all over the floor, before the other grabbed it back to do the same.

When it was empty, Tom threw it into the trash across the room, yelled, "Two points!", wrapped his arm around Terry's neck in a chokehold and dragged him out the door.

Joseph and Cam cleaned up the mess. They knew they would catch hell if Glen came home and found the kitchen like this. Then they walked across the street to the University campus. The field house was closed for the month, until the Hawkeyes returned for training. The boys knew the maintenance workers would let them in if they wanted to shoot some hoops but decided to walk around before the July heat and humidity beat them up too bad.

"It's so weird now, man," Joe said. "Just last year, you'd see people sitting around smoking grass, frisbees flying, peace flags everywhere."

"Naked people climbing the lampposts…" added Cam, making them both laugh.

"End a war, and life just snaps back to normal," Joe mused.

"If you don't count two dead cousins and few neighbor kids too," Cam said. "It ended just in time or you, Sam and the T's might have been called up next."

They walked for a while in thoughtful silence.

"What are you gonna do, Joe? How long are you gonna stick around and get the shit kicked out of you every time Glen gets mean?"

"I don't know," Joe responded. "I'm thinking maybe take a job with the Connolly's at their garage, fix up some cars, get a little place downtown. What about you, little bro?"

"I'm not that little, asshole, stop calling me that. I don't know either. Maybe go check out the recruiting office when I graduate. Get the fuck outta dodge."

"I'd miss your ugly face," Joe said, throwing a soft punch at Cam's other eye, then grabbing him around the neck and giving the top of his head noogies with his knuckles.

They fell to the grass, wrestling and laughing; then lay there in comfortable silence, staring up at the blue sky, sweat dripping off their summer buzz cuts.

A week later, Cam found himself sitting in the front seat of Mike's dad's car hurtling down the highway. Keith and Randy were passing a joint to each other in the back seat.

"Hey, bogarts, pass that doobie up here," Mike said, having to yell over the Styx 8-track that was blasting out of the speakers.

He took a long drag, and holding it, said in a choked voice to Cam, "Want a hit?"

Cam took the joint, hit it and passed it back to Randy. As he slowly blew out the blue smoke, he watched the giant billboards go by. They were even more entertaining when you're stoned, he thought.

"RCA Color TV! Live life in living color!" read one slogan on the highway advertisement, with a lightning bolt shooting off the A.

"I'd walk a mile for a Camel!" read another, with actual smoke rings blowing out of the mouth of the Elvis look-alike.

"Stuckey's! Pecan Rolls!"

"Stuckey's! Breakfast anytime!"

"Stuckey's! Snack bar, candies, Arkansas souvenirs and gifts!"

"Schaefer is the one beer to have when you're having more than one!"

That jingle flashed into his head and wouldn't go away. It made him thirsty, so he popped the tab on a can of Pabst Blue Ribbon from the case under his feet.

"Hey, me too," yelled both the boys from the back seat.

Cam handed each of them a beer, and then cracked one for Mike, who grabbed it, tilted his head back and slurped half the can down.

Hours later, the empty box crushed under his feet, the crumpled cans scattered around the floor of the car with the candy wrappers and potato chip bags, they pulled up to the parking lot of the beach in Biloxi, Mississippi. Keith and Randy were leaning on each other and snoring.

Cam and Mike got stiffly out of the car, stretched, and walked to the shoreline of the Gulf of Mexico. The full moon cast an eerie glow to the soft sound of waves washing up. After a few minutes, they walked back to the boardwalk, and crawled under it, digging nests for themselves. They slept until the sun came up.

The boys spent the better part of that day playing in the water and lounging on the sand in their boxers. Hundreds of families, many spilling out of cars with Iowa, Missouri, and Illinois plates, filled the white sand beach with colorful umbrellas and blankets; and filled the humid air with children's screams and tinny music from transistor radios.

As the sun went down, and the beach emptied, Randy finished the last can of Pabst from the two cases they had picked up and let out a long slow burp which made him smile proudly.

Keith, chewing a large bite of hoagie with his mouth open, said, "I think we should have a night on the town, boys."

He licked the mayo from his fingers, wiped his hand on his Iowa Hawkeyes shirt, and shoved the rest of the large sandwich into his mouth. A piece of boloney fell on his lap, and he picked it up and crammed it in with the rest.

Cam threw a pickle at his face in agreement.

As the other boys stood up and began walking to the car, Cam called, "Hey, you gonna leave this mess on the beach?!"

When he got no answer except a lifted middle finger from Randy, he stuffed all the garbage into one of the empty beer boxes and put it in the rubbish can near the car.

They sauntered up to Howard Avenue. Some of the store fronts on the main street in Biloxi were empty, and all the shops were closed. They heard loud music coming from a block over and headed that way. The bar was so packed, there were people standing on the street holding drinks and bopping to a pretty good Eagles cover band.

The boys shoved their way through the door and up to the

smoky, lively bar, and ordered four beers. It was so loud they did not even try to talk, raising empty cans over and over again to signal the bartender for another round.

Cam looked over the crowd of dancers hopping and jumping to the thumping music. He spotted a girl in a mini skirt holding hands with three other girls, all of them swaying in different rhythms. Her long brown hair brushed her waist, her eyes were bright, and when she turned and saw Cam watching, her smile widened, and she waved at him.

Squeezing through the throng, he boogied his way over to her, and giggling, she grabbed him around the waist, and they danced together. Seeing this, the other three shoved their way to the dance floor and started bopping with her friends. Every time the band started a new song, the dancers roared approval, fists up and pumping in time to the beat. Keith and Randy went back to the bar several times, balancing full beers for all of them, sloshing some as they got jostled by the crowd on the way back.

Midway through a good rendition of the Eagles' newest hit, "Lyin' Eyes", one of the girls turned her head as she danced, and squealed, pointing. A group of young men dressed in Navy whites was entering the bar. All three of them walked straight and tall over to the bartender and ordered whiskeys neat, before leaning on the bar to survey the place.

The girl who had squealed grabbed one of the other girls' hand, and they quickly made their way over to the sailors, giggling, batting their eyelashes and twirling their hair. Randy elbowed Keith who elbowed Mike who elbowed Cam, who was busy trying to get a kiss out of his dance partner.

Mike shouted, "Come on!" and Cam reluctantly let go of the girl's waist.

A bit wobbly from the beers, but held up by the jammed

crowd, they puffed up their chests and moved towards the sailors.

Mike poked the tallest one on the shoulder and shouted in his face to be heard over the racket.

"We were talking to these girls first, man."

The sailor brushed at his shoulder as if there was a speck on his spotless uniform.

He shouted back, "Well, I guess they want to talk to us now, *man.*"

He turned his back on Mike.

"I said, we were talking to them," Mike repeated loudly, shoving the man so hard he stumbled against one of his friends.

At this, the three of them turned to the boys and one of the other sailors gave Mike a solid shove, pushing him into Keith and Randy.

"Hey, take it outside!" the bartender yelled.

He picked up the phone receiver, held it to his ear and started dialing. "I'm calling the cops."

Mike gave the bartender a poor excuse of a military salute and gestured to the sailors. "After you."

"No, we insist, after you," the tallest one said, beginning to unbutton his shirt.

The boys filed towards the door. Mike, Keith, and Randy stepped outside and started rolling up their sleeves. Cam was next, the sailors on his heels.

As he crossed the threshold, Cam suddenly turned without warning, fist cocked back, and delivered a solid right hook into the mouth of the young man who was right behind him. He rocked back into the other two, who roared and jumped onto the boys, fists flying.

The sailor that Cam had punched came for him, blood staining his snarling teeth. Randy and Keith tackled the tallest one to the ground, fists and feet pummeling him while he fought back viciously. Mike and his sailor were trading hit for hit like boxers, both bleeding from knuckles and noses. Mike got in a good roundhouse punch and knocked the sailor's front tooth flying into the screaming and cheering crowd gathered around them.

Sirens blared rhythmically in the background of the melee, growing rapidly louder. Four Biloxi police cars screeched to a halt in the street.

The eight police officers who stepped out of their cars took a moment to size up the situation. They went to work separating the sailors from the boys, pushing the Navy men away into the crowd. In minutes, the boys, bleeding, sweating, and huffing hard, were in cuffs in the back of the cars and heading for the precinct.

"Y'all shouldn'ta come down here from Ioway and messed around with our Seabees, boys," the cop said to Cam and Randy through the cage between the seats as he drove. "We love our Navy and don't take kindly to Northern idjits bothering them. Or our ladies either. I reckon if we see you 'round these parts again, there'll be H-E-double hockey sticks to pay. Am I making myself clear?"

The boys just rolled their eyes.

They were, not gently, thrown into a jail cell.

Keith yelled out, "Hey! I know my rights! Phone call?!"

One of the cops handed a telephone through the bars of the cell. Cam picked up the handset and, under the watchful eyes of the police officer, dialed his home number. He closed his eyes and prayed that one of his brothers answered.

When he heard Sam say, "Yeah?", he let his breath out.

"Hi, *DAD*. Listen, *DAD*, we got in a little trouble down here in Biloxi. I'm gonna need you to wire some money to the Biloxi PD."

A suddenly-deepened voice responded, "Okay, *Son*, I'll do it right now. How much do you all need?"

Cam and the boys knew they'd be paying more than money for this favor, but they had no choice. After a night spent in the Biloxi jail, they were back in Mike's dad's car racing north, and laughing about their Mississippi trip.

"H-E double hockey sticks, y'all! Best not bother the Southern Belles, ya hear!" Randy yelled in a fairly good imitation of a Southern accent.

"Back to Ioway, ya idjits!" Keith joined in, as they zipped up the highway to home.

The rest of the summer went by in a whirl of camping, swimming in the quarry and mowing lawns for a buck a piece in the sweltering heat, to pay Sam back for the bail money. They also had to drive him to the titty bar whenever he commanded them to; and pick him up when he was done.

On Cam's seventeenth birthday, his whole class, which included four of his cousins, turned out at a raging kegger on a farm owned by one of the church families. The party went all night, with kids passing out in corn fields, on the hoods of cars, and on the ground by the bonfire.

Cam and Sergeant Joe's daughter Evelyn were among the last ones awake. The high energy and racket had died down gradually as the kids conked out, and it was now quiet except for the first chirping of early birds and the crackling of the giant fire that still raged in the pit.

"To Senior Year!" she said, raising her red solo cup.

Cam tapped her cup with his and sipped, drunkenly thoughtful.

"What are you gonna do after graduation?' he asked her.

"I'm gonna be an Iowa Hawkeye! Maybe I'll be a lawyer,

defend all the poor saps my dad arrests" she answered boozily, but pointedly. "What about you? You could get into any college, you know."

Cam shrugged and drained his beer; then lay down on his back, still holding the cup, and fell asleep.

Cam's senior year at Trinity High School did not go well. Even though his marks were near the top of his class, Sister Margarite could not tolerate his sneakers, his untucked shirt, the hair that had begun to creep over his ears. Cam, in his turn, could not tolerate the bullshit.

"What difference does it make what I wear on my feet, Sister? Jesus loves me anyway, isn't that what you teach us?" Cam would challenge her when she complained.

After months of his backtalking and arguing, she had had enough. She would turn deep red after each of these exchanges and, tight-lipped, point to the door.

Cam began to cut class, and then began to cut whole days, and by May of his senior year, he stopped going all together. He got a job at the country club restaurant washing dishes, and passed his GED high school equivalency test on the first try without studying.

He smugly tacked the certificate on the wall thinking, *I graduated before my class did, Sister Margarite. Wearing sneakers.*

That summer, he, Joe, and Randy got jobs caddying at the country club. Cam noticed that the drunker the golfers were, the more money they tipped; so, he made it his business to keep their cups filled.

By August, he had a small pile of cash. After a sweltering day carrying heavy golf bags on the links, he and Randy went downtown to the strip club and drank themselves dizzy. Randy kept elbowing Cam for dollar bills to give the naked women dancing above them on the stage.

None of them attracted Cam's attention for long and he stared out the plate-glass window, watching the people walk by. He was amused when groups of girls stopped to check their hair and make-up in the two-way mirrored window, not realizing they were part of the show for the horny men inside the place.

As he was watching a really hot group of college students fixing themselves, he noticed, across the street, a uniformed man come out of a store front, turn to lock it up and walk away.

Navy Recruiting Office, the sign across the door said. A small poster told him, "*Join the Navy! See the World!*" A very large poster in the window had a cartoon drawing of Uncle Sam pointing directly at Cam and saying, "*Uncle Sam is calling! Enlist in the U.S. Navy! I want you in the Navy, and I want you now!*"

This time Cam elbowed Randy. "Hey, man! Let's sign up for the Navy. If we don't get the fuck out of here, we're all gonna wind up in prison."

Randy, who was distracted by an overweight woman of at least forty shaking herself in his face, lifted his drink and said, "Sure, man, why not? This place sucks. Let's do it."

"Tomorrow, man, I mean it. We're signing up tomorrow."

Randy tipped his cup towards Cam's, tapped it in a toast and said, "Tomorrow!"

Cam, satisfied, finally turned his attention to the naked dancers.

In the morning, Cam got up and saw his father passed out on the couch. He grabbed a piece of bread that was spilling out of the open bag on the counter, and walked three blocks over to Randy's house, chewing. He knocked on the door and, getting no answer, knocked five more times, louder and louder until he was banging with the side of his fist.

"Fuck it," Cam said to himself.

He crossed the bridge over the Iowa River and made his way downtown. The door to the recruiting office was held open by a triangular wooden block jammed at the bottom. It was witheringly hot inside, but the young man at the desk was not even sweating.

"Come on in, my man! Are you ready to change your life?" he asked with an authoritative cadence.

Cam was.

He signed whatever the man put in front of him, glancing up repeatedly at the impressive coolness of this sailor, who appeared to be about his age. The young man took back the stack of pages, looking over each of them and nodding his head at the information. Suddenly, he hesitated.

"Oh, you're not eighteen yet," he said.

Cam's heart fell.

Fuck, he thought, I have to wait another month.

He knew what kinds of trouble he could get into in the next few weeks, and defeated, began to turn and walk out.

"Hey, that's no problem. You just have to get your mother or father to sign you up."

"My mom's dead," Cam said. "But maybe I can get Glen, uh, my dad, to do it. What time do you close?"

"I'll be here until nine tonight," he responded.

He stood up tall to firmly shake Cam's hand and gave him a smart salute.

Cam took the folder that the sailor handed to him. He wanted to run home but the blast-furnace outside made even walking a challenge. When he arrived at the house, he grabbed a pen and shook his father until Glen mumbled a stream of curses and slowly sat almost up right.

"I need you to sign this, Glen." Cam tried to imitate the commanding but respectful tone of the recruiter; not too forceful, as he did not want to push his father into one of his rages.

"What is it?" Glen asked, rubbing his eyes and forehead to shake off the miserable pain he felt there.

Cam responded in the same tone, "I'm joining the Navy. I got my GED, and all I need is your signature. You tell us stories about being in the Air Force, dropping bombs, killing all those Krauts and Japs. I want to check it out for myself."

He held his breath, fists loosely at his side, ready for what might come.

"Good! About fucking time someone is this family shows some balls. Do you good anyway, get away from those assholes you hang around."

Glen slapped the paper on the table, scribbled his signature, and lay back down, hand over his eyes.

In the time it took Cam to pick up the paper, he was snoring. This time, despite the blistering waves of heat, he ran all the way back to the recruiter.

His brother Joe was not happy.

When, a month later, Cam was packing up his duffle bag, Joe sat on the bed, watching. "I never thought you would really do it, little bro. You're leaving me here with Glen in this shithole town. The fuck am I supposed to do without you to push around?"

"You're gonna miss me, huh?" Cam said, throwing a pair of fairly clean boxers at his face.

"I didn't say that," Joe responded.

But he folded the boxers neatly and placed them in the bag. "When do you have to be in Chicago?"

"Tomorrow morning," Cam said. "I'm gonna take the four o'clock Greyhound. Probably sleep in the bus station or crash on a bench at the Navy pier. Hey, that's funny, huh?"

"Bullshit. Sam and the T's and me'll drive you. We can all fit in Dad's Cadillac. We'll have a night in Chi-town to send you off."

"Better not get me arrested, Joe," Cam said, only half-joking.

"Hey, not a bad idea. Then you won't be able to join the Navy after all."

But he was only kidding, and they both knew it.

They made the three-hour ride to Chicago, music blasting out of the radio the whole way. Patti Haze on WMET, in her sultry, cigarette-raspy voice announced the Rolling Stones, Janis, Jimi, Led Zeppelin; and when she spun Lynyrd Skynyrd's Free Bird, Sam and the T's sang along pointing at Cam: *"For I must be traveling on, now, 'Cause there's too many places I've got to see."*

Then the DJ announced, "A brand new tune from Styx, just released last week: 'Come Sail Away'!" and all five of them went wild as they caught on and belted out the chorus in pretty good harmony.

They spent the night drinking beers on the concrete stairs facing Lake Michigan, Sam philosophizing about life while the other boys listened to their oldest brother in rare somber thought. Cam leaving the family to join the Navy was literally a sea change for them all, and they all felt it.

In the morning, they dropped him off at the Recruit Training Center in Great Lakes with a few awkward hugs and soft punches.

"Kill it, little bro," Joe said, as they got ready to head back home.

"Stop calling me that, asshole," Cam said back, and gave him a good shove toward the car.

He watched them pull away until he could no longer see the Cadillac before heading into the building.

Cam breezed through boot camp. The drill sergeant singled him out a couple of times and always nodded his head in approval at Cam's willingness to do everything right, hard, best. A few of the other recruits also vied for attention, and there were many fist fights after training, out of the watchful eye of the sergeant. He did notice the new bruises the day after and pushed them even harder.

After a brutal training one day, Cam was called into the recruit division commander's office.

"What do you want to do in the Navy, son?" he asked, after Cam tried to smooth his wrinkled blues and saluted.

"I don't know, sir! I was thinking of being a bosun's mate, sir!" he responded, standing straight and tall and looking over the man's head.

"Custodial work? Anyone can do that job, Seaman Recruit. I signed you up for an aptitude test in an hour. The Vietnam War decimated our ranks. There are a lot of career paths open, especially to anyone with half a brain. I think you have almost a whole brain. Put it to work for yourself, Callahan. Be showered and back here by six. Bring a number two pencil. Dismissed."

"Sir, yes sir!" Cam saluted again, ran to the barracks to clean up, and was seated promptly at six at a desk in a room with the other recruits he often fought after-hours.

A few months later, Cam was sitting in the air-conditioned radar room of an ammunitions supply ship, sailing out of Virginia, and headed East across the Atlantic. Once they reached Rota, Spain and entered the Mediterranean Sea, they began performing practice maneuvers, and stopped to offload millions of pounds of ammunitions onto the smaller destroyers.

Everyone on board, except for the officers, was under twenty years old; and for many of them, it was their first time leaving the country. For many of them, it was the first time leaving their hometowns; and the excitement was obvious as the ship approached the dock in Naples, Italy.

"Men, you represent the greatest country in the world," the chief petty officer stated to the sailors standing before him just before they left the ship. "Make sure you represent well. We are guests in this country. Behave as you would expect a visitor to behave in your own homes. Remember decorum, remember your duty hours, and for crying out loud, remember the condoms."

With that, he released them. They ran in a mass, whooping and hollering down the gangplank into waiting U.S. Navy vans. Cam gave a high-five to his buddy from the radar room, Johnny, as they filed into one of the overloaded vehicles.

The short drive off base took them to a seedy part of the city. Bars lined both sides of the narrow streets, which were covered in litter and cigarette butts. Loud American jukebox music competed with Italian pop pouring out onto the street in assaulting waves. Overhead, laundry fluttered in the breeze on lines hung from one building over the street to the other. Graffiti covered the surfaces of many buildings, obscuring ancient architecture. Skimpily dressed, overly made-up women stood in doorways between the bars, calling to them.

Cam and Johnny, both overwhelmed, walked shoulder to shoulder around the neighborhood to check it out. One of the alleys was so narrow that Cam stood in the middle and was able to touch both sides at the same time, while Johnny took a photo with the Kodak Instamatic he kept in his pocket.

A centuries-old cathedral towered over them as they passed by on a cobblestone street. Several older men dressed in rags sitting on the stone steps held out filthy hands with black nails, calling, *"Americani, Amercani, Dammi dei soldi."* They tossed some American coins to the beggars and kept walking.

They turned a corner and were almost run over by two young men on Vespa scooters, who yelled, *"Idioti Americani! Guardi dove va!"* and flipped up middle fingers.

"Did you see that coat?" Cam asked. "That is the coolest jacket I've ever seen. I want one."

"I saw us almost get killed!" Johnny yelped, wiping his brow in overly dramatic relief.

They walked on and found themselves wandering in a maze of alleys with the smell of cooking garlic wafting everywhere. Johnny kept pointing at the cars driving by with wonder. He had his Kodak in his hand and was taking picture after picture.

"Look at that. Oh man, I love all the Fiats! *Click.* That's a BMW 520! *Click.* Look at that Peugeot Wagon. Oh my god, that's a '62 Ferrari 250 GTO. I might cream myself. *Click click.*"

"You'd get along great with my brother, Sam," Cam said. "He rebuilds cars like they're Lego sets. You should see the Mach 1 he's been working on. Sunny yellow sex machine."

What struck Cam most were the young women. Fashionably dressed, long shiny hair, little make-up to cover perfect faces, they walked past him in twos or threes with confident steps. Men whistled and catcalled. The women always acknowledged them with a wave and a smile.

"We ain't in Iowa anymore, Toto" he said, as he stopped to stare.

A brunette with light brown eyes caught him looking and blew him a kiss. He almost fell over.

"Hey, you heard the chief, no Italian babies and no diseases allowed," Johnny ribbed him as they continued on.

Finally getting hungry and thirsty, they meandered up a steep alley and found a quiet patio restaurant where they could look over the port and the city, with Mount Vesuvius in the distant haze. The odor of garlic was even stronger here, merging with the smell of olive oil, tomatoes and burned bread.

The menus were already on the table when they sat, and a waiter came over quickly to greet them.

"I'll have a beer," Cam said, trying to decipher the Italian words to pick something to eat.

"No beer, solo vino," the waiter said in a patient and friendly tone.

He was used to American servicemen wandering in here, and they all asked for beer.

"Come on, man, broaden your palate a little. We are travelling the world; you have to taste it too," Johnny chuckled and ordered for both of them.

The Spanish he had learned growing up, from both his grandmother and the Pilsen neighborhood in Chicago he called home, was somewhat helpful.

"What did you order?" Cam asked, a little nervous.

He was used to everything coming out of a can, a jar or a box; and they never got food out, except for the occasional Maid Rite loose meat sandwich or hoagie.

"You'll see, my man. I promise it won't hurt too bad," Johnny replied, laughing again.

The waiter brought two small water glasses and a carafe of deep red wine. Johnny poured it for both of them with a fancy flourish, then raised his glass and said, "To seeing the world, and tasting it too!"

Cam clinked his glass, and cautiously raised the wine to his nose and sniffed. It smelled a bit like Welch's grape juice, so he sipped it. The face he made, eyes wincing shut, lips puckered and head shuddering, almost made Johnny spit out his mouthful of wine.

"Yuugh! How can you drink this stuff?!" Cam sputtered.

Johnny told him to try again and, squaring his shoulders, he did. He was surprised to find the second sip was not as bad; and the third was even better. By the time the waiter returned and placed their food on the table, the carafe was empty, and they ordered more.

"This looks like a pizza," Cam said, "But what is up with the puffy burnt crust, and what are those green leaves?"

"Oh my god, bro, you really are from Iowa," Johnny said, taking a slice onto his plate. He cut off the steaming triangle at the top and blew on it before forking it into his mouth. Cam followed his example, and instantly rolled his eyes up in his head with a big grin.

"See, told you!" Johnny said.

Cam felt like his life would never be the same.

The fact that they were radarmen meant that they did not have to report back to the ship until it was ready to sail. They took full advantage of the week, exploring all of Naples. Cam bought a tour book and read aloud to Johnny about the palaces, cathedrals, and classical architecture as they walked. Everywhere they went, they never lost sight of Mount Vesuvius.

"Man, that volcano is calling to me," Johnny said on their last day.

They boarded a tour bus and rode out to the ticket office, where they got a map and started the hike up. The day was sunny and clear and warm, but as they approached the cone, a frigid gust of wind whipped at them.

"Damn, should have worn my new Italian leather," Cam said, hugging himself as they came to the edge of the volcano and looked in.

Steam rose from several small vents, wafting the rotten-egg odor of sulfur.

"Did you know a whole city was buried right here after a big eruption?" Cam read the facts on the trail guide.

"Yep, and I also heard the ash and lava make the soil great for wine grapes!" Johnny answered with a grin.

On their way down, they stopped at the restaurant on the slope and drank two bottles of wine made from vines grown right on the volcano.

"So good," Cam sighed.

"Spoken like a true convert to the religion of the grape! You're a real connoisseur, look at you," Johnny chuckled.

"A conti-what?" Cam asked.

Johnny shook his head and poured the last of the wine into their glasses.

The ship sailed on to Souda Bay on the island of Crete. The liberty there was short and quick, but Cam had his first taste of the Greek liqueur called ouzo. He tossed back a dozen shots and passed out on a park bench for hours. When he came to, Johnny and another guy from their berthing area were sitting next to him stuffing gyros and French fries down their throats and slurping on bottles of Amstel beer.

"Here," Johnny said, around a mouthful of fries, tossing a paper wrapped sandwich onto Cam's chest.

He ate it laying down, expressing his enjoyment by chewing noisily, and then passed out again.

Over three days, they managed to walk a few miles around the hilly white towns and spend an afternoon on the pink sand beaches in the warm turquoise water, before the ship sailed on to Palma, Spain.

The radar room kept Cam busy while the ship was cruising. He worked eight-on, eight-off shifts; but sleeping in his berthing area next to where the helicopters took off and landed was not easy. During the eight-off, he usually played a few rounds of spades or cribbage; by the time he finally crawled into his berth, he got about four hours of shut-eye before it was time to man the radars again.

In Palma de Majorca, Spain, Cam found a whole other world. The streets were spotless, and automobiles shared the roads with horse-drawn carriages. He soaked up history at the many ancient sites and monuments. Standing outside the Royal Palace of La Almudaina, he placed his hand on the stone blocks and felt it almost vibrating with hundreds of years of life. He was awestruck to realize that there were people standing here, right where his feet were planted, in the fourteenth century. *Who was standing in Iowa City back then?* he wondered.

He and Johnny learned to snorkel and spent whole afternoons in the shallow blue-green waters at the base of the cliffs at Cala Llombards. The sheer variety and quantity of fish and other sea life that he saw beneath the gentle waves left him dumbstruck.

Over the next three years, sailing on to ports throughout the Mediterranean, Cam tried everything he could. In Yugoslavia, he tasted cheese made from donkey milk. In France, he climbed spectacular mountains he had never dreamed existed. The parties were epic in Barcelona and Ibiza. In Tunisia, he swam in crystal seas of a color he had only read about.

And the girls; holy mother, the girls. Brown skin and matching eyes; green-eyed blondes; red heads with freckled noses and bright white smiles; Cam thought, *if this is a dream, let me sleep*

The ship returned to the states after his third med cruise and was sent to dry dock in the Brooklyn Navy yards. The radarmen were free from duty for the duration and took full advantage of the time.

The red brick buildings of the Navy Yard were crumbling and deteriorating, exactly echoing the neighborhood outside the fences and gates. Burned out buildings shared the filthy side streets off Flushing Avenue with the apartment housing where most of the sailors lived.

Cam had never been to New York City before, and this first impression did not bode well. Compared to the exotic places he had been he found Brooklyn disappointing. Thinking of the stories he had heard about the dangers in New York had him nervous.

He and a couple of the other guys walked the neighborhood and found dive bars like the Red Awning and the Blue Pinto filled with sailors and local girls. The juke boxes played Charlie Daniels and Linda Ronstadt songs as everyone danced, and the bartender locked them inside at four a.m., until they could legally reopen at six in the morning. Always walking in small groups, the sailors watched out for each other in the crime ridden neighborhood.

Cam and his friends took the graffiti-covered, trash-filled, and rat-infested subways into Manhattan. As they walked up the Bowery, they had to step over stew bums, lying prone across the sidewalk in their dingy trench coats clutching brown-paper wrapped bottles of Thunderbird or Mad Dog 2020, to sit in dark, dank places, and listen to live music. The jazz and blues and rock were the best he had ever heard.

Cam loved the little pubs in Greenwich Village, and hanging out with the hundreds of high school and college kids at

Washington Square Park late into the night. Guitar music, flying frisbees and the wafting odor of pot made him feel more at home.

He and his friends enjoyed the hole-in-the-wall Chinese restaurants in Little Italy and Chinatown, and often wound up at three in the morning stumbling down the stairs at Wo Hop with the other late-nighters to slurp down greasy Chicken Chow Mein.

They wandered around Times Square, which reminded him of Naples, with its seedy nightlife and ladies in doorways. They went into one peepshow, when they could not shake off the man hawking it as they tried to walk past. It was dirty inside, and the girls were young and sad. Cam felt like he needed a shower by the time they got out of there.

Cam visited the famous museums he had read about, spending hours soaking up the mind-numbingly diverse art and artifacts. His favorite was the Metropolitan Museum with its ancient Egyptian objects, American wing and maze of halls filled with famous works of art.

He went to mass at Saint Patrick's Cathedral in midtown, thinking about his mother for the first time in a while. He whispered a prayer for her and told her he was doing his best to be the good man she wanted.

New York City had *everything*, Cam decided. It was like the whole world packed into one city; and he quickly learned to love its exhilarating, fast-paced, endless happenings.

One night, his roommate Jeff invited him to take a ride to Queens. Jeff had met someone at the Red Awning bar that he was seeing pretty regularly, and he didn't want to make the drive by himself.

Cam had not ventured out to Queens yet, so he jumped in the car for the thirty-minute ride. Jeff parked in front of the garden apartments where she lived, in a spot barely big enough for the car with impressive parallel parking moves, and they went inside.

After a few beers and small talk, Jeff and his girl started making out on the couch, while Cam sat in a chair, red plastic bong leaking smoke in his hands, bored.

The girl noticed and said, "Hey, why don't I call a friend to come over and party with us. She lives right next door."

Cam shrugged and watched her dial and then hang up.

"She's coming," said the girl and went back to kissing Jeff.

Cam looked at the New York Mets poster on the wall, the black and white television in its walnut brown cabinet, the china dishes in the hutch next to the small dining room table, the plants in hanging baskets in the front window, the chipped and peeling paint on the apartment door.

Then the door opened, and standing there was a girl.

She wore a red flannel man's shirt under bib overall jeans. Her pin-straight light brown hair came down past her waist. Her light blue eyes twinkled, matching her big smile. She was barefoot, and she was holding a baggy stuffed with Panama Red pot.

"Cam," said Jeff's girl. "This is Tessa."

Part Two: Hers

1937-1979

Hannah's Story

The glasses of wine, champagne and beer circulated the packed room of beautifully dressed men and women of all ages. The chatter was loud, joyous and unfettered. Although it was a celebration of the newest surgeon in the family, it could have been any Saturday night in 1937 Berlin. The chandeliers sparkled, matching the jewelry which dangled from every woman in the room; the older the woman, the more opulent her display. The sixteen- and seventeen-year-olds, who would soon be married, gazed at the gems with anticipation. This was to be their future as well.

The men, in their immaculately pressed suits and bowties, with their yarmulkes perched on the backs of their heads, clinked their glass steins and shared the latest news. The *Berliner Tageblatt* was again sounding off on the National Socialist party antics.

Several of the men grew more serious than the others and tried to bring up the rumors that were growing about Hitler's designs for Germany. But the vast majority laughed them off with a wave of the hand and a chug of beer. They were in their prime years; strong, smart, and handsome; and surrounded by strong, smart, beautiful women. They had been in Berlin for generations, hundreds of years, and had inherited the confidence which carried them forward in their prospects.

They were high society Berliners; doctors, lawyers, business owners, opera singers and entertainers, on the top of their world. They felt invincible and carried on as if they were.

Tucked away upstairs in her perambulator and oblivious to the party below, four-month-old Hannah slept in her white satin dress and leather booties. Her mother, Lena, would not come to check on her until they were ready to leave for home, in the very early hours of the morning. By then, the gaiety had subsided a little. Many of the celebrants stopped to admire Hannah as her father, Karl, pushed the baby buggy proudly to the door. The little family walked home in the waning darkness.

It was barely a week later that Karl came home at the end of the workday, obviously perturbed. This was Lena's first hint that something was very wrong.

Karl was a gentle man with an easy-going and relaxed attitude towards life. He had to be, in order to be married to Lena, who was stubborn, hard, and intelligent, and not afraid to make sure everyone knew it. One of his running jokes was: "It doesn't matter how often a married man changes his job; he still ends up with the same boss."

At their wedding, his new father-in-law had given a speech that included at least one important gem: "Lena is very much like her mother, so I have some advice for you as my daughter's husband: When you have a discussion with her, always make sure you get in the last words: 'Yes dear'".

Over the past year, Lena's strong personality and Karl's quiet one had melded quickly into a solid marriage and produced a healthy baby girl on whom Karl doted.

He took it upon himself, and not without Lena's complete endorsement, to feed Hannah's bottles to her and even change her diapers. He often dressed her in the morning before he left for work, while Lena supervised the kitchen and household help. He held her on his lap as soon as he walked in the door in the late afternoon. Lena had said more than once, "You'll spoil her," but not very forcefully; so, they both knew the arrangement was mutually satisfactory.

As he walked through the door that early evening and accepted the glass of beer from the young serving girl, he waved a folded copy of the *Tageblatt* in Lena's direction.

"More bad news?" she asked, as she took the newspaper, and accepted his kiss on the cheek.

She sat back down on one of the pair of graceful armchairs in the well-appointed sitting room. Instead of taking his seat next to her, as was his custom each day, he paced the hand-woven Persian carpet as she silently perused the news. When he almost sloshed his beer over the top of the glass, he placed it on the credenza without having taken a sip.

She finally looked up, her eyes troubled, her brow furrowed, and her lips pursed to one side. For a long moment, they watched each other, neither wanting to be the first to speak. She broke the silence.

"We have to leave."

"Leave," he repeated.

The word felt foreign in his mouth and his head shook involuntarily as he said it. "Leave? What do you mean? Leave the house and go to the country until things calm down? We can go back to my family home outside Hamburg, there is always room for us there."

As he said this, he knew it was not what she meant. He did

not want to hear the words she was getting ready to say. It would not be the first time he felt this way during serious discussions with her; and it would not be the last. But it was the first time Lena's as-yet-unsaid words worried her as much as they did him. He knew his wife: by the time she actually said what was in her mind, she would have thought out an initial plan and be ready to put it in motion.

"We must take Hannah, our parents, my brother and his wife. We must leave Germany. Now. Tonight, if possible. Tomorrow at the latest. Hitler has made his decree: arrest all Jews, men, women, children, even the old ones. Everyone is to be arrested. How soon do you think it will be before it is too late? We cannot wait to see. We cannot risk our lives. Hannah's life."

She said this last looking directly into his eyes. While she had been speaking, she saw only argument, disbelief, nearly ridicule; but at the mention of their beloved daughter, his eyes instantly changed. Pain crossed his face, which he covered with his large hand.

Lena sat silently, waiting. She knew her husband as well as he knew her. It usually took him a short bit of time to come to the same conclusion as her, even if with slightly less conviction. He wasn't there yet. How could he be?

"The business, the house, the servants, the dogs, all of our things…" he listed, running his hand over the small table between their chairs. He finally sat heavily at the edge of the chair, as he began to accept that she was right.

She did not like the defeat that curved his shoulders. She knew they would both need all of the strength they could muster to do what needed to be done.

She spoke at length then, a plan forming as it was coming out of her mouth.

"We will tell the servants we must return to Hamburg for a family emergency. They will take the dogs with them. In the morning, I will go to the train station and buy tickets for all of us. We will stay with your parents at the house until we figure out where to go and how to do it, a few days at most. We can leave word for the manager at the office that we will be gone for several weeks." A silent beat and then she added, "He must close down the company quietly so as to not arouse suspicion. This will not be easy."

His head nodded in assent, but he found he had no words. He did not need them; the plan was set.

Through the night, both wide awake, they hammered out the details in whispers. The house staff slept nearby, and sound carried through the flat easily. When the eastern sky was a barely perceptibly lighter shade of dark, Lena rose, splashed water on her face and dressed in an unremarkable day dress. She placed the still-sleeping Hannah in the perambulator and pushed it to the Berlin station. She expected that some of their friends and neighbors, having read the news last night, would be making preparations as well. She knew that the later she went to the train station, the more crowded it would be.

As she turned the corner, she nearly walked into two soldiers who blocked the path to the glass doors that led to the ticket booth. Their posture was tense, rifles held rigidly at the left shoulder, helmets tightly strapped under the chin, gray-green pants tucked into shiny black boots. Their unfriendly expressions did not cause her to show fear. She had a plan, and she was ready.

"What is your business here?" the younger of the two Wehrmacht demanded tersely.

"My father-in-law in Hamburg is very ill. I am buying train tickets for myself, my husband, my father and mother and my brother and his wife to travel there to spend his final days with him. His only granddaughter will see him for the last time," she stated simply, indicated the infant in the carriage.

"*Nine,*" the other soldier responded. "You may buy tickets for your husband and yourself and the child. You must leave on the afternoon train and return to Berlin by the end of the week."

Knowing that it was useless, even dangerous, to argue, she assented, and they moved apart to let her through. For a moment, she thought about purchasing the seven train passes anyway but saw that there were several more soldiers stationed inside. Not wanting to draw any more attention, she obtained the tickets and returned home quickly.

Karl was packing their travel bags with basic clothes and shoes in the dim light of the small electric lamps on their nightstands. The maids were preparing breakfast and travel food and getting the dogs ready to go. Hannah woke fussily and Lena handed her off to Karl to finish the packing. She quietly told him what had happened at the station, and they decided she should go see her parents and brother as soon as breakfast was done.

Her brother lived only three blocks away. When she knocked on the door, unexpected and so early in the morning, Hans opened the door cautiously. When he saw Lena, he leaned out and looked both ways down the still-empty street and motioned her inside.

Cut from the same cloth as her, he did not waste time: "What is wrong?" he asked in a hushed voice.

"We are leaving Berlin. This afternoon. We are taking the train to Hamburg and then will find passage out of the country. I tried to buy tickets for you and Ruth and Father and Mother, but the soldiers stopped me. You must go right now to the train station and buy your train passes. I am going to Father next and tell him the same."

"You cannot be serious," Hans' tone was incredulous.

"Did you not read yesterday's paper?" she responded, knowing full-well that he had.

"This is our city. This is our country! Our family has been here for two hundred years. These empty threats are meant to scare us. Hitler and the Third Reich cannot possibly follow through. Arrest all Jews?! Our neighbors and friends and business associates would never stand for it. You are being foolish."

"*You* are being foolish. Do as you wish, Hans. We are on the afternoon train and I intend to make sure that Father and Mother are on it as well. I suggest you give this some more serious thought and change your mind."

With that, she stood and walked to the door. Turning to look at him, not knowing it would be the last time she saw him, she added, "Please…"

When his expression did not change, she walked through the door and continued on to her Father's place.

As she had known the case would be, her mother was more difficult to convince than her father. "You said Hans thinks these are mere threats to frighten a bunch of innocent people. I believe that as well. How could they not be? We have done nothing wrong."

Lena was prepared. "Come to Hamburg. Then decide if you want to leave the country with us. What is the harm? At worst, you will have a few days by the Elbe River and can return to the city after."

With her mother's reluctant agreement to meet them at the station, she returned to the flat to find the servants and dogs gone, Karl feeding Hannah, and the Mercedes pulled up in front of the door. The travel bags were placed in the foyer, waiting. His usually cheerful demeanor, which Lena found both irritating and endearing, was not in evidence. She felt sorrowfulness for a brief moment, and then pushed it away harshly. This was not the time for pity; but for action. Sorrow could come later.

With the breakfast dishes cleaned and put away, a job that was foreign to both Lena and Karl, they took one last look around the flat. Karl walked around the rooms, looking slowly at each object that they were leaving behind. His large hand brushed over the finely carved tables and the embroidered cloths that covered them. In the living room, he stood before the floor lamp, one of the first electric floor lamps in all of Berlin and tried to memorize its details.

Finally, he stopped in the nursery to take a last look at Hannah's crib, her fancier dresses hanging in the armoire, the framed painting of a clown and elephant that hung on the wall above the dresser. He noticed a pair of knitted booties there, and even though they no longer fit her feet, he put them in his pocket before coming back to the foyer.

There he found Lena trying to find a place inside the larger travel bag for a rather sizeable wooden box.

"Your grandmother's silver?" he asked, puzzled. "I thought we were only taking absolute necessities."

"I think we should take at least one valuable item with us, but this box will not fit."

She lifted the lid and took each of the silverware pieces out of its fitted space in the dark blue velvet interior and placed it inside one of the items of clothing. In this way she was able to fit the large serving spoon and several forks, knives, and smaller spoons; the serving platter would have to be left behind.

After closing the buckles on the bag, they loaded up the trunk of the car. Karl got into the driver's side, and Lena held Hannah on her lap. They sat in thick silence for a moment. Then the car's powerful engine roared awake. They pulled away from their home, their street, their neighbors, their life; and drove towards the unknown.

The station was crowded with other families who had tickets for the afternoon train or were lined up to purchase them. As they passed by the glass doors to walk onto the platform, Lena noticed the same two Wehrmacht soldiers blocking the entryway, harshly questioning each person. She averted her eyes but watched peripherally.

The soldiers seized a woman with a perambulator and took her off, crying and screaming, to a waiting truck parked nearby. The baby carriage was left at the front of the line. Two more soldiers stepped in to replace the others, pushing it roughly to one side, and demanded the next person step forward.

Lena forced her eyes to look forward towards the packed station, her heart pounding.

She began to scan each face, looking for her parents. Karl did the same, as they moved forward into the horde of people. It was difficult to push the carriage and carry the bags, so they found a place for Lena to stand, while Karl went to locate her Mother and Father. He was gone so long, Lena thought about the Nazi truck waiting outside. She began to think about what she would do if he did not return.

When she finally saw him, tall above most of the others, she let out a breath she had not realized she was holding.

"They are not here," he said, with a mix of irritation and concern. "I went to every corner of the station and almost to the street, but the Wehrmacht turned me back."

Lena could feel her body vibrating with anxiety. The train

would be boarding soon. They would not be able to move between cars to search for them, once they were seated.

Karl looked into her eyes and said what she was already thinking: "We have to board the train. We will have to find them when we arrive in Hamburg."

She assented, as the conductor blew the whistle and the doors of the train opened. They found the last two unoccupied seats together and watched out the window as the slow-moving mass of people and bags moved towards the train. The cars filled up to the point where those standing were pressed against each other with little room to spare.

As the doors closed, there were still people waving tickets and trying to board. Their angry yells turned into despaired wails, as the train pulled away. Lena saw the uniformed men descend on the unfortunates, and roughly push them back off of the platform. When one young father resisted, the nearest soldier cracked him in the face with his baton.

Once again, Lena forced her eyes forward.

The heat in the train was already unbearable. A low moaning, punctuated with a baby's cry, floated on the humid air. Directly next to them, a small boy stood on his father's feet, arms wrapped tightly around his father's knees. Lena whispered to Karl, and he lifted the boy onto her lap next to Hannah, who gurgled happily to have company. Karl stood up and offered his seat to an elderly woman who gratefully sat. She then reached out to another nearby family, taking their two small children onto her lap. This happened throughout the car they were in; until nearly all those standing were young men, and those sitting held numerous chatting, sweating children.

When the train pulled into the Hamburg station, it took nearly an hour to get off the train onto the seething platform. Lena and

Karl found a place to stop by the exit to the street, scanning the sweltering faces that streamed past them. When the last group of people had left the area, Karl looked into Lena's face to see what she was thinking.

She said firmly, "Let's get the next car to the house. We will figure out what to do then."

Karl gently affirmed, "We will send them a telegraph as soon as we can."

When they arrived at Karl's family home in Hollern-Twielenfleth, forty-five kilometers from the Hamburg station, dusk was setting in. The sound of an unexpected car driving up the gravel road brought his father and mother to the door, and when they saw Karl and Lena they ran to help with the baby and the bags.

"We are so happy to see you! But we had no idea you were coming, not even a telegram! We will have to see what we can do for your supper and I will make the beds up for you. Here, give me the baby," Karl's mother said all at once, before she looked into their faces and stopped cold.

"We will explain when we get inside, Mother," Karl said, not wanting to speak in front of the driver.

The baby was fed and fast asleep in a large dresser drawer. Everyone had a glass of beer in hand, and all explanations had been made. A silence settled over the sitting room. The low gas lamps lent the room a cozy yellow glow that made Karl sleepy, and calmed Lena's frayed nerves. Soft music played on the gramophone. Since it was nearly midnight, Lena would have to wait until morning to get the telegram out to her parents. Knowing that they were safe for the moment, she allowed herself to drift off a bit as well.

The sudden pounding on the door made all four adults jump

to their feet. Karl's mother dropped her glass, which shattered. Karl placed his beer down on the table, squared his shoulders and walked firmly to the door. His hand on the doorknob, he took a deep breath and opened it slowly.

Lena's father and mother stood on the porch, luggage all around them, as a car pulled out and drove away.

In the morning light, over an early breakfast of eggs, potatoes, thick slabs of bacon and strong coffee, the discussion quickly became heated. Lena firmly kept to her plan to find a way out of the country. Her mother just as firmly wanted to go back to Berlin in time for Friday Sabbath. Their journey to get to Hollern-Twielenfleth had been every bit as stressful as Karl and Lena's had been, and she could not see her way to continue on. Karl, quieter but no less adamant, sided with his wife and wanted his parents to start packing. His parents fussed over everyone and let them talk it out.

Their one contribution was: "If Karl and Lena think we should go, then we must go. There have been rumblings here as well, since all of the Berliners began arriving in Hamburg this week."

In the end, Lena's mother was finally convinced to acquiesce. They began to plan their escape.

In order to keep it quiet, Karl's father went alone to speak to his neighbor, a trusted old friend; a fisherman who made his living on the Elbe River. The fisherman's idea, to get them passage on a freighter out of Bremerhaven to the country of Colombia in South America, was met with stunned silence. They had all thought to find a safe place to hide out the war in Europe. According to the nightly radio reports, Switzerland and Sweden were neutral, and welcoming Jews who needed temporary refuge.

"Colombia!" Lena exclaimed, horrified. "Those people are savages. They still live in trees there! What would we do in Colombia?"

"We have no choice, Len," Karl said. The use of her nickname, so rarely heard outside their marital bedroom, pierced her. Lena's posture deflated momentarily, but she very quickly recovered, and took over the planning.

The fisherman had told them they could take none of their belongings; only what they wore. The freighter was not built for passengers and they would be spending the next two months in a small interior cabin with several other families. The ship was scheduled to disembark tomorrow morning at first light. The captain had given instructions to come quietly on board just after midnight so they would not be seen.

If he got caught harboring them, they would all be arrested immediately.

Passage would cost them all of the money they had between them, leaving them with nothing to spare. Lena, dressing herself and Hannah in all of the clothes she could, stuffed the silver pieces she had brought between layers. The fisherman was waiting for them at the dock on the Elbe River just after full dark, ready to sail through the canals and locks to the port at Bremerhaven. They would arrive just in time, if the lock operators were not asleep and need to be awoken.

"Word has been sent ahead to Colombia," he informed them as they settled below deck on the fishing boat. "When you arrive, there will be a man from the HICEM agency to meet and escort you to your new home. He will explain everything to you when you arrive."

Karl and Lena knew better than to ask how the fisherman knew exactly what to do to help them. They expressed their gratitude before he went up to get under way. He waved his hand to stifle their words.

"Just be safe and make a new life for little Hannah there. This is all the thanks I need."

With that he climbed the steep stairs and could be heard moving ropes as quietly as possible.

When they arrived at the port and came up from below, they got their first glimpse of the freighter waiting to sail them across the world. Standing at the base of the gangplank was a small group of people: the other families that would be traveling with them. The captain came down the gangplank and took their money from the fisherman with a strong, silent, meaningful handshake. He led the group up on the deck and then down into the hold. The cabin where they would spend many weeks was dark and close.

It took some maneuvering to get them all inside, and then the Captain pointed at the bunks, two on each side and said in accented German, "One family to each bed. Two meals each day. You can come on the deck any time you want, unless you hear three bells. Then you must stay here and be silent."

The family groups chose their bunks. Lena's parents lay with Hannah on one end of their bed, with Karl's parents on the opposite end. Lena and Karl settled on the floor with several of the others. In this way, they slept fitfully until they felt the ship begin to move away from the port.

The next two months held a mix of deadly boredom and too little to eat. The cloying stench of sickness pervaded the cabin, as nearly all of the passengers felt the effects of the rolling waves during storms that tossed the enormous ship like a toy. Lena and Karl dragged the family up onto the deck every day for fresh air and exercise. It was there that Lena befriended a sailor, and eventually gave him several pieces of their precious silverware to get a bit more food for the old ones and the baby.

During this time, with nothing to do except think, Lena's mind could not help but imagine many scenes where this attempt to escape one horror led to another. When she occasionally thought back to their old life and all that they had lost, she chastised herself for wasting time lamenting the past.

She and Karl had many quiet talks, up on the deck to maintain their privacy, about what was to happen to them. They also expressed fear, but only to each other, for those left behind. They wondered when and how they would get news of what had become of their beloved city, friends, and family.

They were up on the deck on a sunny, clear day when the first shouts came. Even though the sailors were yelling in Spanish, it was clear that they had spotted land. The coast of Colombia was a brown smudge barely visible on the humid horizon, but it brought Lena almost to tears. They had made it; they had escaped with their lives and made it to safety. Unaccustomed to the hot feeling of emotion, she blinked it back stubbornly; and began issuing instructions to the others.

They had all of their belongings either on them or in their arms, as the ship came alongside the dock. The Colombian heat made even the thought of overdressing unbearable, and one of the other mothers began to sway, dangerously close to fainting. A splash of water brought her back as the gangplank was hauled into place. They descended as a group and stepped for the first time onto the soil of South America.

All of the adults searched the enormous port for someone who looked like he was sent to meet them. The older children held hands, jumping up and down, yelling *Hier sind wir! Colombia, Colombia,* until one of the elders told them to hush.

A man walked rapidly over to them from a truck parked by the road, and spoke words of welcome, in German, to their collective relief. He wore a light button-down shirt and linen pants, and after one look at them in their layers of wool suits and long dresses, bade them follow him to the waiting vehicle.

There they removed all of the clothing they could, throwing everything into the bed of the truck in a pile. They climbed in, sitting on top of it all.

The truck drove slowly along the coast on the cobblestone road. It turned onto a narrow street and wound its way through a labyrinth of low buildings. They came to a stop in front of an unremarkable door.

Everyone climbed out, standing along the thin sidewalk. The man introduced himself as Benjamin Mellibovsky, originally of Poland. He shook all of their hands, even those of the elderly and the older children. He made a formal bow before Hannah and gave her a warm smile. She rewarded him by patting his face with both chubby hands.

The office of the HICEM was only large enough for a single table and two chairs. Lena, Karl and two of the other fathers crammed inside as Benjamin sat down and pulled papers out of a wooden box from under the table. The rest of their group wandered down the street to have a look around, careful to keep an eye on the office so they would not lose sight of it in the maze of buildings.

"I arrived here just last year," Benjamin explained in excellent German. "HICEM grew out of the Hebrew Immigrant Aid Society in Paris. It has been helping Jews fleeing persecution relocate all over the world and begin new lives. There are agents like me in Asia, Africa, and the Americas. There are very, very few of you here in Colombia, and in the other South American countries. The going will not be easy. But at least, you will be safe."

Lena's shoulders sagged imperceptibly. She knew that they were going to have to adjust to a new home; but she had never imagined finding themselves facing such an overwhelming and unsure future.

Benjamin had nothing but admiration and concern for this latest group of compatriots. They had fled for their lives, leaving everything behind. They had arrived in a subtropical, inferior country with little infrastructure and poor educational systems; with almost no Jewish population to speak of.

He continued. "We have made arrangements for you to travel on to an area called San Juan de Pasto. It is in the mountainous region, so the climate is much more bearable than in the lowlands. Outside of Pasto there are acres of farmland. You will each be given a small house on the farms, and cows, goats, and chickens to help you get started."

At this, Lena visibly bristled. "Farms? Chickens, cows? We are to be farmers? I have never in my life touched an animal other than our dogs!"

Lena choked up a moment before continuing. "It is impossible. There must be something else for us. My husband owned a business selling fine home furnishings to wealthy Berliners. Look at his hands."

She grabbed them and held them up in front of Benjamin's face. "Do these look like a farmer's hands? I run a household, managing the staff, the finances. We could never, would never, work the land like peasants. We need to live in a city where we can find my husband a place to restart his business, where there are civilized people who dress in civilized clothes…"

Lena gave Benjamin's informal shirt a disdainful look to

emphasize her disapproval.

"We left to save our lives, not to ruin them and destroy our Hannah's chances for a proper future with a prosperous Jewish husband. This is impossible," she repeated resolutely.

The men remained silent but stared directly at Benjamin to show him they felt the same. The thought of manual labor, of working the earth, of raising, slaughtering and preparing animals to eat was beyond their sphere, beyond their ability to even imagine.

Benjamin, although he sympathized with them, was firm and nearly curt in his response. Others before them, especially those with daughters, had had the same reaction.

"You will stay in the flat next door tonight and leave after breakfast in the morning. There is nothing else for you here. Not at the moment. Perhaps not for a long time."

It was a subdued group that, next day, began the journey. They sat in rattling cars, as the drivers took them through unpaved terrain and over perilous mountain tracks. They by-passed dismal, mud-soaked villages. Lena watched naked, sun-darkened children splashing in wide rivers, chewing on coca leaves from overgrown bushes. The rocking and heaving caravan of vehicles went on endlessly. The families swatted mosquitos off of the little ones, barely listening to the friendly foreign chatter of the drivers. The journey ate at the small reserve of hope left to Lena and the others.

At last they passed through the small mountain town of Pasto itself. Lena carefully observed the dingy market and few free-standing stores selling locally grown goods. They drove by coffee plantations out onto dirt roads through open fields of sugar cane, corn and tobacco.

The dusty vehicles stopped in front of a wooden shack. Its few windows were shuttered, and the door was propped over the opening. Several scrawny chickens toddled around the yard, squawking as they pecked at the earth and each other. The driver smiled, his few teeth brown and crooked, and indicated with a gesture that this was Lena and Karl's new home.

At the opportunity to stretch their legs, they all dismounted to look around. The children ran after the chickens, causing them to flap and scold and scurry away.

Karl carried the small bags that Benjamin had given them for their belongings. Inside them, the agent had added some lighter frocks for Hannah, two bars of soap for washing people and laundry, and a single bottle of beer. Pulling the door off the opening and leaning it up against the wall, they all walked in.

In the darkness they could make out the kitchen, which was furnished with several cooking bowls, pans, spoons and a coffee urn. One of the men began pushing open the shutters to bring light into the house. It became easier to see the fairly large front room and its passable furniture, and the two bedrooms, also furnished with basics. Just outside the door stood the well pump for water. The outhouse was several meters beyond that.

The other families did not linger long. They wanted to settle into their own places as quickly as possible. Lena noted with disdain that the drivers did not seem to be in any especial hurry. This was her first glimpse into Colombian culture; and she was hardly impressed.

As soon as they had departed, Lena's mother and father went to lie down on one of the two beds in the smaller of the two bedrooms. The entire journey, from agreeing to arriving, had taken it nearly all out of them.

Karl's mother looked on the shelves in the kitchen and found a tin of coffee, a bag of rice, another of corn flour, and a smaller bag of sugar. She took down a large can labeled *frijoles rojos*, which she read in German as "feriyolis royos"; the r's sounding like she was clearing her throat. At once she began to prepare a meal for the family.

Karl and his father went to get the lay of the land, each holding a skipping Hannah by the hand.

Lena walked to the outhouse, closed the door behind her, and allowed herself a long, bitter cry.

In the morning, Karl was dressed and out of the house at first light. Two large brown cows were already softly lowing in the barn. He let them out into the field to graze the green grass nearest the road. One of the cows ambled over to where he stood, staring helplessly at them. The cow looked at the man in his fine suit of clothes as only a cow can: dumbly, innocently and almost silly. Karl said to her, "I know how you feel."

I'm supposed to know how to milk this giant thing?? He thought to himself. *I'm supposed to survive out here on a farm? I'm from a big city. I know about parties and concerts and museums and business. What do I know about chickens and goats? Nothing, that's what.*

Just then he heard a dull rumbling noise and turned around. Coming down the dirt road was a horse and cart, driven by a diminutive coffee-colored man in ragged clothes. Seated next to the man were two small children, a boy and a girl, each holding a wiggling, pink piglet. In the back of the cart were several goats and a load of hay. When the cart came alongside the city man, the driver stopped. He smiled a toothless but friendly smile.

"*Hola, vecino!*" the man greeted Karl.

Although Karl did not understand, he knew the other man was being friendly, and lifted his hand in a wave. Then he pointed to the cow and shrugged his shoulders. The little man in the cart looked at the cow, looked at the fancy suit the man was wearing and began to laugh. He got down from the cart and pointed at his own shabby clothes and then at the suit. The German man understood: *first go change into something that can get dirty; then I will show you how to milk the silly cow.*

Karl caught on quickly to dealing with the cows, but milking the goats was a whole other thing. They were hard to catch as they scampered away from him. The only thing that helped him keep his senses about it was hearing Hannah's delighted laughing at their antics.

There were always repairs to be done to make the house more livable, crops to be tended to, and chickens to kill and prepare for meals. He traded in his suits for linen button-down shirts with the sleeves rolled up. He even took to wearing a straw hat in the sunny afternoons.

"If our friends could see us now…" Lena said to him on a day he returned carrying a dead goat to roast, sweating and brown like a native. They looked somberly at each other, realizing simultaneously how much they missed their friends and their life in Berlin.

Karl's father helped with chores, and his mother did most of the cooking. Lena's parents rested in the shade of a tree by the pastures, watching Hannah play with flowers and a wooden toy train that had been found in the barn.

Lena spent the days walking.

She walked two miles into town to the little stores where a variety of products were sold. She would carry along any milk they had not used the day before, to sell or trade for other goods. Often, even without speaking the language, she got the better of any deals she made.

She would go to a stall that sold pork first, trading her milk for a large slab of meat. Having never eaten pork in her life, she had no intention of bringing it home. She would take the pork to the corn seller and trade for a large basket of corn. Finally, she would make her way to the general store that sold dry goods.

There she would negotiate enough coffee, sugar and flour to last the family a week; all with hand gestures, head shakings and the occasional attempt to use some Spanish: *"Nine, no, no…ocho, no uno."*

In the first week, the merchants, who mostly seemed amused by her, learned the meaning of the German word *nine*.

Almost every day, she went to one or two of the neighboring shacks where the rest of their group now lived. Over coffee, she would not stop talking about how to get out of Pasto, and to one of the larger cities they had stopped in on their travels here from the coast. The one that struck her the most had been Cali.

"Did you see the temple we drove past off the main road?" she would repeat to anyone who would listen. *"Union Cultural Israelita,"* she would say carefully with her heavy German accent. "We cannot stay here and be chicken farmers. This is not how my daughter is going to grow up. I had already started planning her debut, and who will she meet here, a goatherd? We will be finding our way north as soon as possible. Will you go with us?"

Most of the families agreed with Lena, although one husband and wife with two older boys were learning to embrace this life and decided to stay.

"Sure, you have sons," Lena said to them. "You might get a nice horse for a dowry when they choose one of these *bauernmädchen* for a wife."

It would be another year before the families finally made the move to Cali. A small group of them had undertaken a day's journey north to the city, which in spite of Lena's initial excitement was unimpressive, dirty and filled with signs of poverty. They met with the rabbi from the *Union Cultural* to see what arrangements could be made. One of the women in the group had become fluent in Spanish and made all of the translations. The group made it clear that they were preparing to relocate to Cali, with or without the support of the small Jewish community there.

The Sephardic Rabbi, olive-skinned with dark eyes and a long graying black beard, had never met such pale, blue-eyed Jews before. He was put off by their assertive demeanor; but in the end agreed to help them. They would each be given a home to live in, and a small sum of money with which to begin their new lives in the city.

They returned to the farms triumphantly and made immediate arrangements for the move.

"Cochina!" exclaimed Karl's mother, now rapidly becoming frailer after just two years in their adopted home city. She had wiped a finger across the top of the credenza and held it up in the face of the young servant girl, showing her a single speck of dust. The girl quickly took her apron and ran it over the entire piece of furniture, before escaping through the open courtyard to the kitchen. In the three years that they had been in the country, Karl's mother had learned just two words of Spanish, both heavily accented. *Cochina,* pig, was her constant refrain as she followed the maids around looking for a missed spot of dust; *frío!* meant the soup, coffee, meat or rice needed to be brought back to the kitchen and reheated to nearly boiling to satisfy her.

She would walk the halls of the house, crisscrossing the courtyard for exercise; expecting Hannah, now a content, sweet-tempered and stunning green-eyed five-year-old, to hold her hand and keep her steady. She was too proud to use a cane as she shuffled around; and Hannah was happy to help her beloved, if curmudgeonly, grandmother, *Omi*.

The two of them went to see their very first full-length feature film in a movie theater; King Kong, poorly dubbed into Spanish. Hannah whispered German translations into her Omi's ear. When the giant ape grabbed Faye Wray, climbed the Empire State Building and dangerously waved her around while being attacked by airplanes, they both grabbed each other and screamed in terrified delight.

"That was a terrible movie! Terrible!" her grandmother repeated over and over on their slow walk home.

They stopped in at the little store Karl and Lena had opened. The shop, called Tienda el Barato, stood on a corner at the base of the Loma de las Tres Cruces mountain. They opened the low wrought iron gate with its Jewish star and walked through the wooden door into the tiny space overflowing with goods.

Lena was belting out a bawdy German song to the delight of the patrons shopping or just stopping into chat. When she ended with a low, long, deep and dramatic note, they applauded and shouted for more.

Hannah, a favorite to the regulars at the shop, was offered cookies, candy and ice cream by all.

One man yelled out, "I have a son waiting for her to get a little bigger, and then they will be married!" which Hannah translated for her mother, without really understanding.

"Ha!" responded Lena, which needed no translation.

The life they had made for themselves in Colombia was only marred by the updates from Europe. Although it took months for any word to arrive in this country, news of *Kristallnacht* had nearly done in the will to survive in all of them. As soon as they settled in Cali, they had telegraphed word of their new location to Hans. They received, in return, a single letter written in shaky handwriting on onion-skin paper, begging for money to help Hans and his wife flee Germany. They sadly telegraphed back that no money would be coming, as there was none to share. It would be years before they heard of the tragic end Hans and his wife both met in the Auschwitz concentration camp.

Over the next ten years, all of the old ones would become frail or sick and pass away. Each was buried, in turn, in the tiny four-acre Cementerio Hebreo de Cali, one of only four cemeteries in the entire country where Jewish residents were interred.

The hardest for Hannah had, of course, been the death of Karl's mother at ninety-three years of age. Although the others had been always kind and loving of the only granddaughter they would have, Omi would have an influence on her that left a permanent mark. Omi's headstrong nature inspired Hannah's own independent streak, leading to many arguments with Lena.

Hannah, too young to remember the journey they had undertaken to arrive here, thrived in the tropical city of Cali. She would always be the one to fill the tin plates of the dirty, bedraggled beggars who came to the door every evening after supper to ask for their leftovers. She loved chasing after the man on the bicycle who came through the streets early every morning with a basket full of pan de bono for sale. She would eat one of the warm chewy, cheesy rolls on her walk home, carrying a small brown bag filled for the others' breakfast.

Hannah would help the youngest of the maids do some of their housework, and then play with them in the gated front yard. One of their favorite games involved trying to push each other onto the huge fire-ant hills. The winner got to watch the loser jumping around and brushing the biting large, red insects off her legs. Afterwards, they would roll on the ground, laughing and hugging, until Lena caught them and screamed at the maids to get back to work. She would scold Hannah roundly, make her change into a clean dress and have her practice handwriting.

Hannah did well enough in primary school to be accepted to the private *Colegio Femenino Del Valle* high school halfway up the Loma when she was just twelve. She and her girlfriends would often be found during the lunchtime siesta sitting on the tile floor in the courtyard, playing with the chickens or dancing to music only they could hear. This would test Lena's patience to no end.

"You need to act like a young lady at all times," she would tell the barely chastened child. "A wild girl never finds a husband," was the constant refrain.

Hannah should not have been surprised, on her return from classes at the end of school one day, to find two strangers in the sitting room with her mother. The well-dressed man sat bolt upright in front of his china cup of coffee, and elbowed the young man sitting next to him to do the same when Hannah walked into the room.

"Please come here, Hannah, and say hello to Mr. Johann Solomon and his son, Maarten. They have come from Jamundi just to meet you. Come sit and have a piece of cake with us."

Lena could not hide her eagerness as she spent the next two hours expounding on Hannah's accomplishments and good behavior, with a few well-placed remarks on her occasional demonstrations of silly willfulness. She asked Mr. Solomon several questions, mostly about Maarten. She also managed to get in some thinly veiled queries as to his own business dealings and family history.

The youngsters sat silently almost the whole time, studiously avoiding looking at each other. Hannah fought the flush she felt rising to her cheeks as she realized what her mother was doing.

As the maid showed Mr. Solomon and his son out, Lena proudly patted Hannah on the arm. "You did very well. But you should have been wearing your best dress. Next time, I will have you change before coming in to the room."

"Next time? Mother, I am barely fourteen. Are you trying to find me a husband? I don't want a husband!"

"You do not know what you want, so it is my job to do it for you. If you are not married by the time you are seventeen, you will be considered an old maid. We do not have a big dowry to offer, so I will be bringing many suitors here to meet you and hope for the best that we can do. It is not like in Berlin, where you would have been presented this year to the entire society."

At this, Lena paused, remembering her own debut, and the many balls she had attended in the old country. Hannah took the opportunity to stamp her foot once at her mother, then turn and flee, humiliated, to her room.

Her mother was true to her word. For the next year, there were a dozen such visits. Some of the young men were tall, handsome and full of themselves. Others were overly thin with acne covering their noses, hunched over and not meeting anyone's eyes. They came from as far away as Argentina, always with a well-dressed father, for these meetings.

After each, Hannah would find fault with them in one way or another. The last straw for Hannah was when Lena introduced her to a twelve-year-old boy, whose father wore diamond rings on both hands and a gold Rolex watch on his right wrist.

When they left, it was all Hannah could do not to raise her voice at her mother, which would have likely resulted in a hard slap with that heavy hand. "Mother, he is a child! Do you want me to marry a child?"

"His father owns a diamond business, the largest in Bogotá,

maybe the largest in this whole country! You would never want for anything, and the boy will grow into a man. Three years is not that large of an age difference. You need to think with your head."

"I prefer to think with my heart. I like Sebastian, if you want to know the truth. His parents own several buildings in Cali and a sugar plantation in Popayán, since that is what matters to you."

"That *polaco*??" Lena nearly spit the derogatory term she used for any Jew she met who was not from Germany. "Never. He will, like his father, have at least two mistresses with their own families. Is that what you want?"

Once again, Hannah turned on her heel and left the room, seething.

Shortly after this, Hannah found herself on an airplane to Quito, Ecuador. In spite of the fact that this was a mission to meet another prospective suitor, and in spite of the fact that her mother sat next to her, severely upright, holding on tightly to the armrests and with a look of unbridled fear on her face, Hannah could not hide her excitement. An airplane, to a country named for the Equator! She could not think of a bigger adventure to tell her friends about when they returned next month.

A Studebaker convertible, driven by a tall, thin, friendly man, met them on the tarmac and helped them into the back seat. He loaded their luggage into the trunk, which would barely close over the bulk. Hannah's dresses, mostly chiffon and satin with full or crenulated skirts and wide velvet bows, took up most of the space in the baggage.

Hannah enjoyed the wind blowing her long hair around her face as she gazed in wonder at the city unfolding in front of her. The first thing that got her attention was the towering volcano looming to the west, reaching 15,000 feet into the bluest sky she had ever seen. They passed a neo-gothic cathedral telling stories of lives long forgotten; the palaces surrounding the Grande Plaza; and the open-air markets filled with colorful handmade goods and colorful people. Quito, she sighed to herself, the highest capital city in the world, the closest city to the equator. She decided right then that she had to explore this beautiful place during the month they planned to stay. She hoped against hope that this latest boy her mother was determined to marry her off to had even one scintilla of adventurousness in him and would take her, unchaperoned and unfettered, around his home city.

She sighed again, knowing how unlikely this was.

As the car pulled in front of the villa where they were to be guests, several servants were already lined up waiting to assist them. A man dressed in black suit and bowtie, wearing white gloves, bowed welcome and bade them follow him inside.

They were led through the large marble foyer, with halls leading away on both sides, and taken to the open courtyard in the middle of the house. The family awaited them with warm smiles.

"Welcome to our wonderful city of Quito!" boomed the man of the group, whom Hannah took to be the husband of the beautiful woman sitting next to him, and the father of the three children squeezed onto a low French linen settee.

The little ones were squirming in impatience to get at the china platters of delicate cookies and cakes laid out on the hand-carved table before them. "This is my wife, Martena, and these are Karena, Lis and little David. Please sit and enjoy some coffee from our own trees, grown on the side of the Pinchicha volcano you passed on your ride from the airport. I hope you enjoyed the Studebaker; it is the newest model, very hard to obtain here in South America. But if you know the right people, then anything is possible. Ah, here is our son, Richard now!"

This last was exclaimed as a young man, so strikingly handsome it was hard to look at him without staring, came towards them. He walked directly to Lena and Hannah and shook their hands firmly and warmly.

"I welcome you both to our beautiful country and city, and I look forward to getting to know you well over the next month. May I offer you some cakes and coffee? Father has arranged for us to tour our factories this afternoon, and we would not want you too hungry to enjoy them."

Lena, struck uncharacteristically dumb by his appearance, could only nod her head. Hannah politely answered, "No, thank you."

For the next several hours, Richard and his father, also named Richard, entertained them with stories of the business and the antics of some of their favorite employees.

Several times, Richard's mother chimed in, confidently recounting their arrival twenty years before from Hamburg. She told of their involvement in creating a sanctuary community for the Jewish refugees who came after them, while establishing their growing company that made straw hats.

"We have found true artisans among the local natives here who create the most exquisite formal straw hats, as well as the more casual type used by the general public." She used a word, *equatorianísimo*, several times, which Hannah had never heard, but quickly discerned was a term of cultural pride.

As the families chatted, Lena shared highlights of their own arrival in Colombia, the success of their store in Cali, and Hannah's excellent education. The sun passed high overhead, brilliant yellow against the perfect azure backdrop, and began its long slow descent towards the west. The temperature on the patio was perfect due to Quito's nine-thousand-foot altitude, as they sat for hours, becoming more familiar and comfortable with each other.

The younger Richard asked Hannah very direct questions, including her opinions on the current political state of Jews in South America, the latest dances in Cali, and what she might know about other places in the world. Hannah answered his questions just as directly and even dared, ignoring her mother's barely hidden horror, to ask him a few of her own.

When at last the manservant arrived to inform them that the cars were ready to begin their tour, Richard came to stand next to Hannah and offer his arm to escort her to the door.

"We would like a moment to change and refresh ourselves," Lena stated, as she stood. "Our travel clothes just will not do for this afternoon's adventures."

"Of course," Martena said. She directed the maid who had come to clear the coffee urn and platters to show them to their rooms.

As soon as they were inside the richly decorated bedroom where Hannah was to stay, with a connecting door to her mother's equally ornamented chamber, Lena pounced. "He is the one. They are perfect, and Ecuador is not far to come visit each other regularly. The airplane took less than five hours, even with the stop in Bogota. Did you see the dress the mother was wearing? Those were actual pearls sown onto the hems. And those darling little ones! You and Richard will have children even more beautiful than them. We will be the envy of everyone at Club Shalom! Hannah, even though you were a bit rude, Richard did not seem to mind you at all," this she exclaimed while roughly grabbing both of Hannah's arms and giving her a shake to make her point.

"Are you done, Mother?" Hannah said, as she firmly removed

Lena's strong hands from her shoulders. "Richard is very nice. And so handsome too. There is just one thing…"

"Oh, what could it be, you willful girl?! Are you trying to die alone and kill me along the way? What could you possibly find to dislike about this one?" Lena's rage was barely contained.

"First of all, I did not think you enjoyed that airplane ride so much that you would do it 'regularly.' And as for Richard, it's just that…I don't think he likes girls." She said it simply, repeating something one of her school friends had told her. She watched the color drain from her mother's face.

"What does that mean? I do not even understand you, what are you saying?"

"I mean that I think Richard would prefer if my name was Hans instead of Hannah," she replied, with a hint of mirth that she covered with her hand, feigning an itch on her nose.

"Why would you say such a thing?! It is utterly ridiculous! Men like Richard Rosenblatt do not raise abominations, and furthermore you could never tell such a thing from a simple conversation, and finally, I don't care if he prefers cows. His father is hoping that you two will marry, and if at the end of this month he still feels that way, then you will do just that! Get dressed and hurry, we do not want to keep them waiting any longer. Wear the pale pink taffeta gown. It brings out your eyes."

As they rejoined the family, Richard stood and again offered his arm to Hannah, who took it with a pretty smile. "Your dress is lovely," he said, as they led the group out to the waiting line of cars. "It brings out your stunning green eyes, and the rose shimmer of the satin hem is perfect against your remarkable skin tones."

Hannah smiled to herself as she thanked him for the compliments.

A long while later, they walked through the third factory, the main building with the largest production floor, housing the offices where both Richards spent their days. Hannah's eyes were glazed over, and she stifled yawn after yawn. They had just spent hours listening to the history and description of each style of hat, and each employee. Lena pinched her viciously on her hip more than once to bring her back. What got her attention were the words, "our last stop on the tour," as they were escorted into the spacious rooms with oversized windows that served as the men's headquarters.

At each of the four smaller desks lined up in the open space, sat a young man working. When they heard the door open, they looked up for a moment; then jumped to their feet when they spied the women behind their bosses.

"Introduce yourselves, men," commanded Richard, the father, with authority, but also with obvious affection.

"Henry, at your service!"

"George, pleased to meet you both!"

"David, good day, ladies!"

"Pieter!" said the last with a flourishing bow; and when he stood upright again, he held a single white rose in his hand, which he held out to Hannah.

She and Lena laughed and clapped delightedly, as young Richard wryly said, "Ah yes, our fair Pieter. Trusted right hand man and all-around good chap to have in your corner. You will see him often at the house over the next month, I am sure."

With that, the group turned and walked towards the exit; but not before Pieter somehow caught Hannah's eye again. He gave another bow, tipping a second rose to his forehead and then to her.

Over the next few days, it became apparent that Hannah was

only to see Richard at supper time, high noon each day. After two o'clock, he and his father returned to the office and worked until seven. Martena explained that she and Lena would spend the afternoons occupied with society gatherings and charity work; Hannah was to be shown around Quito by one of the young men that worked for the company. "Pieter, if you remember him. He of the white rose," she said, with a fond smile.

The first day that Pieter arrived to pick her up, he opened the door of the light blue Renault, a boxy flat-sided van with large tires, and helped her step up into the front seat. She laughed in delight at the unusual vehicle.

Pieter laughed too, as he explained, "This beauty was originally built for the French military, and later the French police. The high clearance was designed for the poor road conditions in France. Of course, most of our roads are paved here in Quito, but it's a perfect company car; great at moving materials and also, apparently, at transporting hats."

This last was said in a wry tone, and she laughed again.

"Where are you taking me today, Sir Pieter? There is so much to see here in your fair city," Hannah sounded ready with a list, and Pieter sensed it.

"What would you like to see first?" he asked, after climbing in to the driver's seat and turning to look at her with a direct and frank gaze that she returned.

"The market," she said firmly. "Then the cathedrals, and then the volcano."

"We have almost a month! Why don't you pick one for each day, and we will go from there?" Pieter said, not hiding his intrigue at this unusual girl.

"Done! Today the market, tomorrow the rest, and after that we will see!" Hannah exclaimed, as he put the van in gear and headed into town.

For the next several weeks, Hannah had the time of her life. Mornings, she played with the children at the house. Supper was a formal affair, with all dressed in their best as they ate and then enjoyed their early afternoon coffee. The afternoons she spent with Pieter. They crisscrossed the city, and headed to the outskirts to visit the volcano, the coffee farms and the people who lived in the tiny towns surrounding Quito.

Often, they would stop for a light picnic of some local fare that he picked up. They ate fried plátanos and llapingachos, which reminded her of cheesy latkes. She even tasted cuy, which they held carefully by the four little legs to tear the greasy meat off the bones with their teeth.

When they drove to a historical spot, Pieter knew all the details. When they stopped to speak to people, Pieter could communicate with everyone. He was fluent in five languages and learned new words easily. When they had their little picnics, Pieter told her stories of his family's war time experiences that had landed him in Ecuador with his mother. Hannah often had to blot a tear while he spoke about the camps in Indonesia. She was unaware that it was the first time he had spoken of such things to anyone.

Of the Rosenblatt family, Pieter had nothing but praise: "A wonderful and generous family," he exclaimed emotionally. "They have done much for us and for many others in the community. Richard himself is very nice. I know you were brought here to meet him as a prospective husband; but maybe you have already noticed, he's a little light in the heels. If you know what I mean."

Hannah's little smile told him she did.

He often entertained her with little tricks, like making small objects disappear in front of her eyes or pulling a handkerchief out of his sleeve. One time he brought something he called a "diabolo". It had two thin batons about the length of her arm, with a long string linking them at one end. He showed her two wooden cups joined at their bases by a short dowel. He held the ends of the batons and got the cups spinning on the string. Then Pieter launched them into the air, caught them neatly and rolled them back and forth across the string. She clapped her hands and asked to try it. They both laughed at her fumbling attempts.

Quickly the last afternoon supper arrived, and the room was filled with emotion. Hannah's air of satisfied and saturated enjoyment was complemented by the family Rosenblatt's pleasure at a job well done. It was no small feat to entertain strangers in your home for a month.

Lena radiated anticipation, eagerness, and some impatience. While the rest chatted contentedly, Hannah expressing thanks to the family for the lovely visit and young Richard smiling cheerfully, Lena struggled to sit still in her chair and enjoy this last repast together.

Finally, she could stand it no longer, and in the middle of Martena expressing her pride in the work Pieter had done showing Hannah their lovely city, she fairly burst, "Are you going to marry my daughter?!"

The instant silence and the change in the very weight of the air lasted a long moment. It became apparent the Martena and Richard senior had the same question as they turned to look at their son.

Hannah's face turned to stone, pale and still.

After a beat, the son stood, turned to Hannah, took her hand, and looked deeply into her eyes. "You are a delightful, stunning and amazing creature," he said. "But you are not a good match for me. I know you will find what your mother is looking for. Unfortunately, it is not here in Quito."

With that, he raised her hand to his lips, kissed it and walked out of the room. Martena, Richard and Lena were stunned mute. Hannah just smiled knowingly to herself.

On the flight home, Lena was silent for an hour or so. Then she recovered and enthusiastically began planning the next visit with prospects for Hannah. In her own silence, Hannah looked at the small piece of paper on which Pieter had written his address and phone number, that she had folded up and hidden in a pocket of her handbag.

Lena noticed, and sharply asked, "What is that?"

"Nothing, Mother," she responded and carefully placed it back in her bag.

On Hannah's seventeenth birthday, the celebration included a large German-style cheesecake made by the maids with Lena's overbearingly watchful eye and barked instructions. Over coffee, Hannah announced to the guests her intentions to finish high school, move to Bogotá and attend the teachers' college there. Her friends cheered congratulations and shared their own plans. One was to study and become an architect. Two were following their families into business. One had an apprenticeship already begun with the local photographer, and one shyly announced her engagement.

At this, the small group of intimate friends screamed in joyful astonishment and ran off to Hannah's bedroom.

"You will have to do…you know…" one of the girls said, blushing deeply. "To make babies you have to…"

They all turned red, except for Helen, the future architect, who had been the one to teach them the word "homosexual".

"You have sex," she stated in her customarily formidable tone. "He puts his penis in you and you lay there and let him do it. Then his seed comes out and goes up inside you, and that is what will make the babies,"

The other girls grabbed each other and screamed again, eyes shut tight, cheeks bright red.

"It's not a big deal," Helen continued. "How do you think you all got here?"

It was too much for them; and they shrieked and jumped on top of Helen to stop her from continuing.

Hannah hugged the last guests farewell and went to her room to change out of her party dress. Lena intercepted her there.

"What is this nonsense about Bogotá and teacher school? You will do no such thing. A wife does not need college. A mother does not need a job. She has already the most important job a woman can have -to take care of her husband and the house staff; and to make sure she properly educates her children for their future, as I am trying to do for you. Although, you seem so ungrateful about my efforts. I have a meeting set up for the day after tomorrow with the Rabbi from São Paolo, Brazil, and his son. If this does not work out, and I hope it does because most of the good ones are already promised, I have two more boys lined up for next week. Take your silly idea out of your head and stop fighting this. I am your mother and I know what is best for you. You will do as you are told, and you will do it with a pretty smile!"

With that, Lena turned and walked out of the room, shutting the door firmly behind her.

Hannah stood for a long moment staring at the closed door. Finally, her shoulders slumped, her body deflated, and she sat heavily on the edge of her bed. Covering her face with both hands, she began to sob bitterly.

After that day, Hannah felt something inside her had fractured. She began to accept that she might not escape the fate her mother mapped out for her. School was coming to an end soon, and all of her friends were preparing for their futures. Hannah saw any control she had over her own slip away.

She became more complacent as her mother became more relentless in her quest. Lena continued to lay the fault of each failure on Hannah; her posture, her demeanor, her lack of proper etiquette, her lack of social grace and enthusiasm.

The rabbi's letter arrived the next day to cancel the meeting, writing that he had already found a match for his son. Lena took it out on Hannah, blaming her for not being content with one of the many young men she had already met. When one of the other two families that had been scheduled for the following week cancelled for the same reason, Lena became desperate.

She began a daily regimen of sending letters to anyone she knew, or had heard of, with money who had an eligible son. Each letter was painstakingly handwritten on the thin, easily wrinkled airmail paper. Each was nearly identical: glowing commentary on Hannah's wonderful attributes and accomplishments. Inside the neat fold in the pages. she placed a small copy of a photo of Hannah taken at a recent wedding. She had paid extra to have them colored by hand. These letters were sent as far away as France, Australia, Canada and the United States; just about any country except Germany, which she swore she would hate until the day she died. In Lena's mind, the prospective husband would relocate to Colombia and continue here whatever business his family owned that gave them their fortune.

In this way, she would help Hannah raise her own family correctly. She had doubts about Hannah's ability to do so on her own.

Most of the letters received no response. A few expressed interest; but also a concern about how to arrange a meeting, since they had no intention of boarding an airplane to Colombia. One was answered by the father of the young man saying that, although his son was just newly married, he himself was a recent widow and was interested in proposing on his own behalf.

Lena threw all of the responses away in disgust and continued her campaign.

Hannah began working more hours at the store before and after school. Each day blended into the next in a routine which, although mundane, became comforting at the same time. She loved spending time there with her father, who, whenever he saw her looking sad, would lift her chin and look into her eyes.

"It is not so very bad, is it, Hannah? Mother wants the best life for you. After everything she went through to get us all to this point, she wants your life to be much easier."

"I am not sure that is true, Papa," Hannah would invariably reply.

But she would give him the smile he loved and needed from his cherished daughter.

As the school year came to a close that November, she resigned herself to the fact that her mother's dreams for her, and not her own, would come true. A war against a force of nature, Hannah began to accept, cannot be won.

Late one afternoon, Lena came walking quickly into the store. She was waving a letter in one hand, breathlessly singing, "This one, this one," over and over again.

Hannah almost felt relief. It was a release from the endless waiting, endless arguing, endlessly unsettled feelings. It had all finally worn her down; and Hannah hoped it was, in fact, the one.

She had stopped caring who she married, where she lived and what happened to her. She just wanted all this to end, and something different to begin. Hannah sat with her mother to hear the news.

Lean took a deep breath, barely able to contain herself. She turned to her daughter and took Hannah's limp hands in her firm ones.

"Hannah, dear, you are going to America! The United States of America! He is there, a doctor, son of a very wealthy man! You are exactly what his father has been searching for as a wife for him. He lives in…"

She stopped to look for the name of the city in the letter, and carefully pronounced it: "Toledo, Ohio."

She proudly, triumphantly, announced to all in the store, "My daughter is getting married and moving to America!"

Applause, cheers and hugs followed. Through it all, Hannah felt like a piece of wood, like a replica of herself, while the real self was somehow hovering above, watching. It had finally happened.

Less than a month later, Hannah's two suitcases were packed and in the car that would take her to El Limonar airport, a short ride from the house. Her mother thought it somehow fortuitous that hers was one of the last flights before this little airport closed permanently. Cali was working to grow its acceptance and admittance into the world economy; and building a new, modern airport would be part of this process.

"Endings lead to new beginnings," Lena said, as they left the house.

Hannah was unsure whether she was still talking about the airport or about her; or maybe, secretly, also about herself.

Hannah thought about the ending of school. Her girlfriends had cried desperately when they found out she was leaving the country.

Even Helen's eyes blinked rapidly for one moment before she roughly wiped a tear away with the back of her hand, declaring, "You will be back before you know it, with your handsome doctor and maybe a bouncing baby or two. You can name your first girl after me."

That had made them all laugh, eyes still teary, as they dragged Helen into a final group hug.

Hannah became nervous as soon as her parents had made sure she was in her seat and then left the plane. Her father turned to wave as he ducked through the exit door. Her mother never looked back.

They were not accompanying her on this trip, as arrangements had been made for a mutual friend of Lena's and the Ohio family to meet her at the airport in New York. She would be spending several weeks there before going on to Toledo to finalize plans for the Summer wedding. *North American Summer*, Hannah reminded herself; just six months away.

As the door closed with a jarring thump, Hannah let out the breath she had been holding, maybe for years; and began to think about all that was to come.

America, land of the free, home of the brave, she sang in her head. Lena had made her practice this song repeatedly over the last weeks, even though neither of them spoke enough English to understand most of its meaning.

As the plane took off and banked frighteningly close to the imposing Farallones mountain peaks west of the little city, Hannah became lost in her thoughts. Eighteen years old, on her way to the greatest country in the world, to the greatest city in that country, for a whole three weeks! Her mind reeled with thoughts of this; and of the arranged marriage to come. When the plane stopped for its layover in Kingston, Jamaica, she was surprised that several hours had passed.

That was when the stewardess came over the loudspeaker and announced, in both English and Spanish, that they would be having an unscheduled night's stay in Kingston due to faulty wiring in the cockpit. A bus was on its way to transport the travelers to a resort where they would be taken care of until morning.

Never in her life had she been alone, unsupervised, with strangers in a foreign place; with a whole evening spread out before her. Her body thrummed with fear and uncertainty as she deplaned.

Three young ladies her age quickly found each other and Hannah, and were given a room to share at the resort. Late into the night, they chatted, sharing stories about family, friends, school; and, giggling and blushing, boys.

The others had traveled back and forth for years to visit American family. They filled Hannah's head with wonderful stories of life in the United States. They told of nights out in the city with large groups of friends; of foods they had tasted that were new and often strange, yet amazing; and, above all, of the freedom they had, exploring unchaperoned wherever and whenever they wanted!

Marta, whose singular adventures made her sound like the most experienced and sophisticated person Hannah ever hoped to meet, exclaimed at one point, "After all, it is 1955! It's about fucking time that we women are allowed to do what we want, without our mothers or some man looking over our shoulders!"

Hannah, who had only heard such language from Helen, was both aghast and delighted. When at long last the other girls had settled down and begun to breathe in the quiet rhythm of sound sleep, she could not stop her thoughts racing and her heart pounding. As the Jamaican birds began their early serenade of another Caribbean day, she finally fell asleep.

After a quick breakfast, the bus came for the travelers, and brought them back to the smiling and reassuring faces of the crew of the Boeing 707. They mounted the metal staircase and returned to their seats. The girls waved and blew kisses to each other as they settled in for the rest of the flight to New York.

Hannah watched out the window as the plane flew smoothly into the air. The island became a brown and green gem in the vast Atlantic Ocean.

With endless blue stretching above and below her, Hannah found her thoughts flowing once again in new and unfamiliar directions.

She opened her purse and took out a folded piece of paper, holding it in her hand a moment before opening it. She looked at it for the hundredth time, with a small smile.

It held Pieter's address and phone number in Brooklyn, where he and his mother had relocated just the year before. Their correspondence had secretly continued over the past year, with Pieter's amusing anecdotes lighting up her darkest days.

Right at that moment she made the biggest decision of her life: she was not going to Ohio.

Her mother was thousands of miles away, she was now legally an adult, and maybe, just maybe, she could finally control her own life.

By the time the stewardess announced the final descent into the New York airport, Hannah felt an unbridled exhilaration unlike anything she had ever experienced. She would begin a new life, as an American girl, just like in the magazines she and her girlfriends in Cali loved; just like Marta.

The plane landed and taxied to the gate. With a thud the door opened and hit the body of the airplane heavily. Out the little window, she saw three men drag the metal staircase over to the opening. She waited in line to deplane, heart hammering in her ears.

Then it was her turn to descend. Her sandaled foot touched the snow-covered tarmac at Idlewild Airport.

She was free.

Dirk's Story

"Waar gaan we?"

"We gaan op een boot, Dirky."

"We're going on a boat ride, we're going on a boat ride, we're going on a..." the eight-year-old boy's chant was shushed by his teenaged sister.

"Be quiet, can't you?! Don't you see this is not a vacation?"

"Let him alone, Melke. He's too young to understand. It's better that way, anyhow."

To the boy, his mother said, "Remember your Hebrew School book, my love. You'll have plenty of time to study on our journey."

With that, the boy bounded away to check his little bag once again.

Melke knew her mother was right, and she finished packing her small valise with a silent scowl. This *really* wasn't fair, thought the 15-year-old, followed by a small almost-adult voice scolding in her head: *Oh, it's worse than that. Way worse.*

Melke felt she was old enough to be included in the adult conversations but had been sent to bed while her father and mother discussed the meaning of the latest news with his two brothers and their wives. With her ear to the door, she could hear drifts of voices, with the tensest moments ringing out clearly.

"Our Dutch forces surrendered yesterday after the bombing of Rotterdam. The royal family has already fled. We must leave as soon as possible. What makes you think we will not have our own

Kristallnacht here in Amsterdam??" Melke's Oom Hendrik stated in undisguised frustration.

There was resounding agreement from her parents, Jaan and Grieta, and the wives, her *tantes*. The lone holdout had been Oom Levi, who did not want to believe that their family diamond business, which had just finally been taking off, would end like this. Oom Levi could not accept that their city, and maybe even their lives, could end like this. He was a man of numbers after all, and his aptitude in this area had been the impetus for their burgeoning success. He thought the odds were in their favor and stubbornly stated so.

Grieta's emotional but firm response floated to Melke's ear: "Levi, my parents agree with you. My four brothers agree with you. My three sisters agree with you. They are all staying here in Amsterdam and hoping for the best. We have Melke and Dirk to think about, and we are making plans to begin the journey within a few days. In any case, our business will be on hold for a while; no one is buying diamonds right now. We can wait things out in Batavia in the Dutch East Indies. Jaan has a contact through Eduard who will help us establish there until things improve here."

Jaan interjected, "The Dutch colony on the coast of Batavia will offer us a place to safely pass the rest of this year, and possibly next year as well. Once things return to normal, we can return to our lives. Levi, you must see that it is not safe here for our families. Most of the Jews in Berlin did not believe what was to happen; only the few who followed their instincts were able to escape with their lives. The rumors are becoming undeniable that Hitler is killing those that stayed behind by the hundreds, if not thousands. Grieta and I have tried to talk her family into joining us, but they have refused. We hope you can see this is the only way to guarantee our survival. Our parents are ready to go," he added pointedly.

The tense exchanges that had begun two days ago had come to a head late last night. Melke heard her uncle stand and sweep his hand in despair across the collection of tiny ceramic delft houses on the mantle, sending them flying in all directions. The others in the room remained silent and watchful, as he came to accept that they had no choice.

The three brothers left the flat then and were gone for several hours. Melke was to find out in the morning that they had gone to speak with Eduard, her father's closest business associate, and their neighbor down the street. Together, they planned the drive to Portugal. From there, they would board a ship sailing around South Africa, and on to safety. It was to be a long journey, one with many unknowns. The men organized the first few stops as well as they could on a moment's notice.

Within a few hours, cars began lining up outside the flat at 19 Sarphatistraat in central Amsterdam. Hushed words were exchanged among the adults while the children played in blissful ignorance. Melke and the other teens sulked in a small group. The elderly fretted amongst themselves.

After a final headcount, and with all of the suitcases stuffed in trunks and tied on the roofs, the children, women and grandparents were seated inside the packed cars. That left the men standing in the kitchen for one last talk.

"Is all ready in Brussels? The telegram was sent ahead?" Jaan asked for the third time. "We must not have a delay in picking up the others and getting on our way as quickly as possible. This will be the most dangerous part of the trip with the Germans' victory last week. We can only hope their troops have not reached this far yet. If they have..."

He did not have to finish this thought. They all knew that the risk they had decided to take might very well end badly.

With a final look around and a silent thought *goodbye home, I don't know when we'll be back,* Jaan walked out of the flat and sat himself in the driver's seat of the bulky Mercedes Benz behind a red Rolls Royce. Sitting next to him, Grieta tried to reassure him while Melke, little Dirk, and their grandparents fanned themselves in the back seat of the already stifling car.

If he had patted his coat pocket, Jaan would have realized that it was empty. The handkerchief full of diamonds, meant to help them get a new start in Batavia, had fallen out of his pocket and slid under the kitchen table.

His two younger brothers walked through the two-story flat. They closed the bedroom doors, used the WC one last time, and blew out a candle left burning in the cozy kitchen. They locked the front door behind them. Finally, they climbed into the front seat of a green Citroen, telling their wives to quiet the two bickering cousins sitting with them in the back. Ahead of them, the neighbor in his Fiat, waved that he was ready.

The four automobiles in the convoy set out.

In the front car, Eduard led them east through Utrecht, the interior route to Belgium. Even though it was closer to the German border, they hoped that the Wehrmacht focus was still on the West as they marched into France. Eduard's wife held their five-year-old son on her lap as he sang *Berend Botje ging uit varen* ("Berend Botje has gone sailing"), which his mother had taught him to get him excited about the journey.

Their first stop was one hundred twenty miles away in Brussels, where the final two carloads of family and friends were to join them. It was mid-May, and the European spring sun heated the inside of the crowded vehicles to an unbearable degree, even with all of the windows open. The men lit cigarette after cigarette, and the children began to whine. The silence emanating from the women and the teenagers, the first due to worry and the second to brooding, made the atmosphere feel thicker still.

The ride to Utrecht went quickly and smoothly. They stopped momentarily there to check the luggage straps, before continuing on towards Breda.

More and more vehicles, all overflowing with people, trunks and luggage joined them on the road. Grieta remarked quietly to Jaan that these must be German and Dutch Jews, fleeing south for safety. The tension in the cars grew as the congestion on the highway slowed them to a crawl. Beads of sweat formed at Jaan's hairline as he drummed his fingers on the large steering wheel, face set grimly, feet impatiently pumping clutch and brake. The front bumper of the Mercedes was mere centimeters from the rear of the Rolls.

Grieta, trying to distract them all, began humming *Korenbloemenblauw*, a popular light-hearted song often crooned at family gatherings. Jaan's mother began to sing the lyrics "Cornflower blue, are your eyes that bind me to you. Cornflower blue, heaven is where we are. That's why, my love, I swear allegiance to you," gently elbowing her husband to join in. By the time they got to the final chorus, *T Komt door die kijkers van jou, Korenbloemblauw,* Jaan's father was belting out the last notes while keeping beat with his feet on the floor.

Grieta was happy to see that even Jaan and Melke had relaxed just the littlest bit, when she realized the thumping sound she was hearing was no longer coming from her father's feet. In fact, it was not a thumping sound at all. A low rhythmic buzzing grew rapidly into a vibrating hum. She looked out the window for the source but could see nothing except lines of automobiles creeping along the road. Jaan craned his neck out of his window as the vibration became a throbbing, pulsing din. Confusion turned into fear as the volume of the racket quickly ratcheted up to thunderous levels, shaking the cars violently. Melke and Dirk both began to scream, as they covered their ears and tried to crawl to the floor.

That was when the first round of ammunition rained down out of the sky onto the line of vehicles.

The car just next to Grieta jumped crazily as the strafing bullets combed it from back to front. Just before the windshield exploded, large spatters of deep red hit it and flew out of the open windows in an insane scarlet shower. The shattered glass blew in all directions.

When shards flew into Jaan's car, it spurred him to action. He grabbed Dirk by the collar of his little shirt, hauled him over the back of the seat, threw open his door and leapt out. He yanked open the back door of the car from outside as the attack continued. His yells were swallowed by the roar of the Messerschmitt fighter planes sweeping over the cars on their way to the front. Grieta wrenched herself past the steering wheel. She grabbed Jaan's mother out of the back seat and, ducking low, ran after Jaan. Melke pulled her grandfather from the car and followed behind them.

They crossed the empty oncoming lanes of the road, splashed through a knee-deep canal and threw themselves into the high grass, hugging the ground and hoping to become invisible to the pilots and machine gunners above. Even with their hands over their ears, the thrumming of the plane engines and the staccato rhythm of rapid gunfire overwhelmed them, endless. The children's shrieks were lost in the howling din.

After long minutes the attack ended. The sound of the planes quickly vanished towards the west.

Left in its wake, screaming, sobbing and moaning clearly rang up and down the column of automobiles. It was several minutes before Jaan and Grieta warily stood and looked around. The cars they could see, those in the left lane including their entire caravan, appeared untouched; simply stopped as if because of a traffic jam. Grieta's eyes swept forward and back, trying to comprehend how the world could look normal after the terror they had just lived through.

Then she looked beyond, to a scene of horror.

The automobiles in the right lane were blackened, riddled with holes. Some were on fire, and many were bespattered with crimson splashes. Beyond these, caught in their attempts to escape, she saw bodies, dozens of them; large and small and all covered in blood.

The initial wailing subsided a bit. Now panicked voices began to call names, as people searched for those in their party they had lost in the chaos. A mix of pleading and shouting floated through the thick haze of smoke. The stench of burning accompanied the piteous sound of the discovery of death. Wretched voices, one after another, became a howling as the number of casualties grew. It seemed to go on interminably, enveloping them and threatening to overwhelm them more completely than the attack itself had.

"Mama?"

The quiet whimper made Grieta drop to the ground, pull Dirk onto her lap and rock him, singing baby songs into his ear. He put his thumb into his mouth and, unbelievably, fell into a deep slumber.

She looked up at Jaan and said, "We must find the others. We must get out of here before the next wave."

She had no doubt there would be one, as the Luftwaffe made its way to the French border.

Not knowing what they would find, if they would soon join the grieving, they slowly began the walk toward their vehicles, the grandparents holding each other up. As they waded back through the shallow canal, Melke moaned loudly, hand slapped over her mouth, head jerking to the left. A body floated to her right, missing an arm, its clothes tattered and leaking blood. She splashed to the grass on the other side of the canal, fell to her knees and threw up. Her grandfather gently helped her up and they re-crossed the empty side of the road together.

As they did, they heard a shout: "Jaan! Grieta! Over here!"

Standing in the middle of the lane the rest of their group huddled, clinging to each other desperately. One of Melke's cousins leaned heavily on his father, Oom Levi, who was shouting and waving to them. The boy's leg looked twisted and his face was pale with pain, but he bore it silently.

After frantic hugs, the adults began to talk over each other.

Oom Hendrik's voice rose above the rest. "We are lucky to be alive, all of us! Look around you, we have to leave now!"

"We have to help these people," his wife, Tante Cori, whispered. "How can we just turn our backs on them? But for the grace of God, that could have been us."

Grieta hugged her shivering sister-in-law with one arm, the other still awkwardly cradling Dirk, who barely stirred. Jaan and Oom Levi nodded agreement with their brother.

"We can make Brussels in two hours and be on our way to Normandy by nightfall." This from Eduard, who continued, "We will drive through the night if we have to. It might actually be safer. We will be harder to see from the air."

At this, the men began to herd the women and children back to the cars. Grim-faced, they did their best to ignore the wailing that continued up and down the road. Cori joined the children in their quiet crying, as they crawled back into the automobiles.

The men drove the cars into the empty oncoming lanes. They were not alone. Slowly more of the undamaged vehicles crossed over the line in the road, passing around the long stationary line of ravaged cars. Eyes averted from the massacre, they all stared straight ahead as they made their way into Belgium.

The two cars that joined them in Brussels added Grieta's cousin Elias with his wife and teenaged daughter; and a family friend with his wife and her elderly parents.

The relief that they had made it out of Amsterdam, followed by the smooth pick-up in Brussels and the safe drive around Paris was only tempered by nagging anxiety about the road ahead. They arrived at the hotel in Bayeux, Normandy, late at night and immediately went into their rooms to sleep, their exhaustion exacerbated by the trauma of the day.

In the sunny morning, the children played with the complete abandon limited to the very young. There were only four of them, but they made enough racket for a dozen. They gleefully explored the grounds outside the hotel, chasing each other along the Aure River, then back to the others, only to turn and do it again.

The teens brooded amongst themselves, watching the younger ones with veiled envy; thinking only of what had been left behind. They were at the stage in their lives when friends meant more than family, and even the presence of the German soldiers on the streets of their cities only meant they had had to find other ways and places to meet. They, like the majority of people in Amsterdam and Brussels, had not really believed things would come to this. Abandoning homes, belongings, friends, entire lives, to go on the run. *Ungelooflijk*! *Incroyable*! Unbelievable! After what they had experienced just the day before, they grieved for the loss of the lives they knew.

The men stood together smoking, and the women repacked their bags. They were all silent, deep in their own thoughts; planning, praying, or reliving yesterday's nightmare. Grieta prepared breakfast, pouring Hagel Slag chocolate sprinkles on buttered white bread for the children; laying out coffee and croissants for the adults. As soon as she turned her back, Dirk snatched the small box of Hagel Slag, tilted his head back and poured sprinkles into his mouth until it was full. He happily chewed, his teeth and lips chocolate brown, making them all smile in spite of themselves.

As soon as they finished, the families climbed into the cars and got underway; on to Bordeaux, eight hours to the south.

The drive, on crowded highways over creeks and rivers, on empty roads through small towns with large ancient cathedrals, lulled them into an ease that, for now at least, all was well.

In Bordeaux, they were to remain for several days to map out the rest of the trip to the coast in Portugal. German soldiers had not made their way that far south in France, and they thought it a safe enough plan.

As they neared the crossing over the river Dordogne late that day, thirty kilometers from their destination, the monotony of the ride had set in. Most of the passengers were dozing comfortably and the drivers, one and all, were keen to have a few days' respite.

The caravan came around a sudden tight curve in the road. Lying out of sight and useless on the grass, a sign warning of the hazard had been knocked over earlier that day. The red Rolls Royce took the corner too fast. Its tires hit gravel on the side of the road. Eduard overcorrected, sharply yanking the steering wheel to the left.

The car flipped onto its top, skidding several meters; spun back onto its tires, blowing one, rolled twice more, popping two more tires; and finally came to a stop lopsided on the edge of the road. As the others watched in alarm, suitcases flew in all directions. The trunk burst open spilling boxes all over the road.

No one noticed the tiny boy fly out the window and land in the middle of the road. Large luggage cases landed on top of him, obscuring his small broken body from view.

The eerie silence that seemed impossibly loud after the screeching, scraping, banging madness was suddenly shattered by an ear-splitting wail coming from the front seat of the Rolls. "Luca! Luca!" the mother's voice grew in intensity until it finally pierced the numbness of the motionless witnesses.

Doors on all five of the other cars banged open, and twenty-two people hauled themselves out, some stumbling to the road onto their knees, and ran towards the battered lead car. The teenagers got there first, quickly followed by the men and their wives. The elderly, with looks of despair and dismay creasing their already-wrinkled faces, seemed to approach the disaster as if their bodies moved against their wills. The smaller children, whose minds could not and did not want to let in what was happening right in front of them, hid behind and followed the grandparents.

The driver was unconscious when Melke's father reached him. He was bleeding from a gash on his forehead, and his head lolled back loosely. Jaan carefully pulled him out and laid him on the ground.

Melke and her mother and two other women reached Luca's mother. Her face contorted with shock as she turned to look at them still shrieking her son's name, even though the women were inches from her. They pulled on the door, but it was jammed shut. The desperation on their faces and the straining muscles in their arms as they kept yanking on the door sent the mother over the top. She clawed her way through the open window and fell sprawling onto the street.

Crawling crablike around the car, searching under it, she continued to scream for Luca. Melke grabbed the other teens, and they raced in widening circles around the battered vehicle searching for signs of the little boy.

When the boy's mother came around the side of the car, she saw her husband prone on the ground. She crawled over to him, grabbed his shoulder and shook him violently.

"Get up, get up, you have to find Luca. Help me! Get up!" she yelled in his face.

Jaan crouched, gently removed her hands, and took her by the shoulders. "He's hurt. He can't hear you. We will find Luca."

At that moment screams came from near the pile of luggage laying scattered, on the road. Melke had just discovered a tiny leg, bleeding and twisted at a strange angle, jutting out from underneath a large trunk.

Jaan stood up and saw what she was looking at. He tried to grab Luca's mother before she could make a move, but he was too late. She all but leaped into the road and, coming down in front on the pile of suitcases, threw them off like they were lightweight toys. She uncovered her son and knew right away that he was gone. She sat on the road and pulled his loose little body onto her lap, rocking and sobbing and singing *Berend Botje*, trying to coax him back to life.

The scene was a crazy muddle of people, automobiles, luggage and other belongings, when Eduard began to shake his head from side to side, trying to come out of blackness. Jaan went to calm him, but he quickly became agitated and, holding his head with both hands, sat up.

His first sight was of his wife and broken son, and he nearly passed out again. He moaned as he watched her manic rocking and babbling, with Jaan's strong arm holding him up. Within seconds his spirit was as broken as his baby boy.

Long moments passed before anyone was able to make a move.

Grieta shook herself out of shock and took charge. She whispered to Jaan that they needed to get out of the road before other cars came and they caused a worse accident.

"How could it get worse?" Jaan replied, but he knew she was right.

The thought made him nauseous, and he turned his head to swallow back the gorge rising in his throat. The retching sounds that suddenly came from the twin teenagers as they vomited on their own shoes almost made him lose the battle. Only the knowledge of the need to take control of this situation kept him in check.

Grieta started ordering everyone to move. She herded the elderly to the side of the road out of harm's way. She pushed the teenagers with strong arms; made them pick up the scattered belongings and place them next to the elderly. She got in her cousin Elias' face and told him to get Luca and his mother into one of the cars. She sent Levi to help Jaan get Eduard off the street. Within minutes, they were back in the cars in devastated silence.

It was a sad, slow line of cars that made their way around the Rolls Royce, crossed the river Garonne and pushed on into the town ahead. When they parked in front of the first hotel they saw, it was Grieta who went in to speak to the manager and explain what they needed. The manager gave them the keys to rooms and the location of the funeral home closest to the main road. Grieta got into the car with Luca and his parents. She directed the driver to the funeral home and went in to make all the arrangements.

Eduard carried Luca in, as carefully as a groom might carry his bride across a threshold; and laid him gently on the table.

The director of the funeral home asked no questions about who they were, where they had come from and where they were going. Those were not the kind of questions that were asked or answered easily in those days. Instead he shook Eduard's hand with apologetic tones and told them he would take care of everything.

That night in the hotel no one slept except for the emotionally exhausted children. The funeral for Luca took place early the next morning, and for the rest of that day, the group sat together and mourned.

Much later, in the evening, Jaan and his brothers walked back to the river Garonne and sat on the bank, watching the water flow lazily South. Hendrik threw a stick in, which swirled around in a tight circle and then went floating away.

"We have to move on in the next day or two." Jaan finally broke the silence.

When his brothers made no comment, he continued: "In the morning, we will take the maps and plan the rest of the drive. It should take us no more than three days to get to the coast of Portugal from here. I will send a telegram on to the Dutch consulate in Lisbon, to let them know we are coming and to see what they can do to arrange passage."

After more muted conversation, the three men walked back to their rooms to rejoin their families.

The next day, the travelers sat outside the hotel. It was a

breezy, warm day and they had spread blankets on the grass. The little ones, subdued, sat nearby the adults and quietly played with their toys. Jaan had his maps laid out on the grass, and holding a pencil, began tracing out possible routes.

With the pervasively morose atmosphere pressing down on them, he realized they could not make any decisions.

Folding the maps and tucking the pencil behind his ear, he announced, "Let's take a walk-in town. It will do us all some good."

They wound their way through the open-air market, not truly taking in the tables laden with goods or the invitations, in French, to come sample the wares. As they continued on along the Garonne, the *Gare de Bordeaux Saint Jean* railway station came into sight. Its classical construction, at a right angle with the river, was imposing and comforting at the same time. They stood looking at its length, its high arched entryways, the clock face high above them surrounded by antique carvings.

As they gazed, a buzzing noise disturbed the muted air where they stood. It quickly grew louder, and even the children recognized it for what it was: the dreaded Messerschmitts.

Even as the planes came into view behind them, they grabbed for each other's hands and ran into the train station. All around them, others came charging towards the building as the rhythmic blasts of artillery followed close behind. Hundreds of people found small places within the large, open lobby to hunker down while hell reigned outside.

The attack went on for long minutes, as they sat against a marble wall with their heads tucked tightly between their knees. They prayed and waited.

When all was silent once again, dozens of people cautiously exited the building. Smoke and flames rose up from alongside the river, where the market had been just minutes before; where they themselves had been just minutes before. Standing there long enough to take in the scene, they turned and walked quickly back to the hotel. Their hearts hammered with fear and relief; and horror for those who had not been lucky this time. Again.

Their most recent escape from disaster galvanized Hendrik. "I'm going to the port. Right now. I'm going to book us all passage to London. From there, we can figure out what to do. We need to find a safe place, and we cannot wait another moment."

With this pronouncement, he and Levi left the group and headed back towards town.

Eduard found his voice then. Wrapping his arm around his silent, limp wife, he quietly stated, "We are not going on. It is too much. We have suffered beyond anything we could have foreseen. We should have stayed in Amsterdam and taken our chances there. If we had, Luca…" and he could not continue.

"What will you do?" Jaan asked softly, laying his hand on the shoulder of his business partner, his friend. "Where will you go now?"

"I do not know. We will stay here a day or two and maybe we will take the train back to Amsterdam. At least there, we will be with our family, our friends. We will face our fate with them, together," was Eduard's simple response.

Hours later, Levi and Hendrik returned, finding the group where they had left them. Eduard and his wife sat off to one side by themselves.

"We could only get two tickets," Hendrik said, waving them in the air. "All of the boats are full. We had to bribe the ticket master to get us these. Levi and I have decided to go to London, and join the forces there fighting against the Third Reich. We can't keep running away; we have to go do something."

Directly to Jaan, he said, "Our wives will take our children and continue on with you. They can drive the Citroen as well as either of us. Once we are all settled, we can send word. We leave in forty minutes."

He paused a moment, then added, "It is the only way."

With that, Levi handed Jaan a small stack of money, saying only, "Take this to help you all along the way."

"Where did you get money for the tickets? Where did you get these?" Jaan asked, holding out the paper currency his brother had given him.

He got no answer as the men took their families inside and packed a small bag each. They walked away without further conversation.

It was only later, as Jaan was placing the money in his coat pocket, that he discovered that the diamonds were missing.

That very night, the vehicles moved south toward the French border with Spain.

Jaan had gotten through to the Dutch embassy using the hotel telephone and had been given passage on a ship for them all out of the Praia das Maçãs port near Lisbon. It was scheduled to leave in six days, and if they missed it, there might not be another chance.

The men mapped out an inland route to avoid the dangers of the Spanish Civil War, coming to a breaking point at that very time, on the Basque Coast. This course took them on a harrowing ride, with the full moon casting surreal shadows through narrow, high-altitude switchbacks of the Pyrenees Mountains. The hairpin curves were nerve-rackingly reminiscent of the road on which they had lost Luca.

Two nights later, having stopped to sleep in the cars when

necessary, they arrived at a hotel just north of Madrid. It was with beaten hearts that they unpacked only what they needed and settled into their rooms.

The shriek that awoke the families near dawn did not immediately arouse them from their over-stressed stupor. It took long moments to realize it was coming from the room where Jaan's parents slept. They followed the sounds, stumbling with exhaustion, and found the door standing open. Jaan's mother was sitting up in bed wailing as Grieta worked to calm her. Lying next to her on the bed was the body of the grandfather. His old heart could take no more strain and, near dawn, had given up with a farewell shudder. Jaan stood over his father, head bowed. Melke sat on a chair with Dirk on her lap, her arms wrapped tightly around him. His thumb was stuck securely in his mouth.

Another funeral in another unknown town.

The rest of the journey to Lisbon took two more long days of driving. It seemed that the men were afraid to stop.

The teens, women, and remaining elderly radiated alternating currents of fear, sadness, anxiety and hopelessness. The younger children, sensing those emotions as if they were fire, hot, not to be touched, quietly played in the cars or napped.

They arrived at the port with two days to spare.

The morning they were to sail, the men bargained the cars away for incredibly bad prices. They swallowed their anger and aggravation at being cheated and herded the families onto the large ship amid an enormous volume of crates, trunks and people. The ship steamed out of the harbor, with all the passengers standing at the railing to watch. It was with some feigned cheer that they toasted the beginning of their final journey to sanctuary, with small glasses of Jenever gin that Elias
had hidden in his bag.

Once the ship was out to sea, they all began to relax. The mealtime routines, the fresh sea breezes, and the social exchanges with fellow Netherlanders and Belgians offered them comforts they had been missing. The young children explored the boat with their new friends, running from port to starboard to look at the vast Atlantic sea, or the coast of Africa as it sailed past. The teens basked in the heat of the African sun, dozing, chatting, reading their schoolbooks, writing in journals or drawing on sketch pads.

The adults, having nothing at all to do or think about, found their worries lessen and diminish until they all but disappeared. Even Jaan and Grieta had romantic moments, feeling at ease for the first time in months. The tenderness in their hand-holding and affectionate gazes had the teenagers teasing Melke until she blushed, mortified, and covered her face with her shawl.

At the port in Lourenço Marques, Mozambique, the European passengers disembarked. They moved on to the MS Tegelberg, a brand-new luxury ship, for the final leg of the trip to the Dutch East Indies. Although they had another month crossing the Indian Ocean ahead of them, the atmosphere fairly rang with energy and anticipation. All began to plan their new temporary lives, with thoughts of those left behind at home coming to join them in safety and sanctuary. Optimism ruled the days and evenings, punctuated by nightly sing-alongs led by Grieta and Jaan's mother in Dutch and French.

A week after they had left the African coast behind, Jaan's mother became ill. Fever wracked her aged bones, leaving her shivering uncontrollably under the bedcovers. She quickly became lethargic, refusing food and water; and within two days she was gone. Grieta knew she had passed when the crepe-paper skin on the hand she was holding became cool, and then cold.

Later that day, Grieta held Melke as they stood on the deck with all of the other passengers. Jaan and several other men brought his mother's body up from below on a board, wrapped in a white sheet and steel chains, intoning Kaddish and Yiskor prayers as they walked to the railing. The ship had stopped for the burial at sea and all was eerily quiet, except for the repetitive droning of the Hebrew words. The men tilted the board over the rail, and they watched as the body hit the water with a splash and sank until it was out of sight.

Almost immediately, the ship's engines started up and the Tegelberg was underway once more. Melke stayed alone at the rail for almost an hour, her eyes on the spot where, moments before, her grandmother had slipped into the sea; until she could no longer differentiate it from the rest of the vast, calm ocean.

As they disembarked from the Tegelberg at the port of Batavia a few uneventful weeks later, Grieta was all struck by *green*. Lime hues, olive drab, mossy and bright verdant lushness surrounded them as far as she could see. Behind them the azure ocean and above them the deep blue sky met the emerald and jade countryside in a dreamlike landscape: Heaven. Paradise. Surely here, she felt, was the haven they needed from the hell they had left behind in that other world; the real world. Taking deep, humid, tropical breaths, they carried their belongings into the small island city that waited to welcome them.

And welcome them, it did. The Dutch population, already there for generations and thriving, helped them locate homes and jobs. School for the little ones in Dutch and Malay began immediately. Dirk instantly blossomed back into the happy boy he had been. He easily picked up the new language and befriended anyone that he could stop long enough to engage in conversation. Melke began to take nursing classes. Jaan started working in a printer's office and Grieta took a job in the DEI Bank. Life for the family quickly became a happy routine.

Together with their neighbors and friends Grieta often made *rijstaffel*. They sat at long tables outside in the warm breezes, passing tiny bowls of delicacies around, chatting loudly and contentedly in several languages.

Life seemed like a grand holiday to them all; until the afternoon Jaan came home from the printer's office, disquieted and slightly alarmed.

Monday, December 8, 1941.

News had come across the wire on the ticker tape at the printer's office of the Japanese attack, the day before, on the American military installation called Pearl Harbor. Hushed and serious conversations moved rapidly through the community: What did it mean for the war? What, if anything, did it mean for Europe? What could it mean for them, on their tiny island paradise?

For the next few months, nothing changed for the population of the Dutch East Indies. One morning at the end of the winter, on her way to the bank, Grieta heard the sound of marching feet. She turned and saw, walking rapidly and rhythmically up the street directly towards her, a small column of soldiers. The young man leading the march held a samurai sword stiffly over his right shoulder. A white flag with a large red circle tied to the blade waved in the breeze. The group turned the corner sharply after they passed her, and she hurried the rest of the way to the door of the bank, not breathing until she arrived safely inside.

By the end of the week, Japanese soldiers were everywhere in Batavia. For the most part, it did not affect the daily routines of the Dutch and Belgians. The military men seemed benign to them. Many of soldiers were just teenagers and seemed curious about the Europeans. They were especially interested in the fair-haired, milky-skinned young women their own age.

Melke told her mother how she and her friends were often stopped by the soldiers to pose for a photograph. Their Mamiya cameras, hanging around their necks, took a moment to open, unfold and focus. She and the other girls would remain stock still with pretty smiles pasted on their faces until the men were satisfied; and, bowing deeply, allowed them to continue on their way.

After that, Grieta kept Melke closer to home.

Within a month, senior military officers moved into the area. A distinct change occurred that was to impact them all.

The marches along the streets of Batavia became larger and more organized. Europeans walking in town were made to stop and bow, until they passed. One look at the bayonets and samurai swords stifled any protest.

The few Dutch army soldiers stationed in Batavia, who in the past many years had not been needed for duty, had become just more neighbors and friends to the residents. When the Japanese military moved in, they abandoned their posts and fled to the mountains.

A curfew was set with no warning. People were caught unaware, and mercilessly beaten in the street. Several young men walking in town just after dusk were dragged away from their families, never to be heard from again.

The Japanese troops went into every home, office and place of business; and took away the Excelsior radios the Europeans had brought with them.

Late one afternoon, Grieta and Jaan heard a commotion coming from the neighbor's house and went to the window. The loud crack of gunfire blasted through the open door, making them both jump. Seconds later, soldiers marched out carrying a radio. In their wake, Grieta could hear muffled weeping coming from their neighbor.

The printer's office was shut down, the telegraph machines removed and taken to the new and growing military headquarters. The paper ticker tape full of news and headlines was thrown into a pile on the floor of the small office and set on fire.

The bank was next, with the soldiers carrying away bags of currency. Finally, the schools were shuttered, ending the daily classes for hundreds of children. Melke continued to be allowed her training and work; but had to be home by dark or plan to spend the night at the hospital.

The lack of a common language between the military and the residents was overcome with the sharp end of the weapons, accompanied by barked orders whose meanings were clear enough.

In the dawn hours one late-May morning, the usual cooing of the doves and squawking of green parrots that signaled a new day were suddenly overpowered by the heavy roar of motors and the jolting bangs of oversized tires rolling over sidewalks. They came to a stop with drawn out screeches in front of the still dark houses. Shouts erupted as men poured out of the trucks, threw open doors and charged inside.

They returned quickly, hauling men, barefooted and in pajamas, by the arms. The men, stumbling and half-asleep, were shoved into the backs of the military lorries. The women and children rushed behind them in confusion and shock, as the soldiers entered each home and took husbands, older brothers and young single men by the dozens.

Grieta ran after the soldier who had grabbed Jaan, asking fearfully for an explanation. He brusquely threw a flyer at her, which fluttered to the ground unnoticed. She was still standing mutely by the road surrounded by the others, as the trucks noisily sped away and turned the corner.

When she looked down, she noticed the paper at her feet. Turning her head, she saw identical leaflets strewn along the walkways. She bent down to pick it up and holding it to her eyes with a shaking hand, saw several lines of typed print in Malay, Dutch, French and Japanese written there.

"Mandate: All males over the age of 18 will be relocated to Adek. Families may visit them during daylight hours," she read aloud.

Numbly, still clutching the flyer, she led her children back into the house to figure out what to do now.

Adek was not far, as it turned out. Melke and Dirk were able to ride bicycles that day to the area where the men were being held. Although there was an insubstantial, flimsy fence surrounding them, the men were not allowed to leave, and visitors were not permitted inside. Any items brought to the men had to be passed through guards at the gate; or given to the peddlers, who were allowed to enter and exit freely, to hand on.

That first day, Melke carried a small suitcase with clothing and toiletries for her father. In the following visits, she brought food, cooking utensils, pencils and paper. In this way, for almost a month, the family was able to continue staying in touch regularly. They had no way of knowing how long this imprisonment would go on, nor what it meant.

Money quickly became tight back in Batavia. Grieta did not wish to worry Jaan more, but knew she had to do something. She came to tell him, through the fence, her plan.

"I am taking the children to Tjideng," she told him quietly. "It is more affordable there, and comfortable enough."

"Tjideng is a slum!" Jaan protested. Powerless and frustrated, he fought back his objections. "When will you plan to leave?"

"By the end of this week," she responded. "It is not far. We will still be able to come visit you. Melke and I can find work nearby cleaning or sewing to make some money. It is the only way for us to survive, until you come back to us. Then we can start talking about leaving the Dutch East Indies. I don't know where we will go next..."

This last she said in a whisper, as they had no idea whether they would be allowed to leave the island at all. They touched fingers through the openings in the fence, sharing a look with troubled eyes.

"It will be okay, my love," Jaan said to her. "This is not how our story ends."

She kissed her fingers and reached out to touch his gently, once more. Then she turned and walked back towards town.

The next day when Melke rode out by herself to have a visit, she found the compound empty. The gates hung open, no sign of men or guards to indicate what might have transpired. The yard was still, vacant, barren.

She sped home as quickly as her legs would spin the pedals, burst into the house and threw herself into her mother's arms, as she had not done since she was a little girl.

"They are gone, all gone, there is no one there, it is empty, no one inside, no guards, I don't know where papa has gone, where they have taken him, what has happened," spilled out in a rush.

Her face buried in her mother's shoulder, her words were muffled but somehow very, very clear. Grieta held her daughter tightly and close as it sank in. Standing that way for a long moment, they wept together.

Days later, Grieta and Melke pushed a two-wheeled cart filled with their belongings up the road, muscles bulging with the effort. Dirk sat atop the pile, humming and pointing his little hands, directing an invisible symphony in time to the bumpy ride.

Grieta had told him that Papa went on a trip with the other men, and they were going to move into a new house to wait for him to return. Now nine years old, Dirk had taken the news in stride, believing his mother's words with undiminished spirits. Not for the first time, Melke felt a pang of envy for his innocence; but it was quickly followed by fear for him, and for them all.

They moved into a run-down shack with one bedroom, its water pump just outside the front door. For the work they found sewing and mending, they were paid mostly with food- a little goat milk or meat or some sweet potatoes. Dirk spent his days hunting along the lush mossy grass-covered banks of the creeks nearby for duck eggs to bring home; singing and dancing as he went.

One afternoon, he came back to the shack to find his mother sitting on a rocking chair outside the door with her needles and a large tablecloth, wiping sweat from her face with the corner of her skirt.

"Mama, why are the men making a fence around the town?" he asked, proudly holding out his little straw bucket with two large eggs to show her.

She stood, working to keep the disquieting quiver in her chest at bay.

"Let's take a walk and see." Taking his hand, they set off down the road.

At the sight of the line of men with their hammers in hand, brown backs glistening in the heat, the quiver dropped into her belly. She left Dirk standing back and walked up and down the line until she found a man who spoke Dutch.

"It is for your safety," he told her, "The women and children need protection, now that the men are off working."

Before turning back to continue banging nails into the wooden posts, he added, "*All* of the white women and children."

It did not take long for the meaning of his words to become evident. Even before the fence was completed, more two-wheeled wagons pushed by mothers and children poured into the neighborhood. There were not enough houses for them all, and by the end of the week three more families had moved into Grieta's place. In order to fit everyone, Melke, Grieta and Dirk carried the sofa, chairs and tables out to the street and replaced them with sleeping mats.

And still, they kept coming. Within two weeks, every shack on the block held at least twenty people. The street was so crowded with discarded furniture, it was difficult to walk.

Grieta took in two more families, placing the last of their furnishings out on the road. Finally, there was not a centimeter of open space on the floor. Even the tiny kitchen held several mattresses, and eight people slept there every night.

And still, they kept coming.

The barrier around the neighborhood was completed in a matter of days, with guards posted menacingly by the only access gate. Grieta found herself dividing up the little food she had been able to store, handing a sweet potato and a small bowl of watery rice to the mothers each day. The women took tiny nibbles for themselves, and then passed them on to the ravenous children.

The ducks that lived along the creeks vanished quickly, as the teenagers grabbed them and brought them home to be cooked and shared. Melke ran in one morning with a porcupine wrapped in her shawl, and they had their first meat in days. The dank odor of boiling frogs, turtles, and larger grasshoppers and beetles permeated the humid air, until they, too, disappeared.

The day that she handed out the last scraps in her cupboard, Grieta and Melke walked to the gate and approached the guards.

"Please, we need food. We are all hungry, and there is nothing to eat. We must have food soon, or people will begin to die." Grieta's anguish, as she realized the truth of the statement she had made, hit her in the pit of her empty stomach.

The soldiers laughed. One of them leered at Melke and said, "What will you give us in exchange for food, eh? Will you give us anything for some food?"

Grieta turned around and, gripping Melke by the arm, hurried away from the jeering men. When she arrived back to their street, she found Dirk and several of the other children sitting listlessly on the ground around piles of moss, stuffing small fistfuls into their mouths.

The loud roar of military jeeps and lorries brought them all to their feet. The vehicles stopped at the town square. Soldiers leaped to the ground and began goading and prodding until the entire population of Tjideng was gathered around, wordless and waiting.

"*Kerei!*" the soldiers yelled in their faces.

When no one moved, unsure what they were being asked to do, the soldiers began beating them with batons. As they moved towards Grieta's group, swinging indiscriminately and repeating their command, a teenager nearby whispered as loudly as he dared, "Bow! Bow at the waist, hands at your sides, head down!"

They all did, just in time. The soldier that approached them had his arm up, ready to strike. He stopped and pointed at them, shouting "*Kerei*" at the rest of the cowering people, who stooped over as quickly as they could.

As soon as everyone was bowed to their satisfaction, the soldiers picked through the crowd, grabbing the older teenaged boys and shoving them onto the backs of the lorries.

The woman next to Grieta screamed, "No!" and clutched onto her son's arm as he was yanked away. The baton hit her face with a sickening crack. She fell to the ground and was still, blood trickling from her ear.

The lorries moved out, carrying all of the boys over sixteen, leaving the heavy stench of gasoline and motor oil behind. The women and remaining children stood bowing for over an hour in the blazing sun, while they were carefully counted. Quiet sobbing came from the mothers who had lost their sons. Grieta hushed the ones close by to keep them from winding up on the ground bleeding from their heads.

As the census continued, a little girl fainted at the feet of one of the soldiers. He stepped on her as he walked past, pointing at the line and counting: *"Hachi juu ichi, hachi juu ni, hachi juu yon..."*

Pausing to look back at her prone form, he saw that she was still breathing. Pointing at her, he said: *"hachi juu go"* and then moved on down the line.

Before the men released the group to return to their overcrowded hovels, Grieta and a dozen other mothers were chosen off the lines; and kept in a small group to one side. They were marched over to one of the jeeps, which was loaded with wooden crates. The soldiers motioned to Grieta to climb up and take down a crate. She tried to move it and could not. Another woman clambered up and grabbed the other end. Grunting, they were able to wrestle the box off the vehicle.

She tried to set it down on the ground and felt the light whack of the baton on her backside. They stood, straining to hold up the container until all six were down. The soldiers nudged them into a low structure nearby.

With small crowbars, the women opened the crates and found food: green bananas, large rough-skinned cassava roots, sweet potatoes, canvas bags of peanuts and rice, and even a small tin of salt.

Blinking back tears and biting back the joyful cries that threatened to escape her lips, she and the others put the large metal pots on burners in the makeshift kitchen, and made a watery but chunky stew. With the soldiers' permission, they went back to the shacks and had each person, big and small, take a bowl and line up. Melke and Dirk ran to her when she arrived, with tight hugs of relief.

While not plentiful, food was at least ample enough to buoy their spirits over the next few weeks. The soldiers gave everyone a job to do during the daylight hours. Grieta continued on in the kitchen. Dirk and the other children were made to pick up garbage and put it in the back of a large lorry. The reeking stink, as the truck sat for weeks in the sun, permeated through the camp making the children gag. Melke fashioned a mask out of an old kerchief to tie around Dirk's mouth and nose. The teen girls helped to nurse the sick and dying, which became more difficult each day as the numbers grew.

Malnutrition had taken its toll on many of the elderly; dysentery, malaria and beriberi plagued them all. The girls made shoes out of the canvas bags from peanuts and rice, when the ones they had brought into the camp had worn through. They took scraps of shabby, ragged clothing to make dresses and shorts.

Anyone caught not doing the assigned job satisfactorily was punished. Sometimes, the guards beat the offender to the ground. Sometimes, the transgressor was given the extra job of cleaning out the common cesspool trenches near the huts, by hand.

Melke was sent there once. She had been on her way to visit the patients she cared for, and did not see an approaching soldier quickly enough to bow to him. Moving the overflowing sewage into buckets and dumping them into the back of a truck for hours in the sun, Melke nearly fainted several times. The stink baked on her skin and hair for days.

Every morning and evening, and often at noon, the camp inmates heard the shouting of the dreaded word *Tenko*, roll call.

Dropping anything in their hands, women and children ran to the painted flagpole at the square and formed up. They stood bowing exactly thirty degrees at the waist, arms rigidly at their side, fingers tight and straight, heads pointed north towards the Japanese emperor.

As the soldiers moved through the rows, they struck anyone who was not bent down to their satisfaction. If a child was not in perfect position, his mother was beaten to the ground in front of him.

The prisoners quickly learned Japanese numbers, as they were constantly counting off during *tenko*. Often, especially if the soldiers were unsatisfied, they were made to stand in this position for hours in the hot sun.

One brutally steamy day, an older woman, after two hours, began to cry audibly. She was beheaded by the nearest soldier with a samurai sword. The woman next to her retched, then vomited, splashing the soldier's shiny boots. She was stabbed through the heart with the same bloody blade.

Life became a grueling routine of eating too little and avoiding notice. There were two seasons through the year: humid with monsoon rains that flooded the camp and made a muddy mess; or blazingly bone dry and dusty. But it was always hot, adding to their misery.

On Dirk's eleventh birthday, Grieta made a cake no bigger than her hand out of boiled cassava root, sweetened with a tiny bit of sugar she was able to hoard. His offer to share it with the others was refused. His gift from Melke was a hat she sewed from rags, to keep the sun off his head. They, along with the others living in their shack, whispered the Dutch birthday song to him. The emotion caught in their throats, as the words meant something different now: *lang zal hij leven*, long shall he live.

During the planting season, Melke, Dirk and Grieta worked the fields at the back of the camp. They prepared the dark, humid soil by tilling with their hands, hunching over to spread seeds and keep the weeds at bay.

The food they grew went to feed the soldiers. Any left over after the guards had their fill, usually when the vegetables became soft and grew moldy spots, went into the cooking pots.

Dirk snuck the leaves of sweet potatoes into his mouth when he was sure the guards were not looking; and sucked on them instead of chewing so they would not see his jaw moving. Grieta, with a withering heart, could see his ribs clearly as he bent over the rows in the gardens.

Occasionally would come an evening when the soldiers, in a rare good mood, allowed them all to sit in the shade outside the huts and spend an hour in luxurious leisure. It gave Grieta a small measure of happiness to watch Dirk and the other children throw sticks for the many stray dogs that somehow survived in the camps or play hide and seek, though they ran slowly to conserve energy.

Although dressed in tattered skirts with filthy bare feet, and seated on the ground, Grieta and the other women relished these rare times almost as much as they had enjoyed their social occasions at home; before.

During such an evening, one of the women suddenly said, "I'm making a big pot of *waterzooi*. Would you like some?"

There was stunned silence as the others looked at her to see if she had lost her mind.

Grieta saw she had her eyes closed and a satisfied smile on her face and said "I would love some. I will go get the fish. Do you put leeks or onions in yours?"

"Both," she responded dreamily. "And potatoes, and carrots, and lots of cream. But no sweet potatoes!" she finished with a small laugh.

Another woman joined the game. "I will make the *balletjes* then. My mother-in-law, who is from the South, taught me to make the sauce for the meatballs. I could make them smothered in tomato sauce, or I could even do boulets Liégeois style! Which would you all prefer?"

"I will make the *frites*! The potatoes have to be really fresh to make them crispy," another chimed in.

And for the rest of that hour, the women traded recipes. Grieta thought that it would make her hungrier, since supper that night had been a small bowl of sweet potato stew; but found that somehow it made her feel full inside.

One morning at roll call, a jeep roared into the compound, tires screeching as it came to a halt next to the painted flagpole. Although she could not raise her eyes to see the man stepping down and striding towards them, she could sense the tension among the ranks of guards and stiffened her bow to avoid their wrath.

As one voice, the soldiers announced his name: *"Kenichi Sonei!"*

His powerful footsteps resounded up and down the line, as he inspected the inmates. He left them there for hours as he toured the huts, the cooking facilities, the fields, the fences, the sewage trenches. He kicked more than one dog that ran across his path as he marched around briskly, followed closely by a small contingent of nervous bowing soldiers.

After they were released back to work, Grieta kept a careful, surreptitious eye on this newest threat. She watched him scream with equal fury at the women, the children and the guards. The very day that he arrived, he had the soldiers move the fences in to make the living area smaller for the prisoners. Over the next weeks, he had them tear down one of every five huts and force the residents in with other groups. They now slept three to a mat, shoulder to shoulder.

He had the very sickest left outside to die in the blazing sun, while putting the teen nurses to work cleaning the soldiers' barracks just outside the gate.

On one of his daily inspections, he tripped over a gray puppy that was nearly invisible in the shade, and flew into a rage at having been humiliated in front of his troops. He stomped on the dog until it was a bloody mess. Face a dark red, he ordered the boys to gather every dog in the compound. When they carried or yanked the dogs to the tenko grounds, they found the grim-faced soldiers holding large sticks out to them.

"Kill them all," ordered Captain Sonei.

No one moved. He nodded his head towards a soldier, who stepped forward and beat one of the dogs in the head until it stopped moving.

The smallest of the boys let a sob escape and Captain Sonei picked him up and threw him. He landed broken and motionless on the ground.

"Kill them all," he repeated.

He watched as the boys, moaning and choking back tears, beat the yelping dogs. Dirk, crying soundlessly, shut his eyes and swung his stick, shuddering with every soft thud. Grieta and Melke hid behind the kitchen building with the other mothers and watched in wretched dismay. The horror continued until the last whining howl died away, and the boys were covered in blood.

When it was done, Captain Sonei sauntered through the silent shaking group of boys. He pushed away the youngest, who drifted in shock back towards the huts. He stepped up to Dirk and demanded his age.

"*Juu ichi*," he whispered, trembling.

Captain Sonei nodded and went through the boys, keeping all of those ten or older; several dozen in all. He summoned one of the military lorries, and ordered the boys to climb in.

Grieta saw her son's pale blue eyes staring into hers from his bloody, mud-covered face, as the truck went through the gate.

The vehicle left the town of Tjideng and drove for an hour along rough dirt roads, with the boys clinging onto the rails, the sides of the truck and each other to keep from being thrown off. They were packed in so tightly that no one noticed the two in the middle who fainted during the ride. They arrived at a dilapidated train station and were pushed into small freight car. After several baking hours, a soldier came with three canisters of water, which the boys passed around, each taking a palmful to sip through their desiccated, cracked lips.

There was just enough room to lie down, and most of the boys collapsed into the sleep of emotional exhaustion. Dirk found a spot by the heavy rolling door to curl up. His shoulders heaved as he cried tearless sobs before fatigue overtook him.

The jerk of the train moving away from the station woke him

up groggily; then he slept once more.

When the train stopped for the third time, the doors slid open. The boys were still prone on the floor. A soldier climbed into the car, trying not to gag from the reek of excrement and urine in the stifling air, and prodded them with his baton. Most of the boys rose to their feet unsteadily. Four boys who did not respond were poked roughly, rousing three of them.

Dirk looked at the fourth, one of the younger ones, and saw he was dead.

The soldiers made the boys climb down and follow them through a gate into a fenced-in compound nearly identical to the one they had left. Dirk peeked around, hoping to see his mother and sister waiting.

Everywhere he looked he saw boys, hundreds of them. They were bent over working or carrying heavy stones to a growing pile; or shuffling off to use the pit latrine, which was near enough for him to smell on the humid breeze.

"Tenko!" yelled one of the soldiers, followed by the sound of feet scuttling into lines.

As one, all of the boys bowed and counted aloud. As soon as they were released, the soldiers sent the boys back to work.

Dirk was told to follow the group that was carrying stones from a large pit in the ground near the fence. As he climbed into the hole, he almost tripped over an emaciated leg that was sticking out of the dirt. It took all of his strength to pick up a stone, and climb back out of the hole, where he trailed another boy to the pile.

After working until sundown, the boys queued up with clay bowls. Dirk walked slowly in the line to a low building, where a boy splashed a ladleful of stew into his. He thought of Grieta then and cried as he ate.

Although there were boys who somehow found enough energy to play after eating, Dirk wandered into a nearby hut, collapsed onto a mat between several other boys; and slept all night.

The next morning brought tenko and more work, with no breakfast. At high noon, after a second roll call, the boys lined up with their bowls and were given a scoop of rice. Dirk sat under a shady tree, and began picking maggots out of his bowl, throwing them over his shoulder.

"I wouldn't do that," a voice said above him.

Four boys were standing over him, watching. They sat down in front of him and shoveled small handfuls of rice into their mouths.

The boy who had spoken continued. "The maggots don't taste too bad, and they keep you a little stronger. Just kind of swallow them without chewing too much, and you won't even notice them. I'm Dolf," he said, and put his hand out.

"Dirk," he responded and was surprised by the firm handshake.

"This is Paul, Richard, Gerald," Dolf announced pointing; and each offered a hand to shake. "We have been here for a while so we can tell you what to look out for. And who to look out for too. It's not as bad as the other camp I was in, I will tell you that. Not enough to eat, but at least most of the guards won't kill you."

"The hole where we get the stones," Dirk responded. "There was a kid in there."

"Oh, that's the grave you're digging out. That's where they throw the dead ones. Just do what you're told and eat everything you can; and you won't be one of them," Dolf told him. "After work, come play football with us. They let us, until dark every day."

Dirk's days blended one into the other: work, football, sleep, start again. Some days they were given two meals, but many days they only had one. Dirk carefully carried his stew, on one of those days, to meet his friends under the tree. Suddenly he felt a sharp poke in his shoulder and, fearing it was a soldier, turned slowly around. Two older boys stepped so close to him; he could smell the rot of their teeth.

"Give us your stew."

"No!" Dirk said with a mix of panic and distress.

Before he could move, one of the boys grabbed his bowl and the other pushed him in the face, knocking him to the ground. He sat stunned. His little group, bowls already empty, found him there.

"What happened to you?" Gerald asked.

Dirk sniffled out the story, and pointed to the boys, who were sharing his food nearby. Paul and Richard hauled him up and walked him back to the stone pile to work; while Gerald and Dolf went the other way to their job in the fields. Dirk did not play that night, but sat watching, his stomach clenched in hunger.

Suddenly, he heard a loud cry and, turning, saw the two food thieves on their knees. Two soldiers were hitting them over and over, shouting in their faces; until they both fell face down, sobbing. When he looked up, Dirk saw Dolf watching with a small smile.

"Guess they won't do that again," he said to Dirk.

"What did you do?" he asked, awe in his voice.

"We told the guards they were hiding during work hours. We told them that instead of doing their jobs, those boys were stealing from the garden and making fun of the soldiers for not catching them," Gerald said, proudly.

The next day, Gerald was nowhere to be found.

From then on, Dirk stuck as close to Richard, Paul and Dolf as he could. He saw other groups roaming together. Often, they would tell on each other to garner favor with the soldiers; but they left Dirk's group alone.

One afternoon, instead of joining the football match, Dirk sat off to the side. The boys saw him bent over, playing with something, and came over.

"What do you have?" Richard asked.

Dirk opened his hand to reveal a brown field mouse, its whiskers longer than its body, nose quivering, and tail wrapped around its back legs.

"His name is Hagel Slag. If I can't eat chocolate sprinkles, I might as well have one to play with," he explained, laughing for the first time in a very long time.

Dirk fashioned a nest for "Hagel", as he called him, and came to look for him after work every day. When he could, he saved a grain of rice to feed the little mouse, who quickly got used to crawling onto his hand. Dirk found the workdays less grueling, as he had something to look forward to each evening.

Not long after, meals became even thinner.

Once a day, they were each given a small sweet potato. Dirk and the others ate small nibbles, saving the skins for last. They saw dozens of boys fall still to the ground, to be carried by the others to the grave hole and dropped in. Some of those were still moving when they hit the bottom of the pit; but not for long.

One evening, Dirk returned to find Richard, Dolf and Paul sitting around a bowl.

"We've been waiting for you," Dolf said, "We have meat! It's just a tiny bit, but we can share it."

With that each boy took a stringy greasy piece between their fingers and put it on their tongues. The taste was unpleasant, but they chewed for a long time before swallowing. Dirk went off to retrieve his pet but found the nest empty. He searched, but returned to where his friends were sitting, a puzzled look on his face.

"Hey, stop looking so sad," said Richard. "It could be worse. At least we had Hagel Slag for dinner!"

The other boys laughed and Dolf licked his lips. "You said you were hungry and liked chocolate sprinkles," he smirked.

Dirk's face blanched, and he turned, gagging, and ran.

After that, Dirk kept to himself. It was not hard; the football games had stopped when the food became scarce, and most of the boys went to sleep as soon as they could every night.

One early evening after work, he shambled to his mat by the door and lay down trying to sleep in the heat, mosquitos singing in his ears. He became slowly aware that there was other singing coming from the back of the shack.

In a boy's whisper, he heard, *"Baraju et Adonai hamvorak."*

Other voices responded, *"Baruch Adonai hamvorak le olam va ed."*

Almost too weary and despondent to be curious, he continued trying to fall asleep.

"Baruch a ta Adonai. Elohanu Melech ha olam…"

Dirk rose to his elbow and sighted four boys crouched in a circle and rocking as they quietly sang prayers he had not heard since he was a little boy. Looking around to make sure there were no soldiers nearby, he carefully made his way to them, weaving around the prone forms of the other boys in the moonlit hut. On each of their heads he saw a scrap of potato sack. The biggest and oldest of the boys was leading the call and return prayers. Dirk crouched between two of the boys. One of them noticed and placed a ragged tiny piece of burlap on his head. Dirk began rocking with them, the nearly forgotten words coming back to him.

They recited the prayers in close whispers, for a few dear moments forgetting the world outside their circle. In this way, Dirk made his Bar Mitzvah in midst of a war, in the middle of the horrors of a Japanese prison camp.

Every day blended into the next until another year had passed. One morning, as he and another boy hauled a particularly heavy stone over to the fence, Dirk caught sight of an old man at the fence. No, not a man, a teenager, he realized, who was furtively summoning to him.

Looking over his shoulder and around to spot the guards, Dirk told the other boy, "Let's put this one over there."

They lugged the rock to the fence where he was standing. The teenager shoved a paper through the fence into Dirk's hand and turned and walked rapidly away.

Dirk tucked the paper under his straw hat, warning, "If you tell, we will both get in big trouble."

That night, by the light of a nearly full moon, Dirk crouched by the side of the hut. He unfolded a ripped off page of a newspaper, dated August 15th, 1945.

In huge bold red letters, the headline read, "Japs Surrender!"

He sat stunned, until several boys walking by saw him. They took the paper and read it. Without a word, they began to pass it around until every boy in the camp had seen it for himself.

They feared that the guards and soldiers would be angrier than ever and take it out on them; so, they worked extra hard and stayed out of the soldiers' way as much as possible.

Miraculously, the opposite happened. Over the next week, the boys were given three meals each day; small pieces of bread in the morning with half of a banana, a good size helping of fresh rice with a piece of fish on top for lunch, and a small bowl of hearty stew at dinner time.

The soldiers still made the boys work, but became clearly more relaxed about it; except for Dirk's group. The boys had to now fill in the gaping hole to cover up the bodies at the bottom, as quickly as possible. Once that was completed, Dirk was sent to work in the kitchen.

And, there was no more tenko.

One morning, when Dirk awoke, he noticed right away that the sun was up over the horizon and it was strangely quiet. He sat up and saw the others all around him still sleeping, and carefully stepped around them to walk outside.

The soldiers were gone.

He walked through the entire camp until he came to the gate, which was open and unguarded. Looking around to double check, he slowly stepped toward the opening. His heart quivered in his chest and his stomach clenched as he approached it. He stopped right at the gate, checked around once more and then placed one foot outside. Nothing happened. He put his weight on that foot and brought the other to join it.

He was out. Outside; unprotected, unwatched, exposed…free. As the thought hit him, he stepped back inside and stared out, his brain trying to process and decide what to do now.

Through the hammering in his chest, he suddenly realized he heard a sound: shuffling feet, muted voices.

In front of him, he saw men approaching. His first instinct was to turn and run, but these men did not look aggressive. They were skinny, filthy, ragged, old. There were hundreds of them, and as they came towards him, the ones in front lifted emaciated arms and hands with long grimy fingernails.

Dirk backed up and to one side, as they hobbled through the

gate. Several turned to ask his name.

As soon as he told them, he heard, "Dirk? Dirky? Little Dirk from Sarphatistraat??" and he fainted to the ground.

When he opened his eyes, he was being cradled by one of the withered men, who was rocking him and crying his name.

"Who?" was all Dirk could say.

"I know you don't recognize me. I am wasted away. I am Hans, your neighbor from Amsterdam. We were kept in a camp about a mile from here. When liberation came, we walked here to the boys' camp to get you all. To see if our boys survived. I came to see if my boys were here. Are they? Here?" his eyes welled up as he asked with the kind of hope Dirk had not seen in a very long time.

"No," Dirk said. "Only boys ten to fifteen are here. There is another camp for older boys, they were taken from our camp years ago. So many years ago."

Dirk stopped for a moment to take a breath and then asked, "My father?"

At this, Hans' eyes overflowed, tears tracing through the dirt on his cheeks and down his neck. "I am so sorry, Dirky. He died just last month. He got dysentery and was so miserable. But he kept going because of you and Grieta and Melke. He tried so hard at first but then he lost hope, Dirk. When he lost hope, he died."

He held Dirk tightly and they both cried.

Over the next weeks, British soldiers arrived with supplies. They put up large tents with soft mattresses for each of them, brought in a water tanker truck and set up showers with real soap, cooked pot after pot of stew with meat, fish, potatoes, and carrots; gave out large containers of milk and as much bread as the boys and men could eat. They set up a medical tent for those who needed a doctor's attention. Richard and Paul both wound up there, with diarrhea from gulping the fresh milk down too quickly.

Dolf and Richard reunited with their fathers, crying gut-wrenching sobs of joy when they found each other; and now did not leave each other's side or sight for a single second.

The British soldiers were outwardly kind and friendly to cover how horrified they were by the sight that met them: skeletal boys, shrunken men, filthy reeking thin mats covering the floors of run-down tiny straw huts, open sewer trenches overflowing with excrement and urine along the fence line; and the barely filled-in hole, holding hundreds of dead children.

They gave the freed prisoners clothing, used but in good condition; which hung off of their emaciated frames, but were clean and comfortable. With all that, it was the shoes, with real leather soles, that made them begin to feel human again.

Trucks arrived at the camp to carry the men and boys to Batavia, one hundred forty kilometers to the South, to the prisons where the women and smaller children had been kept. The ride silenced them all; fear and anticipation roiled their guts and more than one vomited over the side as they rode.

After several grueling hours, the vehicles pulled over on the main road where all of the women's camps were located. As the trucks parked, hundreds of women and children poured out of the gates of their camps and surrounded them. They called the names of their husbands and sons. Shrieks of joyful reunions mixed with anguished sobs filled the air, as the British soldiers watched in emotional wonder.

Dirk and Hans walked side by side as they searched for the camp where he had last seen Grieta. Hans, who had no idea where his wife and children were, thought to start with Dirk and hope he could get information about them. The camps all looked the same to Dirk and he miserably sought anything familiar that might lead him to his mother and sister.

Then he saw the painted flagpole; and right beside it, her hands shading her eyes as she combed the gaunt faces coming by, his mother.

"Moeder! Mama! Mam!" he yelled as he charged towards her, wrapping his arms around her so tightly, they almost fell over together.

After a moment, Dirk relaxed his grip on her and looked down into her face; he was now several inches taller than her and this made her laugh.

"Where is Melke?" he asked, and her smile faded.

"Melke was taken last year to a camp where they kept young women. They were called *comfort women,*" she said with bitterness. "I was told that Melke resisted and was shot."

Hans moved in and they all shared a sad and somber and lengthy embrace.

"Papa is gone too," Dirk said, when he could speak again.

"I know. Just before Melke was taken away, one of the soldiers handed me a small box with his fingernail cuttings and a piece of his hair. That is how they gave us the news that our husbands had died. I have kept it, hoping that I could bury it in Amsterdam in a proper grave."

A week later, Dirk, holding his mother's hand, waited on the crowded dock. An old trader ship, Stavanger, would take them to Singapore, where they would board another ship back to the Netherlands.

The week had passed in a blur, and as he stood there, Dirk relived it all. He and Grieta had been given a room at the hotel

Der Nederlanden in Batavia, where they relished hot showers and as much food as they could eat. The privacy alone was a marvel that Dirk adjusted to slowly. The luxury of sleeping when they were tired, including daily afternoon naps with the open windows blowing warm tropical air over them, seemed like a dream.

They listened to the radio: news of the changes happening in the Dutch East Indies and in all of Europe, and soothing classical music; and endless replays of the CBS reporter Edward R. Murrow's broadcast of V-E Day celebrations at London's Piccadilly Circus.

Dirk and Grieta laughed along with him every time he said, "*a few minutes ago, a motorcycle went through with four people on it and now they are throwing confetti on me.*"

The obvious joy in the rest of the world over the end of the war buoyed their singed spirits.

Now, on their way to repatriation, Dirk could not think beyond getting on that boat. He briefly flashed back to their journey here, to "sanctuary"; other boats, another life. He remembered that skinny, joyful eight-year-old, now a skinny, beaten young man; and felt mourning and grief. Then, Grieta squeezed his hand as the ship's horn blew once to signal its readiness to board.

Once in Singapore, the refugees were moved onto the luxury cruise ship Nieuw Amsterdam. Only a few years after its maiden voyage, the ship had been refitted for military service. The hammocks where Dirk and Grieta slept for the next two months were comfortable enough; and although the first-class dining rooms had been redesigned with bolted down long tables and benches, the food was plentiful and helped improve their moods.

The port call in South Africa brought back more memories, as did the route up the Western coast of Africa. For most of this part of the journey, Dirk sat in a lounging chair in the middle of the upper deck where he could turn his head to see the endless Atlantic Ocean on one side and the coast of Africa slide by on the other.

When the ship pulled into the Port of Amsterdam, Dirk was not surprised to see the bombed out remains of the northern part of the harbor. As they took their little suitcases, packed with donated clothes, and walked down the gangplank, what did surprise him was the bitter cold. His years in the tropics had thinned his blood, and both he and Grieta pulled their woolen coats tightly around their necks.

"Look!" Dirk said, with wonder in his voice that took Grieta momentarily back to another time. "They are ice skating on the canal! I can't wait to do that! I wonder if my skates still fit."

"If they don't, I'm sure we can find a pair that do. Maybe your Oom Levi's or your father's…" She choked on the rest of the words.

After the destruction at the port, Dirk was expecting the city to be in shambles; but this was not the case. Everything seemed as if it had been frozen in time. While the world had crumbled, Amsterdam itself was preserved. He felt a sense of welcome from his home as they walked, as if it had just been here waiting for them to return.

They turned onto Sarphatistraat and stopped in front of number nineteen. Flashbacks of their escape, years before, accosted them both; and it was only when the curtain moved and a woman's face appeared to stare at them, that they returned to the present.

The woman's eyes narrowed and then widened. She threw up the window and leaned out.

"Grieta? Dirky?" she screamed, bringing another woman

running to lean out beside her.

Dirk stood immobile as he tried to place these worn faces with mops of blonde hair who knew his name. He looked over at his mother, who had tears running down her cheeks. Dirk heard the sound of running feet and then the door to the flat was thrown open. One of the women launched herself screaming and crying at his mother. The other walked over and looked up into his eyes.

"Don't you recognize me, little Dirky? I am your mother's sister, your Tante Anna."

With that, she gave him an awkward embrace, patting his back lightly. She then took his suitcase and said, "Come, Mila. Enough crying on the street. Let's get them inside. We have a lot to talk about."

His Tante Mila, still clinging onto her oldest sister and babbling, grabbed Dirk's arm and squeezed them all together through the narrow doorway, down the hallway and into the kitchen. As he walked past the living room, he saw that all of the tiny ceramic blue and white delft houses from the mantle and all of the paintings and fine lamps and furnishings were gone. The room was empty, except for two chairs that looked like they had been dug out of a rubbish bin.

While Dirk, Grieta and Anna sat at the table, Mila buzzed around the kitchen, pulling things off the shelves and plating them, while brewing a large pot of coffee.

"Here, have some chocolates from the Leonidas store, which just re-opened yesterday! I got this *filet américain* from the butcher. And look, rusk toast! And herring! And potato croquettes! The vendors are starting to come back! I even found these beautiful flowers in the *bloemenmarkt*, aren't they special? Oh, I am so happy to see you both!"

No one could get a word in until she finally plopped herself down, smiling widely and filling plates for them with everything on the table. In the sudden void, Anna leaned forward.

"Shall I start," she said looking at Dirk and Grieta, "or shall you?"

Dirk looked down at his shoes, and was silent, his plate of familiar Dutch delicacies untouched in front of him. Grieta hesitated a moment, and then pointed at her sister.

"Father and mother are dead," Anna began, her tone intense and her voice penetrating Dirk's tight chest like an ice pick. "Liv tried to stop the German soldiers who came for them. She told them, 'If you take them, you have to take me too!' And they did."

Grieta's eyes welled up as she pictured her youngest sister, barely a woman and always headstrong, step between the Nazi soldiers and their parents.

"Aart, Joost, Jaap, Kees, all dead. Taken by the Nazis a month after Liv and our mother and father."

Dirk heard his uncles' names and bowed his head until his neck muscles strained, and he began to cry quietly, bitterly. Tante Mila moved her chair closer and put her arm around him. He leaned into her warmth.

"Mila and I hid. We dyed our hair and left Amsterdam for the countryside with the help of the neighbors. We had no choice. The Jews, before they were rounded up, were made to wear a yellow star whenever they left their homes. There was no work, no school. Everyone that was left after the round-up was forced to work in German factories; or they were shot dead on the street. We took jobs as tutors for the children of wealthy Christians, who risked their own safety to harbor us. We returned months ago, and we are still learning the fates of the people we used to know."

Anna's folded arms told them she was finished for now. It was plain to Dirk that she resented their escape to Batavia, where, she imagined, they waited out the war in paradise before returning home.

"We became prisoners of the Japanese, not long after the bombing of Pearl Harbor." Grieta began, also aware of Anna's ire.

Anna's eyes widened. "The Japanese? Prisoners? I don't understand." Her bewilderment was clear.

"They took Jaan and all of the men away to a camp. We found out much later that he died of dysentery. They built a fence around our neighborhood. We were all made to work, with no food to speak of. We lived eighty women and children to a hut. Then they took Dirk away to a boy's camp."

Dirk's shoulders shook with his sobs, and Grieta's eyes overflowed as she continued. "He has never told me yet what happened there. Melke..." and then she could not continue.

She put her face in her hands and for the first time in a long time, let the tears come. Anna watched while Mila stood up and went back and forth between the two, comforting them and weeping with them.

When the crying subsided, Anna finally stood. "You must eat something and get some rest. Then we will figure out what to do now. We need never speak of this again. It is the past, and the future awaits us. We survived. Now we have to live."

Wiping her eyes with her large linen handkerchief, Mila nodded. "She is right. Enough sadness for a whole lifetime. Somehow, we were chosen by God to survive, and now we must do our best to show the world what we are made of!"

She pushed their plates closer to them and jumped up to pour everyone a steaming cup of coffee. Grieta and Dirk managed to nibble a bit of each item on their plate, to Mila's satisfaction.

The next morning, when Dirk came out of his room to use the WC and find some breakfast, he nearly tripped over the pair of ice skates that was leaning on his door. The worn leather straps were neatly wrapped around the wooden slats and iron blades. He sat down on his bed with them, placed one of his shoes on the slat and tied the straps around it. A perfect fit, he saw, and smiled.

As soon as he sat down at the table, skates underneath his chair, Tante Mila set a plate in front of him.

"You are not too old for Hagel Slag for breakfast, I think," she exclaimed in her booming cheerful voice.

For one second, those words hit him hard; but he shook his head with a little smile, picked up one of the slices of buttered bread and bit into it, chocolate sprinkles falling onto the plate and sticking to his face around his mouth. This made her laugh delightedly; as did his licking a finger and pecking with it on the plate like a chicken to pick up the wayward sprinkles.

Then he carried his skates to the canal. There were dozens of people of all ages already gliding over the frozen canal. It looked like an ice highway, the way they skated in lanes at a high rate of speed. Dirk sat on a bench to strap on his skates. There was a girl just a bit older than him sitting there, watching the skaters. Dirk saw her adjust her hair and then realized it was a wig covering her head.

"I'm Dirk," he introduced himself. "I just got back yesterday from Batavia. Did you know that there were prison camps there? I was in one for years. What happened to your hair?"

"I'm Ella. We returned from the Sobibor concentration camp last year. I had meningitis and I had surgery. But my hair is growing back, see?" With that she began to pull the wig off.

A man carrying skates was walking by as she did so. He

grabbed the wig and threw it on the ground, angrily grinding his heel into it, destroying it.

"*Moffenhoer!*" he called her, pointing. "Dirty Jerry whore!" And he stalked off, leaving Dirk speechless.

Ella, trying not to cry and pulling her hat over the very short growth on her head, said, "He thinks I'm one of the women who saved their own lives by sleeping with the Nazis. Those women were rounded up after liberation and had their heads shaved to shame them. I should have stayed home until my hair grows longer, like my mother told me. Nice to meet you, Dirk," she said sadly, and walked away.

Over the next year, Grieta began working part time at the Bijenkorf Department Store on the Dam Square. Dirk returned to school. Like all of the other teenagers, he was far behind in his learning. The students, Dirk included, had to work through summer breaks and vacations and weekends to try to catch up. He found that almost all of his school friends had perished in the camps. But he easily made new friends with his open smile, the magic tricks he learned from Tante Mila, and his ability to speak five languages. He was happy to have inherited Grieta's ease at learning new tongues, and these were the only classes in school at which he excelled.

News about their friends, neighbors and family members trickled in. The *Nederlands-Israëlitisch Kerkgenootschap* organization was working overtime to locate and trace each Dutch family affected by the war.

They learned that Oom Levi and Oom Hendrik had joined the British Air Force and were instrumental in victories all over Europe. After the war, they found their families in Batavia; and were able to relocate them to a town on the outskirts of London, where they planned to remain.

Eduard and his wife did, in fact, make it back to Amsterdam. They were captured and died in Auschwitz one year later.

Hans found his wife and children on the island of Java, where they stayed for several months. After surviving an attack by locals in the Dutch East Indies, who were fighting for independence from the Netherlands in the wake of the Japanese withdrawal, Hans took his family and boarded a boat bound for Brazil.

While Dirk thrived in the routine and social interactions of his schooling, he knew his mother was suffering. Her haggard face met him each afternoon, always with a small smile as she listened to his stories about his day. But he knew this life was weighing on her heavily; and he was not surprised when she sat him down one day and took his hand in hers.

"There is nothing for us here anymore, Dirk. You will finish school in just a month, and there is no real work here for a young man. I have made arrangements through the Jewish organization for a move for us. We are going to Ecuador, in South America. There is a very well-established family in the city of Quito that will give you a job. Since we both speak Spanish, we will do very well there. We will stay until I figure out a more permanent situation."

Dirk squeezed her hand and nodded. His heart skipping a beat, he realized that they were to have an adventure and he felt like an eight-year-old again.

Then Grieta looked into his eyes and said, "In the spirit of starting over, and to help you become the man you were meant to be, we will begin using your middle name, instead of your given name."

Slowly and with emotion, she continued.

"A new identity, a new beginning, a new life for us, my darling Pieter."

Tessa's Story

Tessa walked up the concrete staircase that led out of the dingy subway station in a far corner of Queens, into the waning light of a mid-October afternoon. She was musing over her first year, as a seventh grader, at the specialized all-girl Hunter College High School. If they were going to keep teaching meditation classes and giving her unlimited time in the photography darkroom, she was going to love it there.

Besides, it took her out of Halsey Junior High. She had felt absolute terror at even the thought of going to her local school. Being a Jewish kid in a mostly Puerto Rican neighborhood had not been easy, even though she spoke Spanish better than the other kids. This was due to the fact that her parents had spoken Spanish when they did not want her to understand what they were saying, but, having inherited her father's ease at learning new languages, she became fluent quickly.

She could guzzle forties of Colt 45 beer with the best of them; and play handball until her hand swelled to twice its size. But when the gang started to jack cars and get into stealing, she knew she had to find a way out.

When the sixth-grade teacher at P.S. 220 gave out applications for the test to get into Hunter, her mother and father had both said no.

Hannah wanted to keep her daughter close to home. Although she allowed Tessa enough freedom to give Lena a heart attack, she still worried about Tessa's safety in this crazy country.

Pieter flat out told her girls did not need a good education, as all they were good for was cleaning the house and having babies.

"Your mother certainly proves that point every day. I thought she was different when she was younger, but I was wrong."

He went off on one of his usual, hard-to-follow rants, but if Tessa spoke back to him the belt came off in a flash, so she bit on her lips and stayed quiet.

Many times it was just a threat; but not always.

She forged her mother's signature on the application, took the test and passed. Tessa decided the consequences were worth *telling* them, not asking, that she was going to go to Hunter. Hannah shook her head, secretly a bit awed by her daughter's stubborn and confident act. Pieter had yelled at her and then at Hannah, blaming them both for Tessa's willfulness and defiance. In the end, he threw his hands up and stomped out of the apartment.

And look at her now, she thought a bit smugly. One month into the school year, and she was already a pro at taking the train to midtown Manhattan and making the daily walk to 466 Lex.

She was about two thirds of the way up the subway stairs when she felt a purposeful but clumsy hand reaching up under her skirt; a squeeze, a pinch. She stopped as if she had hit a wall. When Tessa turned around, awkward to do on the narrow step, he was standing just below her. Short, dark, to her young eyes old, maybe her father's age; all this registered through her shock. His wide smile lit his round face. He held his right hand to his lips, kissed his fingers tips and held them out to her in one smooth motion.

"Mmmm, beautiful," he said in accented English, gazing into

her eyes.

In an instant her brain began to smolder. This stupid shit, this idiot, this *fucker*.

Before she knew what she was doing, before he obviously did either, Tessa put her hands on his chest and shoved. As hard as she could. She watched his smile change to confusion, then fear. She watched his arms come up, begin to pinwheel. She watched his feet come off the step and she watched him begin the flight through nothingness, rushing towards the dingy tiled floor many stairs below.

And she turned then, went up into the light and began the mile walk home to 110th Street.

She never told her mother about it. Nor did she tell about the two attempted kidnappings, or about the gang of boys her own age who sat around her at the back of the city bus to sexually assault her; or the many other things she endured over the next few years. Something changed in her that day, making her feel more in control and less in control at the same time. Something that told her- *little girl, it's all you.*

Of course, she thought. Her parents had showed her that often.

When she was still in elementary school, her father would sometimes play catch with the boys across the street. Tessa once walked up to them with a baseball mitt on her hand, ready to join in.

He sneered and told her, "Go do the laundry, Tessa. Girls belong in the house cleaning, not outside playing with the boys."

She went home with tears streaking her reddened cheeks, yanked the wet clothes out of the washing machine and pulled the laundry cart two blocks to the laundromat to dry and fold it. Her mother, who had heard the exchange through an open window, busied herself making beds and dusting.

From the time she was little, Tessa loved animals and had often brought home stray cats. Her father made her leave them all outside and feed them on the sidewalk. One time, she snuck a small cat into the apartment. He didn't even notice it until it gave birth to five kittens. Tessa, who hadn't realized the cat was pregnant, watched them being born. She was completely entranced by the process and cooed to the cat to encourage her.

Her father was enraged. "As soon as they can eat, out they go. I don't care what you do to them, but they better disappear. If you don't make that happen, I will."

Five weeks later, she took the kittens in a cardboard box around the corner to the busy 108th Street and begged people to take them. When she got home that day, the mama cat was gone and her father was sitting on the couch reading the newspaper.

"Where is she?" Tessa asked in panic.

"I took her to Flushing Meadow Park and let her go. She'll be happier there anyway," he responded, not looking up.

She screamed at him then. "You're horrible. You are hateful and you are mean. You're a dictator!" and that was when he let out a roar and jumped up.

"I am a dictator?! You don't know what you are saying, you stupid *idioot* piece of shit girl. Get in your room and stay there until I tell you to come out."

"Fuck you! I hate you!"

He came after her, taking his belt off with shaking hands. He swung, hitting her in the arm as she moved back. He swung again, but she was too quick and backed into her tiny room and slammed the door in his face. She could hear him bellowing in Dutch as she slid down to the floor in tears. In just a few moments, a rage grew in her chest. She knew that if she screamed, he would come in. She found a pencil and broke it in half and threw it at the wall. Her door burst open.

"You think we have enough money to break things?" he said, seeing the broken pencil. "You think you have a right to your little feelings? You have no right to opinions until you are eighteen or married, remember that!"

He hit her twice with the belt and slammed the door behind him, leaving her sobbing on the floor. Her mother came home from work, saw Tessa's face and her husband's tense posture on the couch; and got to work making their supper without a word.

That night Hannah came into her room and sat on the bed where Tessa lay on top of the flowered bedcover, arms crossed tightly on her chest. She put her hand on Tessa's arm and said, "Why do you always talk back to him, Tessa? You know how he is, it's better to just do what he says."

"Like you do? I'm nothing like you. I don't know how you stand it or why you stand it."

"One day you will understand, Tessa. Life is not what you think. In America, girls have a false hope that they can live like men. In Colombia, we were taught that is never true. I fought it too, but in the end, my mother was right."

"I will never be like you," Tessa said.

"Your father was not always like this, Tessa. I keep hoping he will find his way back."

Tessa flipped onto her side to face the wall, and her mother sadly walked out of her room.

Another night while they sat at the dining table, with Popeye the Sailor Man cartoons blasting out of the black and white RCA television, her mother asked her about her day.

"*Godverdomme, Hannah*!" her father yelled. "I can't hear my program. Stop talking!" and her mother clammed up.

After the meal, her mother washed the dishes while her father planted himself on the low fabric couch, black-socked feet on the coffee table, watching "Let's Make a Deal".

Before he turned the volume up, he said, "Go clean the bathroom, Tessa. That's what girls are for."

Tessa went into her parents' room and sat on her mother's side of their bed. She moved the book on the nightstand, glancing at the title: "I'm Okay, You're Okay- Changing the Lives of Millions". Then she turned on the bedside clock radio and twisted the dial until she heard what she was looking for.

She closed her eyes as the grim, creepy music lowered its volume and a man's voice could clearly be heard: "Who knows what evil lurks in the heart of man? The Shadow knows!"

For the next half hour, she was transported to a different place and time; away from her father's constant yelling and threatening, from her mother's annoying kowtowing to him, from the converted pantry where she slept. Once a week, she found her escape in the replays of the old radio show.

The rest of the week, she got lost in books; in any story but her own.

During her lunch period at Hunter, Tessa often walked over to Broadway. She felt no fear, only thrill, as she stood in the middle of the melee that was Times Square. In some weird, inexplicable sense, she felt at home here. This dark place was hers, and she its. Liken an unseen phantom, Tessa watched the seedy life around her without drawing attention to herself. She liked it that way. This was, for some unknown reason, the only place men *didn't* bother her.

Young men loudly hawked three-card monte games all along the avenue, working to hustle the businessmen out of a dollar or two. Every movie theater marquis boasted titles like "Behind the Green Door", "Jane's Bond" and "Naughty School Girls". Graffiti, spray painted over drop-down aluminum gates and any empty expanse of wall space, added a colorful complement to the visual and auditory cacophony. A few small but proud "Queen Elizabeth 110" tags, Tessa's own graffiti signature, were part of the landscape. Garbage covered both sidewalk and street, completing the grimy scene.

Most of the time she would walk around alone among the homeless, the crazies and the desperate. At least once a week Tessa and her friend Rosie would make their way into Lou Tannen's Magic Shop. From outside, the black painted glass entrance was all but invisible between the twenty-five-cent peep shows and dilapidated doorways that led into strip clubs. Unnoticed by the up-and-coming professional magicians, they wandered around the cramped store, stopping to watch and listen to the men sharing stories and trading secrets. It made her feel an electric sense of mystery to be in the very room with what Rosie would call "Masters" in an awed, hushed voice.

Rosie usually bought some small item, a sponge ball or shiny aluminum rings that she would take back to school and teach Tessa to use.

"You have to work on your patter," Rosie patiently explained. "Doug Henning…oh I want to marry him so bad, he's so beautiful…would say it's the most important part of magic." As she talked, Rosie made the sponge ball disappear.

Tessa walked over to the vending machine, stuck her skinny arm up through the flap of the dispenser and made a couple of candy bars disappear.

"Now, that is magic," she said, as she tossed one to Rosie.

On a warm Spring day, she got up early to walk to the subway station. Hannah was drinking coffee, getting ready for her workday at the French Cleaners up on 108th Street. She had taken the job out of desperation, when Pieter got fired for the third time. She offered her daughter a slice of toasted, buttered Wonder bread, which Tessa declined with a wave of her hand.

Tessa had her forty-cent allowance in her pocket, and was trying to decide if she should get a salt bagel at the corner, or switch trains at Roosevelt Avenue to grab a still-warm Boston Cream donut at the underground shop. Or, she thought to herself, she could wait until her lunch period to buy an egg salad sandwich from the Horn and Hardart automat across Lexington Avenue. She walked past the bagel shop, breathing in the oniony, garlicky, bready smell that came through the exhaust fan. I think a donut today, she decided. Maybe I can babysit Felicia or some other kid from Temple Sinai so I can have enough to get all three next week.

At Roosevelt Station, she licked the last of the melted chocolate and cold vanilla custard off her fingers and boarded the crowded train. Pushing her way in, she found a spot at the pole and grabbed on. The train jerked its way through the tunnel, stopping at a station every few minutes until it crossed under the river and into Manhattan. At that moment, she felt a hand go under her skirt, rub her and give her a squeeze. She could barely turn around in the packed car, but she spotted him right away; he turned his head quickly and began to smile smugly. He was tall and fairly young, holding on to the bar above the seats.

Not stopping to think, she pulled her fist back over her head and punched him in the shoulder as hard as she could yelling, "Don't touch me, you piece of shit!"

She knew she had the right guy when he did not even react. No one else in the subway car did either, and she was glad when the train stopped at 53rd Street and she could get off.

After school that day, she and a couple of the other girls

walked up to Central Park to throw a frisbee around at the bandshell. Tessa told them what had happened that morning on the way.

"Ugh, I hate that," said Cara. "Last week on the G train I was sitting on the floor with Gabby and some guy stood over us in a long black trench coat. We noticed it was moving in the front and suddenly it opened, and we saw his dick! He was playing with himself right on top of us, yuck. We started laughing at him and he ran off at the next stop."

"When we were on the school bus in fourth grade going to the Museum of Natural History, there was a guy jerking off while he was driving next to us!" Jenna told them.

"The guy who lives with his wife in an apartment on our floor felt me up in the elevator last week," joined Laura.

The girls just shook their heads in exasperation and walked on.

"Look out!" Tessa yelped suddenly.

A woman came at them with her umbrella raised threateningly, yelling a stream of curses. She was dressed in filthy layers topped by a shabby green overcoat, her face covered in bright makeup and her henna-red hair sticking crazily in different directions. The girls ran into the street and zigzagged through heavy traffic, making it safely to the other side where they laughed so hard, they had to stop and catch their breath.

"She almost got us that time!" Jenna said, gasping.

"She's scary, especially when I don't see her coming," Cara added.

When they got to the bandshell in Central Park, they found the usual lively scene. Teenagers by the dozens were throwing 'bees, playing guitars, and roller skating. The odor of pot hung over them all. Tessa took an offered joint from a boy who was sitting on a bench, dragged on it hard and passed it on to the other girls.

They hung out until the sun went down, and then split up to make their ways home.

She walked up the stairs and opened the door of the apartment to the sound of her father cursing in Dutch and shouting at her mother, as usual. A hairbrush flew by her face and hit the wall next to her, followed by the book from her mother's nightstand.

And then a sound she had never heard before.

"Some husband you turned out to be, Pieter! You can't hold a job and your mother pays our bills. You blew the inheritance my parents left us, the only chance we had of getting out of this cockroach-infested hell. You don't want me to go to school because you don't want me to be smarter than you, but school is open to everyone, you know. I'm sick of working with that pervert at the French cleaners- he can't keep his hands off me. I'm sick of this life and I'm sick of you!"

There was a crash as her mother picked up something heavy off her dresser and threw it to the floor. At this her father roared unintelligibly and then a lot of things were flying around their room, punctuated by her mother shrieking and her father growling back. Tessa snuck into her room, closed the door without letting it make even a snick of sound, slowly opened her window and lit a joint, blowing the smoke into the cool humid night.

She woke up to silence, finding her father sleeping on the sofa and her mother gone. Peeking into her parents' room, she was surprised to see everything neat and in its place; except for a couple of spaces on the dresser where something used to be.

She spent the night at Cara's apartment up in Spanish Harlem. Stopping at a pay phone to let her mother know she would not be home until Sunday, she did not ask about the fight. Her mother, who sounded positively chipper and more animated than she ever had, did not bring it up either.

Tessa was not sure what she would find when she got home Sunday, but it wasn't this: her father had moved out.

"Your father and I are getting a divorce," her mother said.

Tessa did not know anyone else with divorced parents and did not know how to feel. The thought of her tyrant of a father and her dishrag of a mother starting new lives left her reeling and untethered.

"If you get a divorce, I will run away from home. I will become a prostitute in Times Square. I will shoot up heroin," she said, trying to hurt and scare.

Her mother smiled a bit sadly and said, "You won't. You are too smart for any of that. Now come eat dinner, and you can stay up a late and watch the Carol Burnett show with me."

Tessa stalked into her room and slammed the door. She opened her window and wondered if she should jump. That would fix them, she thought. It's only the second floor but I would at least break a leg or something and they would have to pull it together to take care of me. Then she realized that it wouldn't work, and she closed the window and went to bed.

Tessa did not become a prostitute or run away or do heroin, but she did do pretty much anything else risky that came her way.

Her mother started a full-time job in an office, began taking classes at Queens College, and attended weekend getaways at "Parents without Partners." Tessa was mandated to visit her father on Sundays, where he would make her sit in his sad little apartment listening to lovesick poems for hours. Between her father's crazy and her mother's sudden drive for the life Hannah had always wanted, Tessa was on her own.

She stayed out all night and all weekend in Manhattan with friends, hanging out in Central Park or just walking the streets, drinking and getting high. Some Friday nights, the girls dropped acid and sat at the Hayden Planetarium tripping on the Pink Floyd Dark Side of the Moon laser light show. Afterwards, they traipsed to Jenna's apartment at the Dakota building on Central Park West to laugh at their hallucinations until dawn.

In the Spring of ninth grade, although she loved her friends and the unique Liberal Arts environment at Hunter, she took and passed the test for Stuyvesant, a specialized high school focusing on Math and Science on the lower East side. She was looking for change and new challenges and found them in the well-worn halls. The academics were meant to foster future doctors, lawyers, scientists; and yet she continued to pass her courses with little effort.

When she was not in class, she was either at the Fugue bar around the corner drinking blackberry brandy sours and playing pool, or throwing a frisbee at Stuy Park, or getting high on the roof of the Stuy Town apartment buildings. With her new friends, almost every Saturday night, she lined up in her Columbia costume at the Waverly Theater in Greenwich Village to see the Rocky Horror Picture Show.

She managed to maintain a solid grade-point average at the school and began to formulate a plan to get out of New York as soon as possible.

"What are you going to do when we graduate?" Laura, who had also made the switch to Stuyvesant, asked her one Spring night in their Junior year.

They were sitting around the fountain at Washington Square Park, and Laura was spinning a frisbee on one finger. Tessa played with her feather earrings and watched her friend hop the disk on her finger a couple of times before answering.

"I'm getting out of this shithole, that's for sure. I don't know where I'm going to go or what I'm going to do there, but I'm leaving the day after graduation."

"Have you ever been anywhere else, like on a vacation?" Laura asked.

"Connecticut, a couple of times, and we go camping every July at Prospect Lake in Massachusetts, but that's it."

"I got my driver's license last month and dad is letting me use his car. Let's go on a road trip this summer! I've always wanted to see California. It's our last chance before we graduate."

"Oh, hell yes," Tessa said. "I have two hundred dollars saved up and could have another hundred by June. I'm in."

Laura picked her up the day after school got out for the summer.

Hannah gave them a box of canned beans and vegetables, "so you won't be hungry. Have fun, girls! Don't forget to call."

Tessa's father had absolutely forbidden this trip, threatening to call the police on Hannah, who hung up on him while he was still ranting.

For two months, the girls explored as many states as they could. They stayed mostly at KOA campgrounds, which cost them five dollars and offered hot showers; or parked and pitched their tent near a creek or under trees in random places. They drove west on Interstate 80 through Ohio and then dropped south onto I-70.

Wide open highways through endless cornfields both impressed and bored Tessa. She had never seen so much uninhabited space, and the quiet was initially alarming. It took her days to begin to feel safe in unpopulated places, away from the city. The people they met were so nice, kind and accommodating, that Tessa was suspicious of their motives.

In one of the campground bathrooms the first week, Tessa sat on the sink counter shaving her legs. The dry scraping noise got the attention of a woman who was showering her children.

"Don't you have soap or shaving cream to help with that? Here, use mine. Where is your mother, you can't be travelling alone, the two of you? You look like you're twelve."

Tessa refused her offer without a word, shaking her head.

Another day, an elderly man at a gas station saw Tessa and Laura counting out nickels and pennies to pay for their snacks and gave the cashier money to cover them. Tessa and Laura walked quickly to the car and drove away.

"What do you think he wanted?" Tessa asked her.

"I don't know. Maybe he was just being nice?"

And they both burst out laughing at the thought.

Then she saw mountains looming ahead and could not take her eyes off of them. They put a John Denver tape in the cassette player as they drove up to Colorado and sang along to "Rocky Mountain High", smoking a big joint out of their shoebox full of pot to celebrate.

They hiked and camped in the Rockies for days. There were other teens on road trips there, and the girls joined them at their firepits; partying and chatting the night away. Some of the other kids had guitars they strummed or bongo drums to bang on; and the music made the nights just perfect. Tessa thought the pitch-black sky filled with twinkling stars of different hues was the most beautiful thing she had ever seen.

They headed south, stopping to stand atop the marker for the four corners of Colorado, New Mexico, Utah and Arizona; and camped in Canyonlands and Monument Valley. Driving mindlessly along the empty desert highway, singing along with the cassette tape of David Bowie and feeling relaxed, the girls did not see the tiny one-man inspection booth at the Arizona border until the state police officer flagged them down.

"Shit," Tessa whispered just before Laura opened the window. "The shoebox with the pot is on the back seat and the LSD is in a photo canister in the cooler."

Trying to smile innocently while quivering inside, Laura said, "Hello, Officer."

He looked at them for a long moment, swept his eyes over the back seat, taking in the mess of clothing with a shoebox sitting on top, and then looked at them for another long moment.

Finally, he spoke: "You are entering the state of Arizona. Are you carrying fruit or vegetables or live animals?"

The girls breathed out slowly as Laura said, "No, sir."

"Open the trunk," was his response.

They got out and walked towards the back of the car. Tessa knew this was the end of the road for them, and that they were going to wind up in jail for possession. Her heart was hammering as Laura opened the trunk, which was crammed with more clothes, the box of canned goods and the Coleman cooler.

"Open it," said the officer, nodding at the cooler.

Tessa thought she was going to shake apart as the top came up. The only thing inside was the canister, floating on four inches of melted ice water.

He stared at it for a beat, then said, "Okay, girls, have a safe trip."

They did not speak for a good three minutes as they drove on into Arizona. Then Laura let out a yelp and started to laugh. Tessa joined her, tears of relief coursing down her cheeks. As soon as they found a place to pull over, they moved both the canister and the shoebox out of sight.

Tucson was, to Tessa, a mind-blowing alien landscape. The

valley with its small city was surrounded by mountains of varying heights. They explored the Saguaro National Forest on the desert floor, the nine-thousand-foot-high Catalinas towering to the north of the city, the sprawling University campus. In the evenings and early mornings when the sun and heat were tolerable, they went for hikes and learned to free climb down cliffs that took them to hidden creeks and swimming holes. It was a liberating feeling to be immersed in nature and relying only on wits and will to survive.

The beaches of California were warm and breezy and beautiful; and San Francisco, crowded with leftover hippies and wannabes too young to have actually been there, drew her in.

Every place they stopped to explore was so different than New York City. It felt surreal to Tessa that all this could be happening out here in her own country, while at home life was so hard and cold. Her city's grimy dangerous grittiness began to look like just a stain on her widening fabric. Her goal of escaping became much more real as they traveled.

Out of all the places they discovered, Tessa fell in love with both the Colorado Rockies and the Tucson desert on the trip. Soaring, soul-encompassing, infinite mountains and tall Saguaro cactuses in the "Wild West Old Pueblo"- both offered her refuge from her grungy, seedy city.

When she got back to New York just in time to start her senior year, she could not decide between the two places. So, she flipped a coin; and Tucson won.

She went through her senior year with a drive she had not had before. This was her last year in New York; all she had to do was finish school and figure out how to get back to the Old Pueblo.

Still, she stayed as far away from the apartment in Queens as she could. On the rare occasion she sat with her mother for a meal, it always ended in aggravation for Tessa. Hannah was living the adolescence she had not had- dating endlessly between classes and work, and flitting about with a happy hum.

When Tessa said to her, "I'm going out tonight, Ma" her typical response was, "Of course, you should! I actually am too- Carlos is taking me dancing. Have fun, Tessa."

Tessa began to join her next-door neighbor on her drives to Brooklyn to hang out by the Navy Yards. They would sit at the Red Awning bar on Flushing Avenue and get free drinks all night. Tessa loved the sailors and their stories of journeys far away. She also liked the way they looked in their uniforms.

The young men took her disco dancing down in Bay Ridge; and when the clubs closed at four a.m., they would stop in at the White Castle and order "ten dollars' worth" for the ride back. They listened to Southern Rock, and Tessa learned the words to every Charlie Daniels song there was. They went to the Nassau Colosseum to see the Allman Brothers, Pure Prairie League and the Marshall Tucker Band in concert, and Tessa bought every one of their albums.

The sailors, mostly a year or three older than Tessa, showed her even more of the world; and she absorbed it all.

It was an odd Saturday night in January, when Tessa found herself alone in her mother's apartment with nothing to do. The girl next door was having her sailor boyfriend over; and it was snowing so hard, Tessa did not want to walk to the subway.

She stood in front of the open Frigidaire freezer, staring at the stack of Swanson's Frozen T.V. Dinners her mother kept for her; trying to decide between the turkey dinner and the Hungry Man Salisbury steak. Finally choosing the salty brown meat patty meal because of the tiny apple cake cobber it came with, she threw the small tin foil tray with its little compartments into the oven.

She decided to fill out the college application for the University of Arizona that the guidance counselor had given her last week.

He had said, "Are you sure you don't want to apply to other schools? A lot of Stuy kids get into Brown, Princeton, Cornell..."

She had shaken her head and told him she was set on going west.

She was sitting at the Formica table in the kitchen, the now-empty tin foil tray pushed to one side, flipping to the fourth page of the application when the phone rang. It was the girl who lived next door.

"Hey, come over. Jeff brought a friend. He's really cute, and really bored."

"On my way!" Tessa said; and hanging up, she grabbed some pot in a baggy from her desk drawer and headed next door.

He *was* cute.

His mop of dark hair set off his bright blue eyes. His short-sleeved close-fitting collared shirt showed solid biceps and clung to his abs. And when she stepped through the door, he smiled a beautiful toothy goofy grin.

He looked at the baggy in her hand and held up the red bong in his, and they laughed together. The four of them smoked and chatted and listened to music for an hour, and then Jeff and his girl started making out heavy; so, Tessa took Cam's hand and they went to her apartment. They sat on the floor in the living room so Tessa could change the records on the record player when they were over, and talked away the whole night.

Cam opened up about why he joined the Navy at seventeen. His stories of losing his mother, and how his father dealt with it had Tessa feeling a strong emotional appreciation for Cam. Her tales of her father's craziness and her mother's newfound freedom had him full of admiration for this tough cookie. She was like no other girl he had ever met; and she felt the same about him.

After that night they spent every minute they could together. On snowy weekends, he used a friend's van to make his way to Queens to see her. When the weather got warm, he picked her up after school on his motorcycle and they rode down to hang out in Washington Square Park with her school friends. He took her to her first drive-in movie in a borrowed convertible. They rode his motorcycle to Bear Mountain to go camping, and on Spring Break, down to North Carolina.

Yet, Tessa held him at arm's length.

"I am leaving New York to head west in July. I got accepted to the university in Tucson, and that is what I'm going to do. You have plans to go to school in Florida after you get out of the Navy in August. I don't know where I'll be in six months, a year, five years. You should stick with your plan. Let's just have fun for now, and then we'll stay in touch and see what happens."

Tessa was on a mission to get the school year done and get started with her life. When her friends cut class, she refused; worried about not being allowed to graduate. When they took their state Regents Exams high as kites on LSD, she made sure she got some sleep, didn't smoke pot on her way to school that day, and even studied a tiny bit. She took a job at a Mini Mart to make some extra money for her plane ticket to Tucson.

Every time Cam told her he loved her, she gave him a kiss and then pushed him away.

One night, as they sat next to the river under the Brooklyn Bridge passing a joint, he turned to her and said, "My ship is pulling out June 15th. We are headed to Getmo Bay in Cuba. I'll be getting out of the Navy from there."

She sat, thinking, and then turned to him and said, "So we have just a couple of weeks. I do love you, Cam." At this, he sat up straight, and she laughed.

"I do love you and I am going to miss you so much it hurts to think about it. Write to me every day. When you get back, you go on to Florida like you planned. Call me from there, and we will figure this out."

Over the next few days, with finals already done, she cut a few classes and they spent every possible minute together. Often, they rode the motorcycle to a quiet corner of Central Park or sat on a bench watching the boats on the Hudson River; and they just held each other and talked for hours.

She took the subway to Brooklyn on the fifteenth and stood on the dock watching his ship sail away. She felt something so unfamiliar, so deeply painful, that it took her a moment to realize what it was: her heart was broken.

But she didn't have time to indulge it. She spent the next few weeks weeding through her things to decide what should go in the one suitcase she was taking to Tucson. She packed her hundreds of record albums in boxes to be shipped out to her later. Everything else was junk, as far as she was concerned.

She had saved up fifty dollars for her plane ticket. The cheapest one took her to Tucson via Los Angeles, which she thought was ridiculous; but she bought it anyway.

She and her friends hung out as much as possible to celebrate the end of this life. They were all leaving New York, going in different directions. Because they had no way of staying in touch, this was really goodbye; and they milked it for all it was worth.

Once she had her plane ticket, she quit her job and rarely came back to Queens; not that her parents even noticed. Tessa spent nights on couches or benches all over Manhattan.

She visited her father for the last time at the end of the school year.

"Dad, I'm leaving in a week for Tucson. I am not planning on ever coming back."

"You'll be back. You're a girl, and girls need their mothers until they get married. Besides, what are you going to do out there? You'll meet some shmuck and he'll make you drop out of school. Then he'll leave you and you'll be on the next plane home."

"Thanks, as always, for solid parental support," Tessa said, walking to the door. Without another look or word from either of them, she left.

The day of her flight, Tessa asked a friend to drive her to LaGuardia. Her mother was at work and had said her goodbyes the night before.

Carrying her suitcase out of the bedroom where she had spent her entire life was not as hard as she thought it would be. She turned at the doorway, and gazed for the last time at her single bed, now bare of the flowery comforter; her narrow dark wood desk and empty shelves; and the tiny closet whose opening was covered with strings of blue plastic beads. Her boxes of albums were stacked inside it, barely fitting.

"Here we go!" she said aloud to it, and left the apartment for good.

Part Three: Theirs

1979-2015

Cam and Tessa's Story

Tessa heard the roof door open, as she lay on her towel with a dozen other freshman Wildcats. Another helicopter of flyboys from Davis Monthan Air Force Base had just passed low over the Coronado dorm to see the topless sunbathers. After waving at them, she lay back and closed her eyes again. She became aware of some

one standing over her.

"Phone call for you," her roommate said, in her usual bitchy tone.

"Who is it?" Tessa asked, puzzled.

The only people she knew were the girls from her floor, since they had just moved in two weeks ago.

"It was the front desk, you have a visitor, didn't say who." The girl turned and walked away.

Tessa threw on a pair of cut-off jean shorts and a bikini top, and took the elevator down, barefooted. She walked up and told the student who was running the front desk her name. He pointed to the door with his pencil, not looking up. As she walked out the double glass exit doors, she saw no one waiting outside.

Then she turned the corner.

Cam was leaning against the motorcycle, arms crossed and that big goofy grin on his face. She could hear the ticking of the cooling engine, and her heart yammering in her ears. She gave a scream that could have been his name and threw herself on him.

"WHOA, ouch, ouch, ouch, no hugging!" he said, wincing and

laughing all at once. "I got a sunburn in Texas 'cause I got hot riding through the desert and took my shirt off. It's a bad one."

He lifted his shirt and she gasped at the deep red, almost purple color of his skin.

Then she regained control of her brain and said, "What are you doing here? Why didn't you call me? Why aren't you in Cuba or New York or Florida? What is happening?"

"Is there somewhere we can go and talk?" Cam asked, looking around the streets lively with students.

They walked two blocks to the Gentle Ben's patio and ordered a couple of beers.

"I didn't want to go to Florida anymore," he began to explain. "I only signed up at F.S.U. because there was no way I was going back to Iowa, and I knew a couple of guys who got out of the Navy ahead of me who told me to come. Tessa, I travelled around the world, but with you I feel like I finally found a home. I know you said we would figure it out. So here I am. Let's figure it out."

"Let's start by finding a hotel room," was her response. And they did.

Tessa's classes had already started so Cam spent his days looking for a place to live. His Navy separation pay would only stretch so far, and he found a converted garage to rent. It was about a mile from the university, with a bedroom so small you climbed onto the mattress at the doorway. He enrolled at the community college and got a job cleaning the professors' offices on the graveyard shift.

Between his schedule and hers, it was a challenge to find time to see each other; but they did so every chance they got. They rode the motorcycle to camp out in the mountains or explored the old downtown part of the city, rich with Mexican history.

Tessa introduced him to the kids she had already become close with.

"I thought you were making up the Navy boyfriend!" Carrie told her, giving Cam a big hug to welcome him.

Money was tight, and there was not much left after he paid his rent. Cam put aside a dollar here and there so he could take Tessa out once a week; and she loved him even more for it.

Their birthdays were two days apart in early September, so they went to the Stumble Inn to listen to a local band and celebrate. They had been there for several hours and their glasses were empty again, so he went for another round. He wobbled just a bit as he came back from the bar, brimming shot glasses pinched in the fingers of each hand. Sweating Michelob bottles hung down from between his pinky and ring fingers. His eyes yo-yoed from the peppermint schnapps shots, trying to keep them from sloshing overboard, and the girl sitting at the small round high-top table watching the band with her head bobbing to the rhythm.

When he made it back, he carefully set down the beers, bringing her attention back to him. Her big, welcoming smile, *his girl, his Tess* made him feel like he'd been gone for weeks and was coming home. His eyes held hers for long enough to send her a private message; and her smile grew even warmer, her nose wrinkling.

She climbed off the stool in the slow careful way of still, but just barely, sober enough to do so without falling; and grabbed his hand.

"Let's dance, Cam!" she yelled to be heard above the country music that shook the very air in the place.

They hopped around with abandon through a couple of tunes until a slow love song played. He pulled her in and held her against him and they melted together. The last sweet note of the tune was fading when they went laughing and stumbling back to their seats. Leaning pretty hard on the table, they picked up their shot glasses and tipped in towards each other.

"Happy birthday to you," she sang over the band, which had started up again.

"Happy birthday to you," he sang back, as her eyes crinkled with laughter.

"Happy birthday, dear us," they sang in fairly good harmony, finishing the song with a long flourishing loud "Happy birthday to us!"

They clinked and drained their fourth shot with a head shake, and simultaneously reached for their beers to chase it down. He leaned in towards her again, and she blew him a kiss.

"Will you marry me?" he asked.

She laughed, thinking she had heard him wrong over the music and yelled, "What?"

"Will you marry me?" he repeated, a bit slower and louder, and with that goofy smile.

It took her exactly a heartbeat: "Yes! I will marry you!" and they laughed and clinked their beers to celebrate.

The music blasted with bass and drums as they let it sink in, their eyes linked together in a new way, their smiles wide with mischief and delight.

Draining her beer, she stood and said, "We need to go tell somebody to make it official!"

He emptied his and followed her through the door to his waiting motorcycle.

She turned as he came out of the bar behind her, the band's bluesy riffs fading only slightly as the door shut behind him, and asked, "Do you have a ring?"

"Not yet," he answered, and she shrugged and continued on towards the bike. Because when you're eighteen, you don't need a ring to seal the deal; the words and the love were enough.

They rode a half mile to a large house so lit up you could see it a block away. As they parked, the rock music blasted out of the open door and windows. Cam helped Tessa off of the bike, pulled her to him and kissed her with such emotion, they both had tears when they finally pulled apart.

"Looks like Kenny has all the speakers hooked up," Cam said laughing.

They held hands and walked into the party. There were a dozen kids in the living room, all holding red cups sloshing over with amber brew. Several were swaying and bopping to the music, and the rest slouched on the ratty couches and chairs salvaged from the used furniture warehouse near the university.

"Cam! Tessa!" they all roared, raising their cups in drunken salute.

One of the dancers staggered over, grabbed Tessa in a bear hug and yelled into her face, "Get a beer and come dance!"

"Later!" Tess shouted back, and Cam helped her get untangled from the overly enthusiastic girl.

They walked through the kitchen, where opened bags of chips lay in varying degrees of empty, and more red cups were strewn about on counter tops and the floor. The back door, standing open, led to the patio where they found the little group they were looking for, gathered around the keg.

"Hey, it's the birthday kids!" the cluster of friends called and sang an off-key rendition of the happy birthday song in a poor imitation of unison. Kenny grabbed two cups from the stack, filled them to the brim and handed them to Cam and Tessa. One of the girls offered them popcorn she was munching from the large plastic bowl she was holding.

They shook their heads and Tess said, "It's all you, Cath!"

"What is going on- why are you smiling so weird?" Carrie asked. "What could you two be up to now?"

Cam and Tess looked at each other for a beat, and then she blurted out, "We're getting married!"

For a brief moment there was silence as their friends gauged whether or not they were joking. Quickly deciding that they weren't, they began to bellow and shriek their congratulations, punctuated with sloppy hugs and back-poundings and handshakes and kisses.

"You fucking nuts! I love you!" Cathy screeched, tossing the entire bowl of popcorn into the air and jumping on Tessa so hard, they would have fallen over if Cam hadn't been right behind to hold them up.

After the initial celebrating calmed down, they stood in a tight circle, tapped their cups to each other *cheers* and upended them, draining them to the last drop. Kenny and Carrie refilled the cups, over and over, until night began to melt into day. As the black, star-filled sky turned gray blue on the horizon, Cam and Tess mounted the bike and rode the mile home to his tiny shack, and fell into exhausted, happy sleep.

When the brilliant desert sun streamed through the bedroom window, waking them both, she rolled over and faced him. Their eyes held for a beat.

"Did you mean what you said last night?" she asked.

"Did you?"

At the same moment, they breathed, "Yes" and smiled.

They made love, between gazes and laughter and heads shaking over the sheer wonder of it. After, they lay in each other's arms.

She said, "I should probably call my mother and let her know."

"Let's eat first," he suggested, and they got up and cracked their last four eggs into the stained aluminum frying pan.

When the edges were sizzling, he placed two on each plastic plate and tossed a couple of slices of white bread onto the frying pan to toast them. She pulled the camping percolator off the stove, poured the steaming coffee into cracked mugs borrowed from the Student Union cafeteria, and placed his in front of him with a flourish.

"Coffee for my fiancé," she said in a fairly good imitation of a French accent.

"Breakfast for my fiancé," he responded in a terrible French accent, and handed her a plate.

They sat at the wooden table on folding chairs and looked out the window at the mesquite tree that shaded the front yard they shared with two other tiny houses. A white-crowned sparrow settled momentarily on a thin branch, before taking flight again. The warm, quiet morning was perfect.

Cam finished chewing a bite and gave her a serious look. "Tessa, one thing you should know. I believe that marriage is forever. The 'until death' thing is for real, to me. Once I say it, I mean it."

"To forever," she said, tapping her plastic mug against his. "I do, too."

After breakfast, she walked to the shopping center three blocks away where there was a bank of unoccupied pay phones lined up between storefronts. Tessa put a dime in the slot of the first phone and dialed the New York number. It was early morning still on the East Coast, but her mother picked up on the second ring. She imagined Hannah in her housedress and slippers sitting alone in the kitchen drinking her second cup of Chock Full of Nuts coffee, waiting for her slice of Wonder bread to pop up in the toaster so she could slather margarine on it.

She could picture the white wall phone hanging next to the Formica-top table by the opening to the small kitchen. There was no room for a door there, and Tessa used to stretch that phone cord down the five feet to her room, so she could have some privacy.

In the last six months before she graduated high school, it was almost always Cam she needed privacy to talk to.

Her mother's "Hellooo" was chipper as usual.

It still amazed her how la-la-land her mother seemed, in spite of the mess of a family they had. Sometimes she wished she herself was more like that. It must be nice not to ever let anything in; not to ever be bothered by anything. Unfortunately, she had inherited her father's temper. Her independent streak and strength, she knew in her heart, came from her grandmother, Oma, and her deceased grandmother, Lena, who died before Tessa was old enough to call her anything. She often found her mother's one-emotion personality a source of rage.

"Hi, Ma. We got engaged last night."

"You just turned 18."

And it began.

Her mother had two goals in life, now that she had sloughed off the yoke of marriage to her husband: to do whatever she felt like doing (Thank you, "I'm Okay, You're Okay" movement, Tessa thought) and to save her daughter from herself. The latter was not something she worked very hard to accomplish; just enough to be annoying.

"I know that. I love him and he loves me."

"You only met nine months ago."

"It doesn't matter. I feel like I have known him forever."

"He doesn't have a job."

"Ma, he just got here two weeks ago and he already got a job."

A pause. Then: "Are you pregnant?"

"What?! No!"

Sigh. "Are you going to finish school?"

"What?! Yes, of course, what does that have to do with getting married?!"

"I just want to make sure you don't make the same mistake I did. Your father…"

Tess tuned out the rest, something at which she was well-practiced. It kept her from responding with rage which, due to her mother's weird inability to comprehend anything negative, would be infuriatingly useless.

Her mother couldn't do much, anyway, from three thousand miles away. That was a big part of the reason, after all, that she had bought herself a one-way ticket to Tucson right after high school. She had legally emancipated from her parents as soon as she arrived, so she could apply for residency and get financial aid. In effect, she had divorced them both so she could begin her independent life.

Your time is almost up. Please deposit five more cents to continue your call.

"Ma, I gotta go, that was my last dime. I'll call you soon." She hung up the heavy receiver as she heard her mother's goodbye, which sounded marginally, at least in her imagination, more subdued than her hello.

Tessa walked around the side of the grocery store building, barely glancing in at the shoppers' carts overflowing with meats, fresh vegetables and cold milk as they waited in lines at the registers.

Following the narrow alley behind the brick shopping center, she saw with satisfaction that the two dumpsters were not only standing open, but also overflowing. There would be no meat or milk, she knew; but a loaf of bread and a pack of tomatoes caught her eye right away. She climbed up the side of the first dumpster. Shrugging her olive-green army backpack off her shoulders, she began to place the few edible items inside to bring home.

A movement and slight noise beside the metal containers made her stop and climb down. The first thing she saw was a tail, and although she thought *large rat* and made ready to run, she quickly realized the tail belonged to a small brown dog. A mother dog by the look of it. It was busy digging at something underneath the dumpster but stopped to look up at her.

"Hi, little mama," Tessa spoke in a friendly tone and was rewarded with a tail wag and a look that might have said *I guess we're in the same boat, huh?* Tessa put her backpack down, took out the loaf of bread, opened it and pulled out two slices.

As she re-twisted the tie around the top of the bag, she said, "I'm sure you'd rather have a steak. Who wouldn't? But this is what we have, so here you go."

The little dog took the slices and trotted off towards the back of the building. Tessa was sure there was a crate full of puppies in there somewhere.

She climbed the second dumpster and was rewarded with a box of graham crackers and a bag of brown potatoes. There was some slime in the bag, but nothing that couldn't be washed off or cut off. Pretty good haul for a Sunday, she thought as she headed back to Cam's place with her booty.

Their weekly routine began early on Monday morning. Tessa spent the weekend at Cam's place, so she got on her bicycle and pedaled to the university for her eight o'clock class. By eleven thirty, she was in her apron and hair net at Louie's Lower Level in the Student Union, flipping burgers and plating French fries. Every time the boss, Jiff, looked away she popped a French fry into her mouth. She knew she would get fired if he caught her, but she had not eaten yet that day and had gotten good at sneaking. Last week, Jiff had sacked one of the other work-study kids for digging a hamburger out of the garbage can and eating it. Every day at the end of their shift, he checked their book bags for stolen food, so they had all learned how to stuff a hot dog in their pants or grilled cheese sandwiches in their bras to get them through the day.

After spending the afternoon in the Library getting ahead on her assignments, she rode back and found Cam asleep on the bed, his books strewn on top of him and around him. He slept until ten at night, grabbed something to eat, and then headed up to the university for his shift.

On Tuesday mornings, Tessa and Cam met at the student union before her classes started, to share one cup of coffee and, if they were flush, one bean tostada.

Often, they were forced to choose between rent and food; and since they needed a place to sleep, they found the dumpster behind the grocery store up the block supplied perfectly good day-old bread and other just-past items that could sustain them. When they splurged on an occasional pack of hot dogs to mix into their ten-for-a-dollar boxes of mac and cheese, they called their likewise financially strapped group of friends and had a dinner party.

Happy times those were. Too young and stupid to know better, they found many ways to have free fun. Camping, hiking, rock climbing and endless parties filled those hungry days and nights.

The two school semesters passed quickly that way, with a lean but joyful Chanukah, Christmas and New Year's Eve; and before they knew it, summer approached. As soon as classes ended in mid-May, Tessa hand-wrote twenty-five invitations to their August wedding on flowery stationary with matching envelopes and mailed them off.

She wondered what each of their family members would say when they opened the envelopes. She was pretty sure she knew. In New York, there would be few shouts of joy; in Iowa, where all of his family still lived, even fewer. Shrugging off these thoughts, she went about buying a simple wedding dress and sandals, and helping their friends plan their road trip to the East Coast.

Cam was flying out to Iowa and driving to New York with his brothers, while Tessa flew back to finalize preparations. Since a Priest refused to marry them outside of the church, and the Rabbi wanted five hundred dollars, a Baptist minister that her mother had met somewhere agreed to perform the ceremony.

Their original plan was to have a potluck in the park after the ceremony. Her parents had had a fit about that idea, and Oma had stepped in to pay for a dinner at a catering restaurant on Long Island instead. The restaurant promised to provide the entertainment: a one-man band to play dance music.

Glen was not happy when Cam walked into the house, but at least he was sober.

"You're marrying that girl from New York. That *Jewish* girl. Your mother is rolling in her grave."

"Mom would have loved her. Are you coming to the wedding? We're leaving in two days, and there's room in the car."

"No, I'm not. And if you were as smart as I thought, you would not go either. It's not too late. There are plenty of girls right here at home that would jump at the chance to be your wife."

"My home is with Tessa. The reason mom might be rolling in her grave is all you," Cam said, and left the house to find his brothers.

Tessa heard almost the same from her own father: "A Catholic boy?! That Popeye the Sailor Man you met in high school?! You are more of an idiot than your mother."

Tessa said, "See you there, dad," and hung up on him.

The day of the wedding was sunny and bright, a very good thing since they had not made arrangements for a different location in case of rain. Their four college friends had gotten to the park early and, with rakes and brooms, fashioned an aisle for the bride to walk down in the fallen leaves under a thick canopy of elms, oak and maples. The thirty or so guests stood alongside the dirt aisle in small clusters. The ceremony was brief, with the Baptist minister friend of Hannah's committing them into the care of Jesus. In spite of herself, Tessa became emotional, exclaiming *Hallelujah* more than once while family members from both sides just shook their heads. The friends among the guests, all in their teens like the bride and groom, were joyous and celebratory. Most of the family members appeared grim, solemn, troubled. Only Oma was calm and supportive.

Earlier, before she walked down the aisle, Tessa had said to Oma, "Nobody is happy for us. Why does our religion matter so much to them all? Why does everyone think we are stupid for getting married?"

Her Oma had responded in her matter-of-fact way, "If he loves you and you love him, it doesn't matter that he is not Jewish. Look what being Jewish did to us. It is your life. Live it the way you choose."

This blessing was one of the longer conversations she had ever had with her grandmother, who intimidated her a bit, truth be told.

Tessa had heard the family stories of holocaust survival and the aftermath. Her father enjoyed regaling her with the horrors every member of his family had dealt with. He pointed out that the flat he grew up in was across the street from the home of Anne Frank and her family. They had gone to primary school together before the invasion from Germany. From these stories, and from her mother's, Tessa had developed a sense of possible impending doom and devastating loss just around the corner. She was awed by the diminutive powerhouse that Oma was; and the bit of advice from her had given Tessa even more confidence that she was right about Cam.

When they returned to Tucson after the wedding, they moved into a larger house down the street, with a roommate to help pay the rent. Money was so tight, Tessa shopped for used dollar blue jeans at the Buffalo Exchange; and gave Cam, for his birthday, a scrawny, sickly kitten she had found on the street. They named it Cinnamon Girl, after a Neil Young song.

Their roommate, Gaye, who did not want to work while going to school, was good at finding ways to make money.

"I'm going to donate plasma this morning, Tess. You should come with me."

They took the bus to a seedy neighborhood in an industrial part of town and walked to a building that looked abandoned. There was a handmade sign on the door that said, "plasma donations" and a long line of homeless junkies waiting outside.

"No way," Tessa said. "How much do they give you?"

"It's an easy five bucks, and you can do it every week!" Gaye said.

Tessa patted Gaye's shoulder, told her to go for it and walked away.

But from Gaye, Tessa also learned how to get "government peanut butter and cheese," which she did once a month, and a few other ways to economize. Every Friday, Gaye found a happy hour with a free hot food table and for the cost of two fingers of Old Grandad whiskey, about two dollars, they ate a full meal. Gaye even lined her bag with plastic to nab some snacks for later. She was a font of wisdom when it came to surviving on little money.

Late at night, while Cam was working, doubts about what they had done, what *she* had done, crept in to Tessa's restless mind and kept her from sleeping.

"Forever," meaningless to a teenager in love, began to take shape. What had she been thinking, getting married so young? How did you get an annulment? What would Cam say if he knew that she had changed her mind?

In the mornings, she began avoiding him; leaving the house before he returned from work even on days when her classes did not start until afternoon. When she did see him, she picked fights about everything he did. It did not take him long, sleep deprived and anxious about taking care of his new wife, to lose his patience.

"You left the peanut butter out again, Cam! And there's a dirty knife in the sink. I just washed all the dishes!"

"What are you talking about? Your clothes are all over the living room floor. Didn't you ever hear of a dresser drawer?"

"It's called a chest of drawers, who calls it a 'dresser?' And I was going to fold those and put them away after I cleaned the kitchen, but now I have to do that again since you can't seem to do it. And there's the cat litter, it is full of shit and it stinks. When were you planning to take care of that?"

"Did I ask for a stupid cat for my birthday? You clean it, she was your idea!"

The bickering went on until either Tessa ran into the bedroom to cry or Cam took off on his motorcycle. They made up after each row, but the quarreling became so frequent they often did not speak for days. Cam could not understand what was causing these fights, and Tessa wouldn't open up. He thought it could be about his work schedule and decided to make a change. The graveyard shift was wearing him down, anyway.

Cam took a job at a construction company and moved his classes to the late afternoons. Things between them improved a bit, since Tessa no longer spent her nights alone, thinking. But the damage had already been done, and the quarreling continued.

They scraped together enough money to buy an old trailer house outside Tucson in the foothills of the small mountains to the south. Tessa had seen it advertised in the Dandy Dime Classifieds and they had ridden out to see it. She loved how close the hiking area was to the place; and the Papago Indian Mission nearby had weekend markets that were open to everyone.

The lot, sandwiched between other trailers, became the regular weekend hangout for all of their friends. The musical ones among them serenaded the partiers with sweet blue grass through the dark desert night, accompanied by coyote yips and howls until the sun came up.

During the week, Tessa rode ten miles to class on her bicycle. Through the cooler mornings in the winter, she enjoyed the ride. But summer came early in Tucson. There was a private joke among locals taking bets on when the ice would melt on the Santa Cruz River; in translation it meant the first one-hundred-degree day. It often happened in the middle of April; and stayed there until October.

On a hot afternoon in May, when she arrived home red in the face and sweating once again, she walked in the door and began yelling at Cam.

"I hate this! It's ridiculous. I can't ride this stupid bike stupid twenty miles every day. I'm not doing it anymore. I quit! I quit everything!"

Cam looked up from his crossword puzzle but did not respond.

"What are you looking at? I fucking hate my life. Are you just going to sit there and stare at me?"

"You hate your life?" Cam asked. "You chose this overheated desert to begin with; not me. You wanted to live out here in the boondocks, 'our own little slice of heaven' you said, and you knew it was a long ride from school. What do you want to do, are you going to quit school now? Do you think I have it easy, riding around town on a motorcycle with a tool belt on?"

She glared at him and stalked into the kitchen. Trying to pull a pitcher of water out of the refrigerator, she knocked the gallon of milk onto the floor. The cap popped off and milk poured out in a rapidly growing puddle.

Tessa let out a scream of rage, and dropped to the floor, trying to put the slippery cap back on. She sat on the floor and began to sob.

"What is wrong with you? It's just milk!" Cam yelled at her.

"It's just milk?! Do we have money for more milk?" Tessa spoke between sobs. "We don't have money for anything. We can barely make the payments on this shithole!"

"Shithole? Tessa, you are being such an asshole! I'm not going to listen to this!" and he slammed the door behind him.

She could hear the roar of the motorcycle, and the screech of tires as he turned the corner and rode away.

Tess sat next to the white puddle for a long time. Finally, she got a dish rag and wiped it up. She took a shower to cool off, and by the time he returned, she was sitting at the kitchen table making a list. He walked in and stood in the doorway; arms folded tightly across his chest.

She turned to look at him. "I am sorry about losing it. I was hot and I am fed up with riding my bike to school. This is not going to work."

"Okay, but I'm not going to get screamed at every time you get frustrated, Tess. That's how I grew up and that is not how I am going to live my life."

They stared at each other, unhappy.

"What are you doing there?" he finally broke the silence.

"I'm making a list of our expenses and our money. It's not pretty; but I think we might be able to afford a cheap car, if I get another job. The Dandy Dime has listings for auto sales and auctions."

"You have to learn how to drive, Tess."

"I know. And while we're at it, I want to learn to ride the motorcycle too."

"Done and done," Cam said.

They hugged tightly as she whispered, "I'm sorry, babe," and cried on his shoulder.

She got a second job scooping ice cream at a small parlor and a month later, they went to an auction and drove off in a five-speed half-ton pickup truck. She almost destroyed the transmission learning how to change gears; but she kept at it until she was a pro.

The motorcycle was harder because it was so heavy; she kept dropping it. But she finally got that too and loved riding to school and back.

It was around this time when Cam's brother Joe called them to say he was planning on driving down to see this desert life they were making for themselves. He arrived late the next night, and as soon as he got in, he and Cam cracked a beer to celebrate.

Tessa gave her favorite brother-in-law a hug and went to bed, to give them some brother time. They wound up talking until morning, and Cam dragged himself to work, leaving his brother snoring on the couch.

They took Joe out to Reddington Pass to hike and do some freehand climbing. When they got to the top of the waterfall, Joe sat on the edge of the rock overhang, feet dangling.

"You know, Cam, after you left home, I lasted a year in Iowa City. Things got worse with Dad; and Sam and the T's took off to California for a couple of years. That left me to deal with him. The last straw for me was when he showed up plastered at Connolly's Garage while I was working. Got me fired, the bastard." Joe shook his head at the memory.

"So, I went to live out in Tama to help Grandma and Grandpa and Uncle Benjamin on the farm. It was great out there. I loved just being outside all the time, and Grandpa put me to work fixing all the machines when they broke down."

This time he chuckled at the thought.

"But the best part was when Grandma would make an apple pie and cut me off a steaming slice as big as my head. And she told me stories I never heard before. Did you know that mom was a nurse in the war? That's where she met Glen. It's hard to believe we never knew that. When mom was on her way to the front for the first time, the military plane she was on with the other nurses and medics crashed in the mountains. The whole crew survived but they had to hike almost nine weeks to the sea where they got transport to the front and went right to work."

"I had no idea our mother was a badass," Cam said, his head shaking in wonder.

Tessa took his hand, with a look of admiration for the mother-in-law that she never got to meet.

"Yeah, well, it was hard for her to be anything but Glen's nursemaid. And ours, too. Hard to believe how she used to do everything with a smile, knowing what I know now. I guess she really meant it when she said 'family first.' I even went to the library and dug up an article and an Army newsreel about that plane crash. It's nuts what she went through. I just don't understand what she saw in our dad, you know?"

"Maybe he has a story that you all don't know, too," Tessa said. "My family was pretty open about the horror show they survived; but not everyone is, obviously."

Joe stayed a week before returning to Iowa. "I don't know what I'm going to do with myself," he said to them the day he left. "Maybe I'll come down here for a while, or maybe I'll check out California for myself. Sam loved it and might go back, too. I'll drop you a line when I figure it out."

When Tessa finished her geosciences program two years later, she got a dream job studying the geologic history of the Tucson valley. Her colleagues were mostly recent graduates as well, and she loved the challenge of working with her team to figure out the story behind the valley they now called home.

Cam found he could not settle on a program and decided to stop taking classes. He started his own construction company, building dozens of houses in the rapidly growing city; and between the two of them, money started to roll in.

Their dumpster diving days were finally over; and they also

happily left behind the adolescent drama of their first years together.

One of Tessa's favorite parts of the job was climbing, with or without ropes, to get samples for the studies her team was undertaking. They explored the volcanic rock to the west of the city, surveyed the nine-thousand-foot-high peaks of the Santa Catalina mountains and spelunked down into the Peppersauce caves on the backside of the range. They investigated the origins of petrified wood, dinosaur bone and clam fossils they found along the way.

One afternoon, Tessa and one of the other scientists were climbing up Sentinel Peak to dig into the igneous rock above the University of Arizona's enormous painted A, when her colleague lost her footing. She hung from her hands just below Tessa, scrabbling with her feet to find purchase. Tessa heard the noise and turned, just in time to see her grasp slip and watch her tumble backwards.

She could only yell, "Janie!" as she watched in muted horror.

Janie flipped over several times on the steep grade and then slid on loose gravel, about halfway down the A, before stopping on a narrow flat ridge. From where Tessa was, about forty feet above her colleague, she could only see that the woman was not moving.

Tessa made her way carefully down and found Janie was breathing, but shallowly. Blood dripped from one ear and a bone jutted out from her thigh. Tessa worked to keep from vomiting at the sight, as she tried to figure out what to do. There was no one else up on the mountain with them and no way to contact the police.

"I'm going for help, Janie," Tessa spoke clearly and carefully, hoping Janie could hear her. "You took a hell of a fall and I don't want to move you. I'm going to put a blanket over you and drive down to a pay phone to call the police. I will be right back. Stay with me, okay?"

As she drove down the mountain road, she spotted a police car parked almost at the base. She pulled over and rolled down the window.

"My colleague fell a long way down the mountain! She is unconscious but breathing. She broke a large bone in her leg and it's protruding through the skin. We need an ambulance right away. I'm heading back up to stay with her until they get here."

The ambulance came quickly, but had to wait for a rescue team to climb up and bring Janie down slowly and cautiously on a stretcher. Tessa stayed at her side, talking softly and reassuringly to her as they worked. After the ambulance took Janie off to the hospital, the piercing sound of the siren dimming as it drove around the switchbacks, Tessa sat in her car, alone, silent and shaken. She drove into town, not exactly sure where she was going.

Turning a corner, she saw a synagogue with its large silver star of David shining in the bright sunlight. Suddenly, for the first time in a very long time, Tessa felt the need to pray. She parked and walked up the stone steps to the oversized wooden doors. She put her hand on one of the bronze door handles and pulled. It was locked. She tugged again, just to check.

"Are you kidding me?" She spoke out loud to the temple. "I need you and you're locked. Unbelievable!"

She turned to walk back to the car and spotted, just down the street, a small white church steeple. Its door was standing wide open to the street. Tessa walked in and found a few other people scattered in the wooden pews, facing the altar. It was cool and dim and welcoming. Tessa sat, put her face in her hands and began to cry quietly.

"Please help, Janie, God. Help her get better, she is a good person. I don't really know how to do this, but I hope it helps. Amen."

She stayed at the church for almost an hour before driving home.

As soon as Cam got there, she told him the whole story; finishing with her utter dismay that her own religion did nothing for her, while his was there when she needed it most.

"Tess, any port in a storm, as my grandfather used to say. The whole organized religion thing is more divisive than helpful. I mean, it would have kept us apart if we had listened to our families. I'm just glad you found a place to say your prayers for your friend. It can't hurt, anyway." He held her close.

After a while, the house phone rang. Maddy, the head scientist on the team, was calling to say that Janie was going to recover after some time and rehabilitation.

"That quick thinking paid off. You're a hero, Tess!" she said before hanging up.

Tessa and Cam held hands and sent up a silent prayer of thanks together.

The first thing Cam and Tessa did, when they had enough money saved up, was to buy a piece of land at the base of the towering Santa Catalina mountains bordering the northern side of Tucson. They pitched a tent every weekend, and walked the property, planning out the house they wanted to build.

There were some arguments over the plans, especially when it came to the kitchen and the outdoor spaces. Cam was all about keeping costs down, and Tessa wanted the spaces in the house to be practical but beautiful. In the end, they compromised on everything; and happily, watched their new home grow and take shape.

It took a year to complete the house and make it ready for them to move in. On the day it was officially done, they bought a pizza and sat on the floor to eat it.

"Cheers to us and our new house!" Cam said, holding up his slice to tap hers.

"Cheers to us, our new house, and our newest venture," she responded.

Cam looked at her, puzzled, until she rubbed her hand over her belly.

He jumped up and let out a whoop, his slice of pizza falling to the floor, and danced around the unfurnished room until Tessa stood to join him. He dropped to his knees, laying his ear against her midsection. Then he put his mouth against her belly.

"Hey in there! Hey, little baby!" his muffled voice vibrated on her skin and tickled her until she pushed him away, laughing.

They sat to eat and Cam kept his free arm around her waist, rubbing her middle. He could barely chew; he was smiling so widely and marveling that they were going to be a Mommy and Daddy.

"I just hope we can do a better job than our parents did," Tessa said, a bit anxiously.

"Are you kidding? That's a low bar, Tess. We are going to be great! You are going to be great," Cam said, giving her a loving squeeze.

They settled into their new home quickly, spending most of their time furnishing the nursery with an animal theme. Tessa had watched and followed along with the television artist Bob Ross and painted a squirrel scene, which now hung over the changing table. They had just finished hanging a print of a baby giraffe and were eating dinner, when the doorbell rang. Sharing a questioning look, they got up together and went to the door.

Glen stood on the front porch wearing a plaid golf hat, holding a small suitcase.

It had been years since they had seen each other, and they had only spoken on occasion over that time.

"Dad?"

"Hi, son. Hi, Tessa."

There was a lengthy silence until he added, "I wanted to see you. May I come in? Please."

Cam checked with Tessa, who shrugged her okay. Glen set his suitcase down in the entry way.

"Are you hungry, Glen? We were just finishing dinner."

Glen looked at her; his eyes glistening a little. "Tessa, you are so nice. I never knew that about you."

"Maybe if you had given her half a chance, Dad," Cam retorted. "What are you doing here?"

"Is there somewhere we can sit?" Glen asked, and they led him to the comfortable wicker chair set on the back patio overlooking the imposing mountains.

Tessa brought out some lemonades in sweating glasses. She had no intention of offering him anything stronger. In any case, he did not ask; he just took a long sip of the refreshing drink. Tessa and Cam held theirs, waiting for him to speak.

"You look great, both of you," he began.

Cam, not sure what to make of his father's compliments, told him, "Tessa is expecting a baby. We are doing great, Dad. No thanks to you. Are you sober?"

"I don't think I have ever been this sober, son," Glen said, passing an age-spotted, heavily veined hand over his eyes.

"I'm here to apologize. To you and to Tessa. Joe has been filling me in on how you are doing, and I am so proud of you both."

The two of them remained silent. Neither was prepared to accept a simple apology and let him off the hook that easily.

"I was a shitty father, Cam. I know for sure you will be a very good one. Tessa, you remind me of Cam's mother Lillian in a lot of ways. She was a strong woman. She had to be, to deal with me. I disappointed her so much. I can't fix that, even though I wish I could. Before she died, she asked me to promise to take care of you boys; and I failed. She asked you to grow up to be good men; and you all succeeded, somehow."

Cam started to speak, but Glen held up his hand.

"Now it's my turn. You won't be surprised that I have cirrhosis of the liver, I think. But it's the lung cancer that will probably kill me in the end. In any event, I don't have long. I won't be around to meet your baby. I hope you won't be too unkind when you tell him about his old Granddad."

A million emotions swarmed over Cam. He could not bring himself to approach Glen; that would have been too far of a reach and Glen did not look like he wanted that either. He was an old man, sick and full of regret. He did not seem to expect forgiveness. That showed Tessa how little he knew his son.

"How long will you stay with us?" Tessa asked him.

"I can stay?" Glen responded with some disbelief.

They made a room ready for him and he gratefully thanked them again for allowing him back into their lives.

As they settled into bed, Cam quietly said, "It's kind of unbelievable. I did not think there was any hope for him and now that he is dying..."

"I know. But at least he is here now, before it is too late." She held his hand as they fell asleep.

When Tessa came home from work the next day, she found Glen in the kitchen.

"I am making my very special, very unique, very ketchup-y Sloppy Joes. I hope that's okay."

"It's great, Glen, thanks."

"Before Cam gets home, I want to say something to just you, Tessa. I was a complete ass about Cam marrying you. You are the best thing that ever happened to him. Just like Lillian was the best thing that ever happened to me."

Glen paused to swallow back sorrow before continuing.

"I am glad he did not listen to his drunk of a dad. I am glad he got away from the situation at home, even though I know it must have been hard for him. He was just a kid, jeez. I realize, now that it's too late, that I made it hard for him, for his brothers, for you. My father-in-law never forgave me, and I understand. He even told me I was the reason Lillian got sick and died. I think he might have been right."

Tessa said nothing as Glen unburdened himself. She was not sure what to say. Her own father had never apologized or even acknowledged how hard her childhood had been. She always thought she needed that from him; but now Cam's father was saying all the right things, and she really did not know how she felt.

Glen looked up and met her eyes. "I have some things I want you and Cam to have. He has never seen these before, because his mother hid them. I think the memories might have gotten in the way of her accepting the life we had, so she put them away, literally."

He was coming back from the bedroom when Cam walked in.

"Smells like Sloppy Joe! I haven't had that since mom passed away."

"You probably don't remember, but I was the one who made it for you. Mom was more of a casserole maker and cake baker. How those church ladies fought over her baked goods! Sloppy Joe was my specialty, on the rare occasion I was home to make dinner for you boys. You did eat a bucketful," he said, smiling at the memory.

He handed Cam a newspaper-wrapped package. Cam sat, pulled the scotch tape off, and moved the newspaper print out of the way. Staring up at him were two framed black and white photos.

The first was Glen and Lillian's wedding picture. His mother, in her starched perfect uniform, her face so young and serious and beautiful; his father in the bed sitting up straight with his leg in an enormous cast, holding her hand and smiling widely.

Tessa watched Cam's face. He could not take his eyes off the fresh, youthful couple, so full of life. Another life, that he had known nothing about. He touched his mother's face with wonder, a tear tracing his cheek. He looked closely at Glen in the hospital bed and let out a little chuckle at his father's expression.

The second photo showed seven nurses standing in front of or sitting on an Army jeep, in field uniforms with their hair disheveled; looking hardy and ready to serve. His mother leaned a bit jauntily back on the jeep, with a small smile, mugging for the camera.

After giving him a moment, Glen told him, "She was one tough cookie back then, it was incredible what she did overseas on the front. I guess it was good training, because she had to be a different kind of tough for the rest of her too-short life. I will never understand why she had to go the way she did; it should have been me. I did not realize how much I needed her and how much I would miss her when she was gone. When she was alive, I ignored her and all of you. When she passed, I just could not step up. I was the weak one, the whole time. Cam, I can never say this enough, but I am sorry, and I'm not just saying that because I'm sick. I've been sick in one way or another for a long long time."

This time, Cam did stand and give his father a hug. Glen, unaccustomed to such display, pounded his back a couple of times before gently pushing him away. He looked at Tessa, who came over and gave him a hug, too.

Glen's eyes glistened. "Thank you both for letting me say my piece. If you let me, I will stay a few more days. I don't think we'll see each other again after I leave."

Glen spent the next few evenings telling them stories about his family. "You didn't know my grandfather, Padraig, but what a spark plug. He survived the Irish potato famine as a young boy, and later, the Depression and Prohibition. He and my granny had dozens of grandkids who all lived in the same neighborhood. My father was the only one who moved away to go to school. They lived a grand life and died within six months of each other. My father always said I was a bit like him, just an American version. Turns out Padraig was a much better man than me, but I guess I inherited some of his charm. I used to spend summers in Chicago with the Callahan clan; what a crazy bunch they were. Those were the best times of my life. I wish he would have met you boys; he would have put you right to work, like he did me. My dad was kind of the quiet one of that brood; but he married my mother, so he must have missed that bit of wildness after all. Now, her side of the family has its own tales to tell…"

Tessa ate up the stories he told. She was beginning to appreciate, and maybe understand a little, that their parents' generation had lived through a lot. What had seemed like boring events and names and dates to memorize in Social Studies class, were actual things that people she knew had dealt with. It struck her with wonder how any of them survived and even thrived to carry on and create the next generation.

Now that she was expecting her own child, her perspective about this seemed to be changing. When she stopped to think about it, as she did more and more often, she realized that it was an inevitable transformation; maybe even necessary to becoming a mother herself.

When Glen left to return to Iowa, he gave them each a hug. His last words to them were, "Keep up the good work, you two."

Cam attended every doctor's appointment with her, but on her sixth-month check-up, he was in Iowa at Glen's funeral. On the drive to drop him off at the airport, Cam had confided in her his feeling of regret.

"I should have gone back to see him once in a while. He was a real jerk, but he was still my dad. I feel like I failed on the 'family first' thing my mom used to say."

"Babe, he was the one who failed; he told us that when he was here. I know what you mean though. I feel like that with my dad too. I keep wishing things could be different before it's too late."

"If wishes were fishes…" Cam had said with a sad smile.

Now she sat alone in the waiting room. Magazines were spread out on the table with names like "Positive Pregnancy" "Parenting for Today" and "Baby and Me". She picked one and leafed through it.

"I Lost My Baby at Birth!" screamed the title of one of the articles. Tessa skimmed the article, her face growing darker as she got to the part where the perfectly healthy baby died of a cord accident.

She stalked over to the receptionist and dropped the magazine on the counter open to the offending article.

"How can you have magazines like this in a room full of pregnant women?! Do you think we need to hear that this can happen right now? It's scary enough being pregnant, this is not the kind of thing I want to be thinking about while I'm lying in bed at night, not able to sleep. You need to be careful what you put out there!"

The receptionist apologized and put the magazine out of sight under the counter, promising to be more careful. It took Tessa several deep breaths to calm down. The doctor did not seem particularly sympathetic about it, telling her, "Your emotions run a bit wild because of the hormones. You'll feel better once the baby is born."

When Cam got home, she told him what had happened. "I don't want to have the baby in a cold hospital with robot nurses and doctors. It's like a baby mill! They don't care about anything but doing their jobs, as if I'm just another thing to check off the list. I'll bet the receptionist put that magazine right back on the table as soon as I left. Maddy told me about the Tucson Birthing Center. She said the midwives are all great, and you have the baby right there in the center, which is an actual house. That's what I want to do, Cam."

"Done and done," he said, and they made an appointment to visit that week.

The midwives, Jody and Deb, welcomed them warmly to the center, and Tessa knew they had made the right decision.

She worked in the field through the pregnancy, in spite of the challenge of bending over to dig. One morning, she crouched down with her hand shovel and heard a popping sound underneath her. Suddenly, a rush of warmth spilled out of her and she fell to her knees. Maddy, who was working next to her, saw what was happening, and held her as she crunched over, gasping through the pain that wracked her.

"Breath," Maddy calmly told her, and then yelled to one of the other scientists, "Go get Cam. Tell him to meet us at the birthing center."

When the first contraction finally released, the second came before she could even fully catch her breath.

"Shit, that's coming fast," Maddy said. "I'm going to help you to your feet, and we'll get in my car. It's only a twenty-minute drive, are you ready? Up we go! Come on, Tess."

Leaning heavily on Maddy, Tessa made it to the passenger seat. Another contraction made her pant and moan, as they drove into town.

Cam was waiting at the entrance to the center with Deb when they drove up. They all helped her slowly inside. Then Maddy gave each of them a big hug and said, "Next time I see you, you'll be a mommy and daddy!"

Deb examined Tessa, and confirmed the baby was on its way.

"To be honest, you almost gave birth in the car!" she said. "This one is anxious to meet you."

It took another forty minutes, but Cam caught the baby and stared at the newborn's face until Tessa finally said, "What did we get?!"

"It's a girl," he sighed, already in love. "It's Lily."

Tessa nodded her approval of the name, and held her arms out to welcome Lily to their world.

"She looks a bit like your mother in those photos your dad gave us," Tess said.

"I hope she doesn't get my mother's nose," Cam said,

laughing.

The overwhelming feat of caring for a newborn was balanced by the emotion they felt when the three of them got a quiet moment together. Sitting on the couch next to each other and staring at the baby brought a sense of wonder and awe, until they heard a wet noise coming from her lower half.

"Not it!" they both called, putting their fingers on their noses. Cam sighed and went to get a cloth diaper from the pile.

"Another one for the toilet," he groaned, as he went to rinse it out before throwing it into the washing machine. "How much can a baby poop, for crying out loud?"

"I would say our girl could win a world record," Tessa said, cooing at the freshly changed infant.

Lily was only a year old, already walking and starting to say words, when Tessa noticed she was having trouble buttoning her pants.

"Still got some baby fat to lose," she told Cam glumly. "I can't even close my zipper."

The next morning, when she woke up, she ran to the bathroom to vomit. Cam, still sleepy, got up to hold her hair. "Hm, pants not fitting, waking up nauseous, do you think…?"

Sure enough, a test confirmed it: they were expecting again. Eight months later, Noah joined them, and they felt their family and world were complete.

They hired a babysitter to watch Lily and Noah during the workday. She was an older Mexican woman who had raised eight children of her own, and Tessa was delighted to have someone to speak Spanish with. Delia cooked them refried beans and freshly grilled tortillas and spicy stews, kept the house clean, and always had a fresh pot of coffee waiting for them when they got home from work.

"Will you marry us?" Tessa asked her one day when she arrived to find the laundry neatly folded on their bed, the aromatic scent of mole enchilada sauce floating on the air.

"What would my husband Ralph say?" was Delia's amused response.

"He can marry us, too," Cam said, catching the conversation as he walked in. "I could use a hardworking old guy like him to keep my men in line."

He grabbed a steaming flour tortilla off the griddle and stuffed it in his mouth with a deeply satisfied moan.

When the kids were a bit older, Cam told Tessa she should take them to New York to meet her family, who had never, in the years since she moved to Tucson, come to visit. She had written her father an emotional, angry letter just after Noah was born, telling him he should want to come see his grandchildren.

His response, when it came in the mail weeks later was a blank greeting card on which he had written, "Thank you for sharing your feelings. Love, Dad"

Her mother always had an excuse why she couldn't travel: work, her Master's Degree program, a sick friend. The latest reason was her boyfriend, who was a controlling mafia-wannabe with no discernable source of income, and Sunday dinner at his Mama's house in the Bronx.

Tessa had no patience for either of them, especially once she and Cam had children of their own that they worked so conscientiously to raise with love and positive guidance.

Cam, however, had that phrase he threw at her when she ranted about them: "Family first, remember? And, Tess, you don't want to regret not being the bigger man, I mean woman, before it's too late. How you deal with them now, reflects more on you than on them…"

She got irritated whenever he said things like that, but he would lighten the mood with, "You can pick your friends, and you can pick your nose, but you can't pick your family."

With a resentful, annoyed sigh, she bought plane tickets for New York.

When she arrived at La Guardia, she rented a car and loaded the children and luggage into it. She pulled up in front of her mother's apartment and sat in the car outside. It all seemed smaller than in her memory- the street, the garden apartment building, even the trees that lined the cracked sidewalk. It also looked dingier than she remembered it.

Her mother opened the apartment door with a big welcoming smile. There were freshly baked cookies on the kitchen table and a box of Legos on the floor.

"Ma, they're too small for Legos," Tessa chided her and moved the box out of their sight, replacing it with toddler toys she had brought with her.

"How long are you staying?" Hannah asked, bouncing both of the kids on her knees.

"A week" Tessa responded.

"Okay, I took off Monday from work since it's the only day I don't have classes. We should take them to the zoo at Flushing Meadows Park that day, they'll love it. I do have to go to John's mother's house as usual on Sunday. I'm hoping you get to meet him while you're here. Do you have set plans for the week?"

"Not really. I will probably take them to Central Park at least once, show them their mom's old stomping grounds. I am hoping to reconnect with some of the girls from Hunter and Stuy, if they came back to New York after college. I lost touch with pretty much everybody, so I'll reach out to their parents and see. Of course, I am going to introduce the kids to Oma. I also want them to meet dad at some point."

"Good luck with that," Hannah said. "Oma says he is driving a limo for an airport car service and she hardly sees him."

"At least he's working," Tessa responded.

"Oma says he spends all his money on lottery tickets, still hoping to win the big one."

Tessa shook her head, pushing away her ire. She set up the portable cribs in her old bedroom. She would be sleeping on the couch, in spite of her mother's offer to share her bed. Too weird, she thought.

She drove over to see her grandmother in the morning and was surprised when she walked in and found her father sitting at the table, waiting.

"There are my grandchildren! Lily and…" he stood up to greet them with open arms.

"Noah, dad. His name is Noah."

"Why didn't you name him after his old grandpa, hm? You look just like me!"

God forbid he is anything like you. Tessa bit her tongue to stop the words from coming in front of the children.

"Look, Grandpa bought you giant bakery cookies! Which one do you want, Noah? Lily can have the other one," he said, holding them out to the little boy.

One had blue icing with Cookie Monster's face, the other was yellow: Big Bird. Noah reached for Big Bird and Lily, thankfully oblivious to her grandfather's blatant chauvinism, happily gnawed on Cookie Monster.

"I hear you're working now," Tessa said, sipping the cup of coffee Oma had given her.

"Yep, your old man found the perfect job. Driving a car on my own schedule. The money is okay, but the best part is the guys I work with. Great guys! That job I had at Lufthansa when you were little, they were a pain in the ass; early mornings just aren't for me."

"What about the job at the travel agency at Alexander's, the auto supply company you sold air fresheners for, the delivery jobs you had for the Bohack's Grocery and the Cort Drug Store?"

"You did love driving around in that brown van trying to sell air fresheners on Saturdays," Pieter responded as if it were a fond memory of her childhood, ignoring her question.

Her father left early, and Oma suggested they walk the kids to Max and Mina's for an ice cream cone after lunch. Tessa ordered her old favorite, Cap'n Crunchberry, and it was just as good as she remembered.

She and Oma sat at the plastic table inside the tiny ice cream parlor watching Lily and Noah lick the drips off their cones. Noah had chosen Peanut Butter Cookie Mess, and was blissfully enjoying every lick. Lily had chosen the Cotton Candy Fruity Pebbles, and her smile was covered in pastel pinks, greens and blues. After a while, the children took their cones and wandered over to gaze at the walls of the shop, which were plastered with colorful cereal box fronts and Garbage Patch Kids cards from the 1970's.

"I know it wasn't easy for you growing up, Tessa," Oma said quietly.

Tessa looked down at her ice cream and said nothing.

"Now that you are a mother, maybe you will understand things from a different perspective," Oma continued. "During the war, your father…"

"I've heard the stories, over and over again, Oma," Tessa interrupted, a bit shortly and bitterly. "Dad made sure I knew how bad it was. What I will never understand is why he was so mean to me, and to mom, too. I think he got stuck emotionally as an angry eleven-year-old. I think he never should have gotten married and had a kid."

It was Oma's turn to look into her ice cream cup. After a moment, she said, "Tessa, I thank God for you every day. I thank God for your mother, as well. I don't know why I survived the war, and lived to be almost ninety now. But maybe it was to see things through until you came along. I don't know exactly what I believe and what I believe in. But I do know that I am grateful to still be here, and to see you as a mother raising my great-grandchildren. It is a wonder to me. Your father never recovered from what he experienced. How could he? He was just a child."

"But you seem okay somehow, Oma. After losing your husband, your mother and father, your little sister, all your brothers, your daughter and, even in some ways, your son..." Tessa looked at her own chatting happy children and could not continue.

"After the war, we tried our best to look forward, not back. This is why I took your father to Ecuador to begin a new life. He seemed to be doing well for a while. Even after we moved to New York and he started courting your mother, he seemed to be on a good track. You should have seen them dance, Tessa. They went out on the town every chance they got. Your mother was like a freed caged tiger."

Oma smiled at the warm memory of hopeful days.

"But then, they got married and things went downhill very quickly. He lost his job at the airlines, and then could not hold one for very long after that. I kept giving him money, hoping it would help him feel more confident; but I actually think now that it had the opposite effect. I think the responsibility was too much for him, and it made him angry. And then you came along. You were a perfect baby, Tessa. Even the obstetrician thought so and asked your mother if she would give you up for adoption."

They both laughed, and Tessa slid her hand onto the top of her grandmother's papery, wrinkled fingers.

"In you, Pieter saw everything that he did not have, everything he could not be and everything he could not control. In his spiraling into a kind of madness, he lost your mother and he lost you. But he is my son, and I will be there for him in a way I couldn't when he needed me most..."

Then Oma could not continue, and Tessa leaned over to lay her head on her grandmother's shoulder.

All four of them held hands as they walked Oma back home.

The next day, Tessa loaded Noah and Lily into the car and headed into Manhattan. She had reached out to old phone numbers and had not been able to connect with any of her school friends; so, she decided to take the kids to some of her favorite spots in the city.

When Tessa parked the car a few blocks from Central Park, the very first thing she noticed was something missing: garbage. There wasn't any. The streets and sidewalks were clean, and there was no graffiti, no homeless crazy people to chase you down the street, no burned out buildings. It was disorienting at first; then just weird. The city felt different, and the families happily chatting away as they explored the park made her think of Disneyland.

She was grateful, though, that there were no empty nickel bags and used condoms laying around the playground as the kids slid down the smooth concrete slide on pieces of cardboard and, shrieking with joy, raced up the steps to do it again. Even the sprinklers were working, and Lily and Noah were a sopping happy mess when she put them in the car to go back to Queens.

That night, when she spoke to Cam on the phone, she told him of her impression.

"Do you want to move back?" he asked.

"No!" Tessa said vehemently. "It's someone else's world now."

But she did enjoy the week. She introduced Lily and Noah to New York pizza, salt bagels, potato knishes, falafel sandwiches, giant warm pretzels and even, against her better judgement, what they used to call "dirty-water dogs" from a street vendor.

She visited Washington Square Park, where a new building had been constructed in the alley where she and Laura had played frisbee through the night. The pot-smoking guitar-strumming long-haired kids had been replaced with hip young NYU students carrying video equipment and interviewing each other around the fountain. The darkest recesses of the park now had playgrounds and dog parks for the local residents to enjoy.

She even took the children and ventured to Times Square, which was full of tourists speaking a million different languages. Not a peep show, three-card monte game or hooker to be seen. *Just weird,* she thought again.

By the time they were boarding the flight for Tucson, she was more than ready.

On a cool winter night after dinner, with both of the kids bathed, read to, and in bed sleeping, Tessa and Cam sat outside on the back patio, sipping beers and admiring the mountain.

Tessa turned to him and said, "I got some news today. A position with a very well-known geology team has come open. Jill Baron is the famous ecologist who heads it, and the work is groundbreaking and exciting. Maddy knows her and already called to tell her about me."

Cam barely hesitated before asking, "Where are we going? I

never liked it here much anyway. It's weird raising kids in a place with no seasons and red chile peppers on saguaro cactuses for Christmas."

"Really?? How about the Rocky Mountains in Colorado?" she answered, with a huge smile.

They road-tripped up to the Loch Vale Watershed for the interview with Dr. Baron. Cam had never been to the Rocky Mountains and could not keep his mouth from dropping open in awe at every turn.

"I could never imagine a place this crazy beautiful," he said.

Tessa agreed completely.

Tessa was offered and accepted the job. They returned to Tucson to close down their life there. Cam sold his company, and their house was on the market for less than a week. The hardest part was saying goodbye to their friends.

Maddy hugged her tightly and cried a little, saying, "Why did I introduce you to Jill? I knew you would leave me for her."

They searched for a place in the fairy tale town of Estes Park, hidden in a tiny bowl at seven-thousand-foot elevation, surrounded by jagged peaks. Tessa thought she might be in heaven. They found a geodesic dome house complete with a pool and hot tub, at the base of Kenny Mountain with a view of Panorama Peak from the front door. Then she knew for sure that she was.

Remembering how, all those years ago as a teenager, she had flipped a coin and gone to Tucson, she smiled to think she now had the other side of the coin to explore. I'm a lucky girl, she thought contentedly.

The first night in their new home, they were sitting outside finishing drinks on the lounge chairs when Tessa heard the sounds of heavy footfalls approaching.

"Shhhh, do you hear that?" she whispered, cutting Cam off in mid-sentence.

He nodded silently, looking around for the source. They both froze when they heard a loud *snuff* just yards away. The warm yellow light coming through the triangular windowpanes of the dome house caught the fur of a very large brown bear coming towards them.

"Shit," Cam breathed, as they both slowly stood up and backed into the house. "Did you put the bear bar on the dumpster, Tess?"

"Damn, I forgot!" she whispered, as the sound of the dumpster being tipped over came to them.

They shut off all of the lights inside, and peaked out the windows, watching the massive furry animal make a tremendous mess of the front yard.

"We are not in the desert anymore, Toto," Cam said, as the bear, satisfied it had found everything of value, moved on.

As soon as they were well-settled, with Tessa exploring the mountains with her new team and the kids enrolled in school, Cam opened a handyman business catering to the Estes Park community. His wide warm smile, and the integrity and generosity with which he approached every job, made him very popular very quickly. Within a year, he opened a remodeling business, which grew over time into a luxury home-building company. His office phone rang non-stop with prospective clients and architects who wanted him to do their projects.

As he sat at his desk paying bills at the end of a busy day, a man walked in. He was wearing a black t-shirt and six heavy gold chains. He had corn rows and wore sunglasses that hid his eyes. He did not remove them.

"Cam Callahan?"

Cam nodded and waited. The man stuck out his hand and said,

"I'm Devone Carter, manager for a very well-known rap artist. I can't give you his name, but he was hanging out here after his gig at Red Rocks and saw your work. He wants a vacation home in the Rockies, and he wants you to build it."

Cam could not wait to get home to tell Tess. This would be his first celebrity client. They popped a bottle of Dom Perignon to celebrate, letting the cork fly high, to the delight of Lily and Noah.

The children blossomed in the fresh air of the mountain seasons. The four of them hiked every summer weekend, Lily carrying a sketch pad to draw the deer, sheep and elk they saw. Her drawings were hanging all over house and getting pretty good, in Tessa's opinion. She had a unique way of depicting the animals' emotions in her artwork, with her teachers commenting encouragingly on her special style.

They all learned to ski together, the kids quickly surpassing Tess and Cam's skills and showing off on the moguls. One of their favorite winter activities was snow shoeing right from their backyard and off into the hills.

As each year passed, it brought a personal evolution for the members of this family. Tessa became the lead scientist after Dr. Baron left for a new endeavor. Cam's business kept him busy and happy and challenged. Lily began to take Art classes at the community college, even though she was barely a teenager. Noah enrolled in every honor's level Math and Science course offered at the Middle School.

And suddenly it was New Year's Eve, 1999.

"Can you believe we are beginning a new century, Cam?" Tessa said with wonder in her voice. The four of them were sitting in front of the T.V. waiting for the countdown. Tessa and Cam held glasses of champagne; Noah and Lily's flutes were filled with sparkling apple cider.

"We will be married twenty years in August!"

In unison, Lily and Noah said, "Wow, you're old!"

"Gee, thanks, kids," Cam said wryly.

"It's just so crazy," Tessa continued. "I used to tell my friends how cool it was that my grandmother was born in the nineteenth century. Now, if we have grandkids..."

"Ewww!" Lily interrupted, clapping her hands over her ears.

"I said, 'if," Tessa laughed. "If we have grandkids, they will be able to say their grandparents were born in the middle of the last century!"

"That is nuts," Noah agreed. "Do you think all the computers will blow up at midnight like they said? I saw some scary headlines this week."

Cam said, "I hope not, but I guess we'll find out in 10...9...8...7...6...5...4...3...2...1...Happy New Year!!!"

They clinked their glasses, hugging and kissing and toasting the twenty-first century; and laughed as Noah ran to check his Apple Mac to make sure it still worked.

On Lily's sixteenth birthday, they took a road trip to the Grand Canyon, stopping at Bryce and Zion canyons in Utah. There Lily sketched to her heart's content, putting her impressive perspective on the rock formations and sunsets.

On Noah's sixteenth birthday, they surprised him with a helicopter ski adventure in Telluride.

Tessa felt content with her life, especially when she looked at her family at the dinner table as they noisily shared the good food and their very opinionated views of anything and everything.

Late at night, she worried. What if things were going too well? What if this is the calm before the storm? What if something terrible happened to one of us? Or to all of us?

One night, she lay tossing and turning, her thoughts churning in her head and keeping her up.

"What's wrong, hon?" Cam asked.

"It seems silly, but I just keep thinking things are too good," she responded.

"Well, they are really good. But too good?" Cam was puzzled.

"First of all, the kids seem so happy to spend time with us and with each other. That's not normal for kids in high school, is it? Aren't they supposed to be mean and bitchy and secretive and hateful? And they don't seem to have many friends, do they? I mean Lily is taking Noah as her prom date, for crying out loud. Isn't that just weird? Neither seems boy or girl crazy, or has ever mentioned a special person that they like, either. I mean that is not hereditary, for sure..."

At this Cam laughed in agreement.

"And," Tessa continued, getting to the heart of her fear. "I keep thinking about what happened to both of my parents. They had a very good life- happy, normal, wealthy, even; and then their reality was completely ripped into shreds. Everyone they knew and loved was killed, and they ran for their lives into insanity. The older I get the more I think, could I do what they did? Would we survive? What would I do if something like that happened, and any or all of you were..."

She began to spiral, until Cam folded her into his arms. He held her, saying nothing, because there really was nothing to say.

Finally, she spoke.

"I think, I hope, that we would recognize the signs if the world went to hell like it did back then. And maybe we would be better prepared than they were, mainly because of what happened to them. I don't know, but I guess worrying about something that could happen is kind of a waste of time. Maybe karma or God or whatever would be kind to us because of what happened to them. I don't know what I believe, but I know how fortunate I feel to have this life, and to have you and Lily and Noah. Whatever happens, at least we have that."

"Truth!" Cam said, giving her a squeeze. "As for the kids, remember what we taught them? 'Callahans stick together. If someone gives one of you a problem, no matter whether the other ate all your favorite cereal or destroyed your treasured toy, you stand together.' Well, they're standing together and what more could we want?"

She gave Cam a long, clinging hug and said, "I think I can sleep now. I love you."

"I love you, Tessa. Forever and always."

And they slept in each other's' arms.

After graduating high school, Lily went off to the Rocky Mountain College of Art and Design. Her teachers had encouraged her to apply to schools in New York City and San Francisco and even Paris, but Lily wanted to stay close to home; and the program at RMCAD had everything she wanted.

In her first year, her work won a Freshman award; and by the end of the program, she had participated in Art Shows in Denver and Colorado Springs.

She found so many friends among her fellow artists, that Tessa's worries about her were put to rest. Lily often brought a half dozen friends home for weekends; and Tessa loved sitting and listening to their youthful enthusiasm and reflections.

One person kept returning to the house with these groups over and over again: a sculptor named Gary.

"See?" Cam said to her after a very late night of sitting around chatting with Lily and her friends. "I told you not to worry too much. I guess our kids just needed to find their own niche and their own people. Estes Park was a pretty small pond, after all."

"Gary seems nice," Tessa added. "I think he and Lily might be a thing."

She was right about that.

Noah finished high school early, not surprisingly, and began a program at the Colorado University School of Medicine at the age of seventeen. He thrived on the challenges and volunteered for any extra undertakings that were offered to his cohort.

"Sleep is overrated," he said to Tessa when he had a rare moment to call her and check in. He sounded exhausted, happy, fulfilled and challenged; and her soul sang with joy and pride for his dream of helping others.

Tessa sat on a lounge chair on the pool patio thinking about the trajectory she and Cam had taken, and sometimes could not believe the life they lived now. She remembered sending Noah off to college, four years ago already; and she shook her head. Enjoying the warm afternoon breeze and the shadows playing on the mountains, she mulled it all over.

How did we get here? she pondered. Two crazy kids, from crazy families, who started out starving students and now we are living this dream. I wonder what our ancestors would think of this life we have. Imagine, Cam's great grandfather barely surviving the potato famine, Cam's mom shipped to the states from somewhere in Eastern Europe, my mom escaping Berlin, and my dad in that labor camp as a little boy; all leading here to this heaven on earth. It's almost like a chain of dominoes; or better yet, like a tapestry. No, neither of those quite works, because this story never ends.

She was still deep in her thoughts when Cam came home, changed into his swimsuit and jumped in the pool, splashing her and coming up to laugh, "How was that?"

"Seven point eight!" she said, and jumped in, too.

Noah finished medical school and took off to see, and to help, the world in the Doctors Without Borders program. His photos from Bangladesh showed a poverty level that Tessa had not imagined possible in the twenty-first century. His pictures of the mountains of Pakistan rivalled their own adopted hometown for beauty. Noah visited distant family members in Colombia, which made Tessa's heart glad. His time in Burkina Faso left her sleepless, as she watched the news of kidnappings and bombings there.

In Kenya, he fell in love.

Tessa got her first hint that this might be the real deal, when Noah began emailing her about a fellow doctor, Ely. That, and the fact that he decided to stay in Kenya for an extra year, made her pretty sure that Ely was special to him. When Noah brought him home for Christmas to introduce them, Cam and Tessa had no doubt.

"Peas in a pod," Cam said to her as they lay in bed on Christmas Day. "Still a bit weird to me; but I'm glad he is happy."

Tess lay her head on his shoulder and nodded. "He's perfect for Noah. All I wanted was for them to meet someone who would love them as much as I do, someone they can hold hands with to go through whatever life hurls at them; and now we have that. It's almost a relief," she chuckled and then continued, "Were we ever that young, Cam? I seem to remember, but it feels like someone else's life that I read about in a book somewhere."

Lily and Gary were married in a small intimate ceremony at the Hillside Gardens in Colorado Springs. Watched over by the jagged peaks of the Southern Rockies and surrounded by endless sculptures strewn about in the maze of the place, they exchanged vows and partied the night away.

Soon after, Lily opened a studio in Boulder, at the base of the mountains near the University where Gary taught blossoming young sculptors. Cam helped her hang the sign over the door: Callahan's Art House.

Noah and Ely were married in a sweet ceremony in the backyard of the house in Estes Park. As the sun set, brilliant orange, red and yellow rays shot through the thin mountain air, creating a spectacular backdrop to their tender vows.

They moved in with Lily and Gary in their cozy townhome near Lily's studio, until they bought their own place not far from Tessa and Cam.

The two doctors opened a medical office in town to serve the small community in Estes Park, but their deeply rooted need to help people was unsatisfied. Within two years, they decided to relocate to Denver and open a clinic in one of the neighborhoods where families had little money and few options for health care. They quickly became local heroes to the many people who had not been able to see a doctor for years.

Noah and Ely often drove the seventy miles to visit Tessa and Cam in Estes Park. One night, they popped open a bottle of champagne.

Puzzled, Tessa asked, "What are we celebrating?"

Noah and Ely exchanged excited and loving looks. Then Noah fairly burst out: "We adopted a baby! The paperwork was finalized this afternoon, and we leave for Kenya next week to pick him up. You are going to be grandparents!!"

Tessa burst into tears and jumped up to hug the men. Cam joined her; his own eyes misty with emotion.

"Can't wait to meet him, son," Cam said, hugging Noah and Ely warmly.

They were still celebrating when Lily and her husband walked in the door.

"What's going on?" Lily asked.

Her brother told her their news; and there was joyous emotional hugging all around. Ely poured two more glasses of champagne. He passed one to Gary and the other to Lily.

"No thanks," she said, holding up her hand with a mischievous smile. "Not drinking right now."

They all looked at her, bewildered, until she added, "At least not for the next nine months."

The yelling, shouting and jumping around in joy would have frightened away the biggest brown bear in the neighborhood.

Yaro was a chubby two-year-old, full of curiosity and with a wide constant smile. When Noah and Ely first brought him to meet his grandparents, Tessa bounced him on her lap, memorizing every feature on her grandson's face.

"What will you be called, now that you need a grandparent name, Mom?" Noah asked.

Tessa took a moment to think about it. There were so many options! Nana, Abuela, Mamita, Grandma, Granny…Oma!

It gob smacked her in the face and she laughed aloud.

"Yaro, I am your Oma! Can you say that?"

"O-Ma!" Yaro repeated, patting her cheek and chuckling happily.

Tessa retired and began to babysit him two days a week, when both of his dads were scheduled to work at the clinic. She read to him, sang and danced with him, took him to the Denver Zoo, and played endlessly with him, delighting in his sweet, inquisitive nature.

"I can't wait to take you hiking in the mountains, Yaro. Did you know that every rock has a name? This one is mica; can you say that?"

"Dis one mai-kah," the boy repeated. Tessa's heart was full.

She was pushing Yaro on the swing at the schoolyard playground when her cell phone went off. She glanced at it, ready to hit "dismiss" when she saw it was Gary calling.

"Hi, Gary," Tessa answered. It was unusual for her son-in-law to call her and she felt a creeping nervousness.

"Now, Tessa, it's going to be fine. But Lily had to be admitted to the hospital this morning. She was having contractions and the doctor wanted her to come in."

"It's too early, Gary," Tessa said, suddenly fearful. "She still has months to go."

"She is dehydrated, and they are trying to stop the contractions with IV infusions. I will call you as soon as anything changes."

The rest of the afternoon, Tessa worked to distract herself with Yaro; but she kept one hand on her bag to make sure she did not miss a call.

On her drive back to Estes Park, Gary called again. She pressed the phone button on her steering wheel and his voice came over the Bluetooth speaker.

"They can't stop the contractions, Tessa. But the baby's heartbeat is strong, so they are going to monitor Lily and see what happens."

"Should I come to the hospital?" Tessa asked.

"Not yet. We'll call if anything changes. Hang in there, Oma! Love you…" and he hung up.

Tessa pressed the phone button again and rang Noah. He was waiting for news and picked up right away.

"Noah, they can't stop the contractions. I'm so scared. Please come to the house and wait with us."

"On our way!" he said.

Into the night, no one slept except Yaro. The four adults sat in the living room quietly chatting. Noah sat next to his mother on the couch, holding her hand and reassuring her.

"Lil's in good hands, mom. I know everyone at the hospital, and they will take good care of her and the baby."

Ely nodded in agreement. Then he asked, "Do you want to say a prayer?"

Tessa hesitated, then assented. They stood in a circle, holding hands. Ely quietly spoke. "God, please take good care of Lily and the baby. Watch over them as they go through the birth, and in the time to follow."

He paused and then finished, "And please take care of Oma and Grandpa too. We are going to need them more than ever! Amen."

With misty eyes, they all answered *Amen* and hugged each other tightly.

They were dozing on the chairs and couch when Tessa's phone rang. It was still dark outside, but the birds were singing as she awoke instantly and grabbed it.

"Gary! What is happening, is everything okay?"

"The baby is here! Lily came through like a champ and is resting. The baby is in the Newborn Intensive Care Unit being monitored and getting oxygen. She is so tiny…."

"She?! Can we come to see them?"

"Visiting hours start at eight. Why don't you all get some rest, I'm sure none of you slept very well. We will see you in a few hours. I promise to call if anything changes."

At exactly eight o'clock, Tessa, Cam and Noah lined up at the front desk to get their visitors' passes. Ely stayed back at the house with Yaro, on the condition they would call if they needed him. Noah greeted everyone he saw in the small hospital warmly as they trooped into Lily's room.

She was awake and looking very worried, holding Gary's hand as he sat on the bed next to her.

"What is wrong?" Tessa said, as soon as she saw them.

"The baby is not breathing on her own," Lily said, and burst into exhausted, stressed tears.

Gary explained, "The NICU nurse thinks they may have to move her to Denver. They want to make sure they give her every chance…" and then he too began to weep helplessly.

Without a word, Noah left the room. Tessa held her daughter and Cam put his arm around Gary, while they waited for him to return. It was not more than twenty minutes, but to Tessa it felt like so much longer.

"She has been diagnosed with Apnea of Prematurity, for now. It is pretty common in preemies, but the doctors want to make sure, and also to keep an eye out for infections. They want to move her to Children's Hospital in Aurora. I think you should let them, sis. She would go today, as soon as you get discharged."

Lily's eyes, already reddened and swollen, welled up as she looked at her little brother. "Whatever you think, Noah."

Gary nodded his assent.

By late afternoon, the new little family was on its way to Children's. Noah rode in the ambulance with them, while Tessa and Cam went home to update Ely.

As soon as they walked in the door, Yaro yelled, "Gwampa! Oma!" and raised his arms to be picked up.

Their busy grandson was a much-needed distraction. When he lay down for his afternoon nap, Tessa and Cam went into their room to rest.

"Do you think the baby is going to be okay, Cam? It would kill Lily and all of us if anything happens to her."

Cam held his wife and they dozed off for a long while. When they awoke, they made dinner, but only Yaro had an appetite.

Noah returned around nine that night.

"The baby needed some help in the ambulance because of the breathing issues. Her heart stopped once, but the EMS got her back right away. She is in the neonatal pulmonary clinic. They have her on a heart monitor and a ventilator, and Lily and Gary will be able to stay with her. You will not be able to see her for now, but I did manage to take some photos with my cell."

He handed Tessa the phone and she held the picture almost up to her nose trying to absorb every millimeter, every baby wrinkle, every eyelash and birthmark. In another photo, Lily leaned over the bassinet and kissed the glass lid.

"She is so tiny," Tessa whispered, passing the phone to Cam to look, who then gave it to Ely.

"The odds are in her favor," Noah said. "Unless she develops an infection, she should be fine. I mean, she comes from some pretty strong female stock, mom."

He smiled at her and gave her a hug, before packing his own baby into the car and heading back to Denver with Ely.

Over the next few weeks, Lily and Gary spelled each other at the baby's side while the other came home for a shower, a few hours of sleep and a change of clothes.

The newborn's heart stopped twice more, and her breathing did not improve. The doctor recommended that a cardiology specialist be brought in to join the team that was caring for her.

While Lily and Gary were watching the cardiologist's examination, Tessa, Cam and Noah stood outside the closed hospital room door. Cam held Tessa's hand, and Noah had his arm around her.

When the doctor came out, followed by Lily and Gary, she escorted them all to a nearby office.

"She has a condition fairly common in premature infants," the doctor said, sitting at a large dark wooden desk with a computer system on one side.

Lily and Gary sat in leather armchairs across from her, with Tessa, Cam and Noah standing close behind. The cardiologist turned her screen towards them, pointing at the ultrasound images of the baby to show an opening between her heart and lungs.

"While in utero, a baby receives oxygen from its mother and the lungs are not yet functioning. All babies have a gap called a ductus between the heart and lungs while still in the womb. Once a baby is born, the gap usually seals. But sometimes, in premature babies, it does not close."

The specialist pushed the screen back around, leaned her forearms on the desk, and looked directly into each set of eyes staring intently at her in the thick tense atmosphere of the office.

"Your baby is already several weeks old, and her ductus is still open. This is a dangerous condition for both her heart and her respiratory system. We can try Ibuprofen to help it close. This often does work. However, if it does not resolve on its own in the next few days, I recommend surgery."

Noah was the only one able to speak at that moment. "What does the surgery involve, doctor?"

"It is a catheterization procedure. She would be sedated, and the catheter threaded to the aorta through her groin area. After we take a look at the size and shape of the gap, we will either place a coil there or plug the opening with a device that will block the vessel. If the ductus is found to be too large for these procedures, we will make a small incision between her ribs and tie it off."

"What are the chances of..." Lily could not finish the question that was on everyone's mind.

"It depends on how strong she is. The risk of complications from any of these procedures is usually low. After surgery, she would be monitored for infections. If the surgery is deemed necessary, the prognosis for normal development is actually excellent."

"Thank you, doctor," Gary said, as they left the room, emotionally drained with worry.

Tessa and Cam did whatever they could to support the little family, but for the most part they felt useless and ineffectual, sitting at home waiting. Every time one of their cell phones went off, it gave them a start. At one point, Cam was holding his phone when it rang, and he jerked so hard it flew out of his hand and landed behind the couch. Tessa laughed out loud, which felt both strange and good at the same time.

Lily texted them photos of the baby, trying to take them with the least amount of tubes, wires and machines showing. Tessa combed each picture for positive signs.

Viewing one of the photos over her shoulder, Cam commented, "Look at that, Tessa. She has your lips. She even has your look of determination."

"She needs that right now. I hope she is as stubborn as her Oma," Tessa said, gently touching the screen with one finger.

Three days later, after the procedure, Tessa and Cam were back in the specialist's office with Lily, Gary and Noah. Tessa felt like she was in a déjà vu. The doctor sat silently looking at the computer monitor, clicking the mouse to enlarge the images, while they anxiously waited for her diagnosis. The cardiologist took her time, comparing the new images with the ones from a few days prior in a careful and meticulous manner.

Finally, she took off her glasses, rubbed her eyes and put her hands on the desk.

Looking directly at Lily, she gave a small smile and said, "The gap is closed."

The joyful and relieved hugging went on so long, Noah finally untangled himself and said, "Okay, let's listen to what the doctor has to say."

"She will be fine. Her heart and lungs should function normally. She is just over five pounds already. We will want to give her one more day of close monitoring, and she should be able to go home tomorrow."

This time there was actual cheering.

The whole family sat on the steps outside Lily and Gary's townhouse. Balloons bumped each other in the light breeze. Signs proclaiming, "It's a girl!" and "Welcome home!" hung from every available space. Yaro danced on the sidewalk to joyful music only he could hear, running over to bop a balloon every few moments.

Tessa spotted the car first, as it came around the corner.

"They're here!" she announced, and they all walked over to the car to help the new family into their home.

Gary unclicked the car seat and pulled it out. They all crowded around, having their first look at the newest member of the family.

Lily stood behind them happily. "We could not decide on a name for her until last night," she said. "Family, meet Isabelle Taya!"

She gave her mother a hug. "We decided to name her after all of the strong women in our family, since she already has shown so much toughness in the face of her first challenge. The I is for Ilse, the L's are for Lena and Lillian and of course, the T is for you, mom."

Tessa gave her daughter a tight hug and whispered, "You're the strongest of us all. I don't know if I would have survived what you just went through."

Then Tessa called to everyone, "Let's get inside! I need to give Isabelle Taya a proper Oma hug."

Yaro grabbed her hand, skipping up the stairs as he sang, "Iz Bel Tay Yah."

It was a noisy joyous bunch that went into the townhouse, lugging bags and stuffed animals and gift baskets and flowers.

Tessa, finally holding her granddaughter for the first time, looked into the wide eyes in the tiny face. Sitting in a quiet corner of the room, she reached a finger out to trace each feature. Tessa whispered to the baby how happy she was that Isabelle was home and safe. She told the baby girl what fun she would have with her cousin Yaro.

She leaned down and gave Isabelle Taya a sweet lingering kiss on the forehead.

Then Oma gave a little laugh and said to the infant:

"Welcome to this crazy family, baby girl. Have I got some stories to tell you!

A Note from the Author

Dear Reader,

Thank you for reading my debut novel. I hope this book, written during the Covid-19 pandemic and begun the very day after I retired, took you on a journey and gave you some things to think about.

Some background information may explain where this tale, or really set of tales, came from. I hope it may inspire you to learn more about the story, or really set of stories, that led you to where you physically are right now, sitting and reading this book. It's likely to be a pretty fascinating journey, I can tell you.

All the way through school, I found Social Studies and History classes beyond dull. I did not connect to the names, dates, wars, and events we were made to memorize. The timelines we studied helped not at all- I could not find any interest in the textbooks we read, or the occasional movie we were shown.

It was only when I became an elementary education teacher that I vowed to find some way for my students to understand and relate to the information they were expected to master. And I found myself learning along with them as we focused on the *people* of history, as we dug into the *why* instead of just the *when, where,* and *how.* We asked more questions than we answered, and this fostered a growing curiosity about how the world got where it is today. This made it real; to them but also, to me.

It became even more real once I married someone from a very different background, and birthed three amazing human beings, who are now creating their own strands of our family stories. But it really hit home for me one day while I was at work as a bilingual teacher.

My classroom phone rang, and when I picked up, it was the secretary at the Assistant Superintendent's office. She hesitated a moment and then told me she was filling out the ethnicity survey for the district employees and did not know what to put for me. It gave me a bit of pause as I realized I was the only bilingual teacher in the district whose last name was not "typically Latino". At the same time, it struck me that she did not call any of my colleagues to ask the same question. I really did not know what to say, so I asked her, tongue-in-cheek, "Is there a box that says 'Spanish-speaking Jew with an Irish name?'" When she, a bit uncomfortable, answered in the negative, I told her to just check "other" and hung up.

As a result of that experience and so many others, and because I love writing and I adore stories, I decided to create this book. The characters and events are mostly conglomerations of stories I've heard, people I've met, research I've done, and a whole lot of imagination. There are also historically accurate people and events included here, which is important to know.

For just two examples, Lillian's plane crash in the mountains of Albania and subsequent hike to the coast actually happened to a group of American nurses on their way to the front. And if you think my imagination is dark enough to create a horror show character like Kenichi Sonei of the Japanese prison camp, then you give me too much credit. He is a perfect example of real-live evil.

Feel free to do a search on any historical event or person in the book. I learned so much during the writing of this book, and as a teacher, I would love to know I inspired further curiosity in you.

I want to end with some hopes for you, Reader. I hope you enjoyed the book, of course. I hope you talk about it with your family and friends, and that if nothing else, it gives you something to think about. But mostly I hope it leads you on your own personal exploration. You truly never know what you will find there.

When a book is written, it is never completed in a vacuum; and so, I have some special people to thank. My husband Pat was my alpha reader and gave me great feedback; as did my beta readers Regina Monaco, Joe and Linda Moore and Jeri Strauss. My small but amazingly productive and supportive writing group was key to the writing of this book, so shout out to Brenda Kahn and Tamara Silberman as well.

Thank you, and be well during these "interesting" times,
Maureen Morrissey
November 2020